WHITE FLAG OF THE DEAD BOOK IV

UNITED STATES OF THE DEAD

JOSEPH TALLUTO

CHAPTER 1

Major Ken Thorton looked at the bodies of two of his men swinging gently in the breeze. They had been hung upside down and left just high enough so the zombies couldn't get them.

Thorton and his men had reached the rendezvous point later than expected, but they certainly had not thought to see something like this. The men did not know what had happened, all they knew was what was in front of them. Ten men had been dispatched to ambush John Talon and all were missing save the two hanging like grim piñatas.

Ken was pissed, through and through. Two of his men were trussed up like pigs to slaughter and the rest were undoubtedly dead. Talon was proving to be a worthy adversary and a royal pain in the ass. Even the thought of Talon's family being murdered was small consolation in the face of losing a third of his men.

Thorton clenched and unclenched his massive fists as he took in the wounds of the two men. Milovich had been stabbed, then shot. That was obvious. Kazinski showed signs of a fight and massive trauma to his eye. It was very clear how he died.

Behind him, soldiers fired on exploring and curious zombies, which led to more curious and exploring zombies. Pretty soon, there was going to be a large battle here.

Thorton was oblivious as he studied the dead men closer. The ground beneath the two had drops of blood that had turned deep red, but not brown like old, dried blood does. That told Thorton Talon had been here pretty recently and was not far ahead. *Perhaps another opportunity might present itself.* Ken thought.

A closer rifle shot interrupted his thoughts and brought him back to reality. It was time to go. As he turned away, a slip of paper in the pocket of the hanging corporal caught his eye. Because of his height, he was able to reach it. Unfolding the note, he quickly read its contents and his temper, which was always ready to erupt, suddenly flared.

Ten fake soldiers,

Came to the party late.
Two were really bad shots,
And then there were eight.
Eight fake soldiers,
Tried to even the score.
Several met with John,
And then there were four.
Four fake soldiers,
Didn't know what to do.
A couple fell out of windows,
And then there were two.
Two fake soldiers,
Wanted to have some fun.
Both died surprised,
And then there were none.

Keep coming and you're a dead man, Thorton.

J.T.

"Son of a bitch!" Thorton cursed, crumpling the paper and hurling it from him. "That does it. No more Mr. Nice Guy! Mount up, you idiots! We're out of here!" he yelled at his men, who were readying to face a charge from a small horde of zombies. The men were more than willing to comply.

"Sir!" A private ran up to Thorton. "What do we do about the corporal and the sergeant there, sir?"

Major Thorton glared at the young recruit. "Leave them. They're useless. Take the truck, though." He said, motioning to the vehicle that was parked over by the bait shop in the trees.

"Sir!" The young soldier bolted for the truck, weaved around a pair of zombies that had come out of the woods for the party. He just barely made the cab and slammed the door shut, fired up the big engine and pulled the truck around, tossing off a trio of zombie hangers-on.

As the trucks pulled away, one of the last soldiers picked up the crumpled piece of paper and tucked it into his pocket. Whatever pissed off the major so bad might be useful knowing, the soldier figured.

The little convoy moved out on Route 50 and each and every soldier had the luxury of watching their former comrades hanging dead from a light pole. Some of the soldiers grumbled quietly, knowing it was a bad thing to leave them unburied, but they were too afraid of the Major to protest. But more than one filed away the insult, to be brought again to the surface should the occasion warrant.

Beneath the resentment, was a healthy dose of fear and apprehension. Ten men had gone to take out a man and his friends in what should have been an easy ambush. But now all of those men were dead and the killer of those men openly mocked and threatened their leader. What kind of man was John Talon and what kind of men did he lead? Was the major in over his head? Would they all suffer the same kind of inglorious end?

As the little note was passed around, the soldiers began to wonder. How many of them were going to finish this trip? They started with forty and now they were down to seventeen. If Captain Tamikara was as successful as the two swinging in the breeze fishing for zombies, then they were truly screwed.

These thoughts ran through the soldiers' heads unbeknownst to Major Thorton. He was sitting in silence, seething over his recent losses and John Talon's insult. He wanted something to destroy, something to tear apart. He needed to send John a message, something he would be sure to understand.

Can't save them all Johnny. Thorton thought as they reached the outskirts of Coolville. The town looked alive, but it probably had seen better days. The cemetery to the northwest of the town and highway had many new graves, most of them looking like they had been hand dug recently. An earthen barricade ran the length of the highway, but did not encircle the town. It was a curious feature but one Thorton was grateful for. He didn't need complications right now.

The trucks rolled over the ground and around the barricade. It was a simple earthen dam, steep enough to be difficult for a zombie to walk up, but easy enough to crawl. The top was flat and wide enough to accommodate a vehicle. In fact, there were tire ruts that showed vehicles had been to the top.

Thorton radioed to the truck behind him to roll along side of his and to make sure all men had their magazines full. This was going to take some doing.

At the center of town, after driving past several curious onlookers and groups of people working small gardens near homes, Thorton called the convoy to a halt. He saw the town was relatively small and sparsely populated, but he didn't really care. He stepped out of the truck and straightened his uniform, figuring to continue his ruse one more time.

"Good morning!" Ken said to the assembled townspeople across the street. There looked to be about fifty of them in the parking lot of what seemed to be the local grocery store.

One man, a gentleman of indeterminate age, walked forward with a noticeable limp. His eyes roamed over the trucks and the assembled soldiers and started to look wet with tears.

Thorton was disgusted by the show of emotion, but kept a smile on his face. "Are you in charge?"

The man nodded. "When we saw the trucks, we hoped the military had finally gotten hold of the zombies. Are you with a scout group or some kind of public relations?" the man asked.

Thorton smiled. "You might say that. Speaking of scouts, you all didn't happen to meet a man heading east recently on Route 50 there, did you?"

The man thought a minute. "Come to think about it, there was a big RV moving in that direction, headed east. Passed by here about three hours ago, give or take an hour. Might have been the man you're looking for."

Thorton mused about that information. That meant Talon was probably twenty to fifty miles ahead, given the terrain and obstacles. In normal times it would have been closer to a hundred miles. *Good. Very good.* He thought. He looked down at the man.

"How are you situated for supplies? Will you be able to make enough for winter? We have seeds if you need them." Major Thorton was doing his best to continue the ruse.

The man grinned. "No, we're pretty well set. We've managed to can a lot of food and save the seeds from previous plantings, so we're actually better off than some. South of here we even have a small pig farm, so there's pork on occasion."

"Well, good. Good for you. You're a better community than a lot I've seen." Ken looked over at the townspeople. "What about defenses? All I saw was that earth dam near the woods as we came to this place. Why didn't you make it go all the way around the town?"

The older man cackled a bit. "You ain't the first to ask that. We built that dam to keep the zombies from seeing us as they walked along the road. We can take out any lone zombie or two that comes along, we just have to be careful. If there's more than five or six, we send up the alarm and all of us go scrambling to the top of the hill. The zombies can't do much more than crawl to the top and then we take them out. Simple."

The strategist in Ken's head found the simple logic appealing, if a little strange. A mass horde would wipe this place out with little effort, but up until now, the town of Coolville had been lucky.

"What about weapons? I was ordered to assess all defensive capabilities of any viable community I came across." Thorton was rather impressed with himself at that little bit of official sounding vocabulary.

"Some handguns and rifles, mostly shotguns. Hunting stuff, pretty much," the man said. "Nothing like what your boys are carrying over there." He waved a hand at the line of soldiers spread out behind Thorton.

"Good. Well, I've seen what I needed to see, learned what I needed to learn. Thank you very much." Ken stuck out his big paw to the little man and shook his hand vigorously.

"What happens next, if you don't mind me asking?" the man said, rubbing his hand a little.

Ken smiled and said, "I need to confer with my men and I'll let you know. You go on back to your people and I'll be talking to you all in a minute."

Thorton and the older gentlemen parted ways and the major walked back to his semi circle of men. As he was talking, a few things had occurred to him. In the first place, Talon was close, but ahead in getting to the capitol. Second, wholesale slaughter of the people he was planning to enslave would mean he would be in charge of exactly squat. Last, unless there was complete surprise, he might lose a few of his men and he didn't have the numbers to take that possibility likely. The best bet was to delay Talon, but the question was how?

Thorton reached his men and spoke in low tones. "Get back into the trucks. We're pulling out in a little it, but we need to create a distraction." Thorton outlined his plan and the men smiled. It was simple, it was devious and would accomplish what they wanted. All to the good, as far as they were concerned. Some griped about leaving behind ready provisions and entertainment, but they were quieted quickly.

After most of the men had gotten back into the trucks, Thorton signaled to Coolville's leader that he needed him. The older man walked over, clearly enjoying his role as representative.

"Yes, Major?" he asked.

Thorton put on his best lying face. "There's a large company of troops to the west of us and we need to signal we have been here and this area is secure. Have your people round up as many used tires as possible and bring them to the top of the hill on the north end."

The man gave Thorton an odd look but hastened to comply. While the townspeople worked quickly to fulfill their obligation, Thorton spent some time looking over the maps. He figured if he swung south and followed 144 to 124, he could pick up 50 again and cross the river into West Virginia before Talon did. After that, it was a straight end run to the capitol, with Talon watching helplessly while Thorton burned the Constitution.

While killing John Talon had its merits, Thorton had come to the realization that letting him live and realize his utter failure, coupled with the probable loss of his family, would be a far more fitting revenge.

After an hour, Major Thorton could see a decent pile of tires on top of the hill. He ordered one of his men to douse the tires in oil and gas, then set it on fire. The oil and gas caught quickly and in a short amount of time the pile was burning well. Thick black smoke rose high into the sky, able to be seen for miles. Ken looked at it for a minute, then laughed. *These idiots just called in every zombie with a good set of eyes within a forty mile radius.* He thought. As he contemplated, it was a nice trap for Talon as well. *Hopefully he'll take some time to get here.*

The townspeople watched the smoke go up and Thorton gave them a thumbs-up for encouragement. Already he could see some of the people looking nervously at the tall pillar of black rising from the hilltop, announcing to one and all that the Coolville Buffet was here and open for business.

Ken's men climbed back aboard and as they pulled out, he shouted to the people. "Good work! You'll be getting some real company soon!" He tried to hide his grin, but it was a wasted effort. Without a second thought, Ken and his convoy moved out of Coolville and onto the twenty eight mile detour which would hopefully put him ahead of Talon for good.

Route 144 wound its way along the Muskingum River, with the water on the right and a heavily wooded area on the left. There was little evidence at all of the Upheaval in this quiet place, save for the occasional wandering zombies. Across the river was a small campground and it had been deserted long ago.

Thorton and his men were able to make good time until they came to another campground. This one was still in use, but a quick look showed shredded tents, scattered supplies and blood splattered equipment. The feeding zombies was another giveaway.

As the convoy came to a slow stop, Thorton was able to assess what had happened. A small group of survivors had taken refuge in the campground and with the water supply nearby it was a good bet. However, they lost when a surprisingly large group of zombies came upon them in the early morning and overwhelmed them. One man looked to have made a run for the river with another person, possibly a child, but the twin blood streaks across the road signaled the zombies had caught them and dragged them both back to the feeding frenzy. Several zombies were on the road, while the rest, about fifteen in all, were hunched over the remains of the travelers.

At the sight of the trucks, the zombies began to move towards the vehicles, shambling in an eerie, groaning dance to destruction. Many were covered in blood and left dark footprints on the roadway.

Major Thorton got out of the truck, followed by the rest of his men. He hated to have to waste ammo, but if they did it right, it should be done quickly.

"Fan out. Pick your targets. Slaughter them." He grinned as the nearest zombies fell. The last time he gave that order was against a living community. *Funny how things turn around*, he thought.

After the last zombie fell, Thorton ordered some of his men to toss the zombies out of the way and the others to look for anything worth bringing along.

A few minutes later, the trucks were rolling again, the men having found a few canned goods and knives, but little else of value. They didn't bother burying the dead, for as Thorton was fond of saying, "Why bury fertilizer?"

Route 144 became Route 124 after emerging from the forest. 124 began in the little town of Hockingport, a small community on a point of land where the Muskingum and Ohio rivers merged. Hockingport had a few businesses scattered here and there, with some homes nestled in the trees along the river. The biggest population center in Hockingport was the trailer park, where the double wide reigned supreme.

As they passed by, Thorton noted the destruction of the trailers, some with big gaping holes ripped in the sides.

"Canned meat to the zombies," he said to his driver who sniggered

"Yes, sir," said the Private.

Route 124 took them north along the Ohio river and as they moved they stopped infrequently at homes which seemed like they might have something of value. One home yielded a goodly supply of dried goods, while another had a decent firearms collection. The owners were nowhere to be found, which, if they were alive, was probably a good thing for them.

As Thorton and his men moved further north, Mustapha Island came into view. It was a wooded island, nearly half a mile long and about five hundred feet at its widest point. Moving past, Ken could see smoke fires of survivors. Among the trees he could see about a dozen shapes moving around and there looked to be a few boats carefully lashed to trees. As far as secure choices went, it was a good idea. Surrounded by water it guaranteed safety from the zombies. But eventually supplies would run out and then the survivors would have to return to the mainland. If they had prepared well, they might actually live to see the end of the zombie plague and return home.

Thorton couldn't care less. If they had what he wanted, he took it. If they served a purpose, he used them. If they were in the way, he removed them and if they crossed him, he killed them. Life was simple for a man without a conscience.

Route 124 swung sharply north and for a while they were in deep woods. The sun was nearly overhead, but the tall trees formed shadows which were hard to penetrate. The undergrowth was thick and Thorton figured hunting zombies in these woods would be a royal pain in the ass.

Travel along these roads was painfully slow. The roads were no longer maintained and as a result, had many cracks and splits. Anyone travelling too fast would find themselves without tires in a very short amount of time. This was why it had taken so long for Thorton and his men to travel from California to Ohio.

The convoy finally came out of the woods into a small populated area. At least, it would have been if the Upheaval hadn't happened. As it was, there was little to see even had it been still living. It looked like one of those end of life areas, where people settle in to quietly finish out their days. A small store was the only convenience and a single gas station served the small population. There wasn't any zombie activity to be seen, but as recent events taught the faithful, things weren't always what they seemed.

124 finally reconnected with Route 50 and Thorton felt like he was getting ahead. After the setbacks and loss of men, he felt like he had finally gained the upper hand.

"Sir! You can still see the smoke, sir!" The driver of the truck pointed out.

Thorton looked and laughed quietly. *We're twelve miles away and that pillar of smoke is as clear as an arrow. Talon has to be heading that way, now.* He thought. Out loud he said, "Slow down, I want to see the maps and figure our next move."

Ken quickly found his bearings and as the trucks slowly moved north, he planned his next move. It was nearly midday and as strange as it sounded, he needed to start thinking about a safe place to spend the night.

As it was, they were on a collision course with several towns of dubious safety and Thorton decided to try and get by the towns and head for the hills of West Virginia.

"When you see signs for 618, follow them. That will get us across the river and reconnect with Route 50. We'll find a place to spend the night after that."

"Yessir!" said the private, swerving around a stalled vehicle and increasing his speed. He had a hard job, watching for road hazards and trying to keep on course. As they moved around a large bend in the river, a huge island came into view. He pointed it out to the major, who dismissed it out of hand.

"I know it looks good, but we may as well keep moving if we can. The further we get to D.C., the better chance we have of taking care of business before Talon. Keep driving."

The island, Blennerhasset Island Historical State Park, was formally the home of Harmon Blennerhasset, a wealthy Irishman once accused of treason by Thomas Jefferson for plotting to establish an empire in the Southwest with Aaron Burr. A large restored mansion lay on the east end of the island, but from Thorton's point of view, the island was just wilderness.

The road wound through a large town and there was a lot of devastation. A fire sometime in the past wiped out a good portion, leaving blackened ruins for blocks. Cars were all over the place, many left with open doors and belongings inside, a sure sign someone fled when the zombies came close. Here and there lay skeletal remains, the reminders of the Upheaval. Some of the remains showed clear signs of head trauma, making it easy to tell which ones used to be zombies.

The deeper the convoy moved through town, the worse the devastation became. Thorton could see where people had made last stands against the hordes of zombies. Rings of bodies around ruined homes and businesses told tales of desperate battles against the undead. One building, an aquarium shop, had dozens of skeletal remains lying around its parking lot. The smashed in windows and scorch marks were a familiar ending to that chapter.

The trucks entered the business district and there was immediate activity. Down every side street and alley had to be dozens of roaming zombies. At the passage of the trucks, they began a slow, measured pursuit, hopeless in ambition, but determined in execution.

Thorton signaled his driver to speed up and ordered the other trucks to close ranks as much as they could. If they were getting this much of a response this early, they would do better to try and run through before zombies ahead of them tried to block their way. It was hard enough with the cars and bodies, but a sizable swarm of ghouls could stop the trucks dead in more ways than one.

The trucks quickly made their way through the rest of the town and Thorton could see the river peeking through gaps in the homes and businesses. Pretty soon they would be in West Virginia and Thorton hoped they would be able to make a clean run to D.C.. He had no idea what waited for him at the nation's capitol, but he figured it couldn't be that bad.

"Sir!" his driver yelled. "Behind us!"

Thorton looked out the rear view mirror and blanched. Nearly three hundred zombies of assorted shapes and sizes were following the trucks at various speeds.

"Shit. Well, if we keep moving, then we should be able to outrun them. If nothing serious is blocking our way, they won't be a problem." Thorton hoped he was right. A horde of that size could easily overwhelm his small band and he didn't come all this way to get slaughtered.

But even as the situation looked grim, Thorton's mind was already running with escape strategies. Push came to shove, he'd make a break for the river, trusting in the zombies' aversion to water and get himself away from the killing. If he had to leave his men to die, so be it. He'd been on his own before and managed pretty well.

The trucks reached the edge of the bridge and Thorton immediately saw a problem. The bridge was blocked by three cars that looked like they had wanted to all get through at the same time. They could clear the cars, but that meant they had to use up precious minutes to do so and they didn't have seconds to spare.

Thorton was about to order the private to ram his way through, when the private spoke up.

"Sir. Why don't we take the tracks, sir? Our wheels are large enough and there's enough clearance under the trucks to pass over the rails."

Thorton looked quickly and saw it was possible. "Do it, corporal."

"Sir, I'm just a private, sir."

"Not anymore. Now get us across!" The zombie horde, over four hundred strong, began their pre-slaughter groaning and wheezing, since they were only two hundred feet away. In the last truck in the line, the men were scrambling to get weapons and magazines ready. They hadn't received the order to fire, but if it was them or the zombies, they were going to sell their lives dearly.

Fortunately, the trucks began to roll away from the stoppage and over to the railroad tracks that ran parallel to the highway bridge crossing the river. It was one of those old iron trestles, rusty brown and black. Corporal Halleman eased the first trunk onto the tracks at the crossing, being careful not to go too fast and bounce themselves right off the bridge. The train bridge was not much wider than the trucks, but since the trucks had to drive over the rails, the left tires were inches away from falling off the bridge.

Halleman opened his door and slowly worked his way over the river, just watching the railroad ties and his front tire. The truck driver behind him did the same thing, followed in turn by the last truck.

The men in the last truck were at their wits end. They had watched helplessly as the zombie horde had nearly caught them once and while the first two trucks were slowly getting onto the tracks, the zombies were coming for them again. At the last second, when the first decayed hand reached for the truck, the vehicle lurched forward, moving onto the tracks. The men watched the zombies give chase, then cheered when they saw the zombies couldn't navigate the railroad tracks. The first two to try it tumbled and fell down the hilly slope to the water's edge. The next few to try were a little luckier, but they also fell. As the trucks moved away, the soldiers began to relax, unclenching their rifles and letting out long breaths of relief. More than one commented on the need to change their shorts.

The lead truck made its way slowly across the river and Thorton found himself studying the town across the bridge. In the background rose the foothills of the Appalachian Mountains and Thorton knew his road was nearly at an end.

Bumping off the rails, Major Thorton and his men took a break, stretching out and looking back the way they had come. The zombies kept trying to cross the railroad bridge and they fell and were washed away by the river. The ones who didn't fall off were stuck in between the ties and had no way of figuring out how to get out.

As the men stretched and eased cramped muscles, the idle chatter began to die away as they looked around. The city was quiet, but every man there felt like they were being watched. Idle bits of debris lay scattered about and the papers picked up by the small breeze seemed unnaturally loud. Nervous hands held ready rifles and the men slowly spread out, guns at the ready. No threat was imminent, nothing manifested itself as danger, but in every man some forgotten instinct was screaming danger.

Thorton felt it himself, but he didn't see it as an immediate danger. It was more of a palpable sense of death and decay. The men had crossed the river and were headed into the Appalachians and that was the barrier that kept back the worst of the darkness.

This land is dead. He thought. *All of it. No one escaped.* He couldn't help himself from these dark thoughts, so pervasive was the feeling of dread.

After a minute he shook his head to clear it and growled at his men. "Get back in the trucks. There's nothing here. Stay sharp." Thorton climbed back into his truck and the engines roared to life.

The convoy moved quickly through the city of Parkersburg, avoiding pockets of zombies that came out to play. This city looked long abandoned to the dead, having been overrun a long time ago. Outside of the city the convoy drove under Interstate 77, still full of rusting and abandoned cars. They had to make a small detour around a jam of about thirty cars. These people tried to get off the interstate and wound up causing an accident that stranded motorists for miles.

Thorton was daydreaming when he thought he saw a flash in between the trees on the north side of the road. He motioned for the driver to turn off the main road. "Thought I saw something. Turn here," he said.

Corporal Halleman complied. A small sign for a subdivision pointed the way and Thorton motioned to follow the road to see where it led. He was hoping for a secluded area where he and his men could set up shop for the night.

What he didn't expect to find was a living community. As they approached the main entrance, Thorton could see several curious onlookers coming out of their homes. The trucks stopped at the gate, which was just a series of chain-link fences lashed together. Thorton though he saw something orange in the trees and when he looked closer, he saw that the people had used the trees as fence posts and had strung up dozens of electrical extension cords as a fence. That was probably the smartest thing he had seen in a while.

He stepped out of the vehicle and approached the gate, noting the two men with shotguns sitting in the beds of large pickup trucks. Those men would already be under the aim of surreptitious guns from the trucks, so he had nothing to worry about. A young man around thirty came forward and Thorton noticed he was wearing a sidearm, a revolver of some type.

"Are you in charge?" Thorton asked as the man approached the gate.

"Yes. Name's Bob Gull." The man was thin but muscular, with graying brown hair and tired blue eyes.

"Major Thorton. Do you mind if my men come through your gate?" Ken asked politely.

"Hell, I never figured to see military again. Come on in. You can park them right over there." He indicated a spot up the street.

The trucks came through the gate and parked over where they were supposed to. The men got out and formed loose groups, awaiting orders. About fifty people were gathering around the area, which looked to be something of a small crossroads.

Major Thorton waved Bob Gull over and the two men walked slowly together down the center street. Thorton was looking things over as he talked to Bob. Already he had seen several women that interested him and a young girl that especially caught his attention. She was a pretty brunette of about thirteen years of age. *Perfect,* Ken thought. Out loud, he said, "Have to admit I didn't think anything would be back here."

Bob Gull shrugged. "That's probably what saved us. People who didn't live around here passed us by and as the years started to go by, we saw less and less of them."

"What about zombies?" Thorton asked, still walking.

"We still get a few from the city, but not as many as we used to. We've been expanding our fence a little each week and we just managed to enclose a pond nearby. Sure was nice not to have to climb the hills for water." Bob Gull chuckled.

Thorton managed a smile. "How many people do you have here? I'm trying to get a tally for the rest of the survivors."

"Right now we have sixty-seven. Sixty-eight if you count the woman who's pregnant as two."

"I will. What about supplies, weapons, that sort of thing, how are you situated?"

"We make runs to the city for supplies and such, but we've had to expand a little since some stuff has been running out. We have a few weapons and are really short on ammo. Could use some if you have it to spare. We've been trying to kill zombies with just hand weapons, lately."

Thorton stopped in his walk and turned around to look at Bob. "Perfect." was all he said.

Chapter 2

We left the two of Thorton's men swinging in the breeze. Nate merely looked at them and grunted and Tommy just smiled and shook his head. Duncan was trying to look tough for Janna, but she was busy poring over the maps to pay him much mind.

I wasn't as badly beaten as I had thought, apparently I had managed to block most of Kazinski's punches or roll with them when they got through my defenses. When you're used to not getting hit, the actual experience tends to make you exaggerate. I didn't think at all about killing those men, they would have killed us and worse, given the chance.

We moved ahead on Route 50, but after a brief bit of driving, I announced to the crew that we were going to spend the day at rest as soon as I could find a decent spot. I had seen the haggard look on everyone's faces and the events of the last day really were taking a toll. We had been through the wringer and I couldn't just throw the team back into the fray without some sort of rest, be it physical or mental.

No one argued with me, so when I saw the sign for Blennerhasset Island, I figured it would be as good a place as any. We crossed the river and I followed a service road onto the island. The gate read 'No Trespassing', but I gently nudged the RV through, not worrying too much about the paint job. I followed the service road for about three hundred yards, then parked the RV in a grove of trees.

I looked back at Janna and said, "What kind of space have we got here?" She looked at me quizzically until Duncan pointed at the map.

"He's asking how big the island is and if there are any more roads." Duncan clarified.

"Ohh, okay. Hold on." Janna flipped through a map and found a detailed section to look over. She did some mental calculation and said. "According to the scale, it's about three miles long, kind of shaped like a wasp."

I looked over at Tommy and Nate. "Works for me. You want scouting duty or water supply?"

Nate stood up and stretched his big arms. "You can walk. I'll get the water. Duncan, you and Janna are on gun cleanup duty. Tommy, you better go with John in case he falls down or something." Nate's eyes twinkled and I blew a raspberry at him.

"Don't get too wet, Granny," I said, placing my M1A on the table alongside the other weapons Duncan was piling up. Janna just looked wide eyed at the weaponry and turned a cocked head at me.

"Where'd you guys get all the guns?" she asked, picking up my SIG. I had an identical one in my holster, only this one was made of stainless steel. It was heavier than my familiar one, but it handled recoil better.

"Pickups from dead homes and towns, mostly." Duncan said, breaking out the cleaning kits. "Sometimes we trade for them. Depends."

"Do a lot of the people you meet have guns?" she asked, as Tommy and I got ready to scout.

"Fact is," I said, "the people most likely to survive the Upheaval had guns or were familiar with them before it all went south. So to answer your question, yes, most of them do."

"We're an armed, polite society now," Duncan said, pulling the rear pin on an AR, opening the rifle.

Janna smiled while Tommy and I exited the RV. Nate had already gathered all the gallon jugs for refilling and was making his way to the river. He had four in each hand and more tucked under his arms. If he fell in now, he'd float to New Orleans before we could get him out.

Outside the RV, Tommy looked West and pointed out a line of smoke rising into the sky. It was thick and black and could be seen for miles.

"Wonder what idiot started that?" Tommy said.

I shrugged. "Not sure, but if they wanted to call in every zombie in the area, that's one way to do it."

"Should we investigate?"

I considered it for a second. "Not really our problem. I'd hate for it to be a fire started by some stupid cat in a tire store and we go charging in to face hundreds of zombies for nothing."

"Suits me. I hate backtracking."

Tommy and I walked slowly along the service road, letting the sun shine on our faces and breathing in the river air that moved through the trees. I wasn't carrying anything heavy, just my SIG and my pickaxe. Tommy was similarly attired. We were taking a chance, but since this was an island and the river was fairly swift at this junction, I wasn't too worried about roaming zombies. If the water was shallow, like parts of the Missouri River, then I'd be more cautious, since the zombies could fairly walk across in dry weather. But since this was Ohio and it rained regularly, then the river was faster and deeper.

We walked across a cleared area, just starting to be regained by the vegetation. A small group of trees were clustered around the barely visible service road, so we couldn't see anything beyond. On either side of us we could hear the river moving past and the thrum of insects and frogs became background noise to the walk.

Tommy and I didn't speak, we just kept ourselves to our own thoughts as we walked along. We'd been through enough that we didn't feel the need to blather on all day. Besides, if there were zombies about, two idiots discussing the weather would draw them like flies.

We moved cautiously through the trees and stopped as we took in the scene before us. Freshly tilled earth, in a swath a thousand feet long and five hundred feet wide, stretched from tree line to tree line. Whoever had done this had spent a good deal of time on it, as evidenced by the scarecrow in the field, standing guard over precious seeds.

"Okay. Well, that answers my first question," Tommy said.

"Yes?" I prompted.

"Is this island inhabited?"

"I'd say so. I wonder what we might find behind door number two?" I pointed to the edge of the field, where two openings could be seen, one going north and one going south.

"One way to find out," Tommy said.

"Yep. Here we go." I loosed my SIG in its holster, just in case. I called back to the RV with the radio and let Duncan know we probably weren't alone on the island and to look sharp.

Tommy and I walked around the plowed field, noting that the regularity of the plowing meant that whoever had done this was using farm equipment and not doing it by hand. We reached the far edge and decided to take the south path first. I pointed out to Tommy that the service road had gotten a lot better. At this point it was paved, with a faint yellow line running along the edges.

We strolled easily on the road and peeked through the south opening of the trees and were surprised to be greeted by a large Holstein cow. The big grass eater was munching long stems along the fence by the road and paused to look us over with her big brown eyes before deciding we were harmless. Our sudden appearance woke up several other bovine ladies who wandered by for a closer look. Tommy patted one on the nose and gave the wooden fence a slight shove. The boards held, but a cow could easily break down a section.

"Smart thinking," he said critically.

"What's that?" I said as I counted fifteen cows.

"The fence is strong enough to keep a zombie from breaking it down, but if the cows were ever attacked, they could break out and escape if need be," Tommy said.

"Wonder what we'll see on the north side." I asked, curious about the caretakers of this island.

We moved quickly, our curiosity moving our feet a little faster than normal. When we emerged from the trees, we were somewhat disappointed to see just a field, but it was apparent this was a grazing land for the cows, rotated so the grass didn't get overgrazed.

"Okay, well, the last place to look would be down the road to Grandma's house," Tommy said.

I looked where he was pointing and the road went due East, disappearing into the woods. Trees lined the road and it had an almost claustrophobic feel to it. I pulled my pickaxe out and kept it in hand, just in case. Tommy saw my move and mirrored it. I doubted we would see any undead on this island, but sometimes you just never knew.

I don't know what I expected to see when we reached the far opening. At most, I figured we might see a caretaker's house, since the service road must have been built for somebody. But since I didn't know anything about this area or this island, everything was a guess.

After a brief walk, we came on to what seemed to actually be a caretaker's house on the left side of the road. It was a large, two story affair, with a couple of sheds near the road. A brief look showed the house to be in pretty good shape, surrounded by thick woods. It would be hard for zombies to storm the place, if they could ever get across the river in force. But since they couldn't, this would make a decent place to hole up for a while. But as interesting as the house was, it didn't answer the question as to who plowed the field and who was taking care of the cows.

What was even more interesting was the white face staring down at Tommy and myself as we goggled around the front yard. Just as I looked up, the face vanished and I turned back to Tommy.

"Did you see that?" I asked, pointing at the house.

Tommy shook his head. "No, what did you see? Z?"

"Not sure, but given how fast it disappeared, I'd say it was alive," I said, staring hard at the house, trying to pull up my x-ray vision superpower. No luck.

"Investigate?"

"Not yet. I want to finish looking this island over. We can come back in a minute."

We left the house and its mysterious occupant and continued down the road. Three hundred feet further, there was a clearing on the left, which wasn't interesting, but through the thinning of the trees, I could see another house and that *was* interesting. My initial glimpse was the house was huge, which really threw me for a loop. What it was doing here and who built it were relevant questions.

We walked a bit more and seeing a walkway conveniently placed, we moved out onto a decently manicured lawn. A large white building was to our left, connected by an open-air walkway to a large mansion. A second open-air walkway connected to another outbuilding and my first impression of the building was it reminded me of Mount Vernon, George Washington's home in Virginia. In fact, if I had to guess, this home was built to resemble Washington's home, so close they were in appearance.

Tommy whistled appreciatively, since neither he nor I had expected to see such a structure out here on an island. But it just goes to show that in this country, surprises lay around every turn.

Which is one of the reasons I wanted to save it so badly, needed to save it from the likes of Thorton.

"I wonder if anyone's home?" I asked, starting towards the front door, but Tommy held out a hand.

"I'd say so," he said ominously, pointing to the second floor.

I looked. "Oh."

There were four windows on the top floor that faced the front and in every one of them, a rifle was sticking out, pointed in our direction. We were in a bad spot and would quickly be cut down if we tried to run or fight.

I put my hands on my hips to assess the situation, but in truth I was turning on my radio and locking the 'send' button. The rest of the crew would be able to hear me and take whatever necessary action needed. I hoped it wouldn't be for revenge.

I tried diplomacy. I raised my hands to chest level and called out. "Hello the house! My name is John Talon and I would like to talk to the man or woman in charge!"

After a few seconds a voice called out. "Why are you here? What do you want?"

I called back. "I just want to talk. Nothing more."

A small, thickset man with dark curly hair opened the main door and stepped out onto the small porch under the front door awning. "If you just want to talk, drop your weapons and come forward."

"No," I said quickly.

"What?" The man was startled and began to get red-faced. Clearly he had not been challenged much in his life.

"I said no, I'm not dropping my weapons. I don't mean you or yours any harm, I just want to talk," I said. I could see some of the rifles shift a bit as the hidden marksmen absorbed my words.

"You plan on dying on my lawn? I can have my people shoot you and your friend down right now." The man seemed sure of himself and I got the impression he might have given the order a few times in the past.

"That's true, you could. But you should know that I take a good deal of killing and I'll surely get one or two of your people before I'm cashed. And for sure I'll kill you first, mister. That much I can guarantee." I decided to match him bluster for bluster.

Well, I could tell he didn't like that at all, since he was as exposed as I was. I had shifted my hands downward and they were on my hips again, just an inch from my gun. I knew from practice I could get that gun out in a hurry. Actually hitting a target from that distance with a quick draw was another matter, but I wasn't about to admit that to this guy.

"You got sand, pal," he said brusquely. "All right. Come up to the house. Let's palaver."

Tommy tapped my arm and mouthed, "Palaver?" as we walked up to the front door. I noted the rifles had withdrawn from the windows. Doubtless the bodyguards would be in force when we reached the main entrance.

I chuckled. "I have a feeling about this. Let me do the talking. Keep your eyes on the guards."

Tommy nodded as we approached the front door. The house was big, but not on the scale of some later generational mansions. But in its day, I'm sure it was amazing.

We stepped inside the main entrance hall and were immediately struck by the simple beauty of the building. A large stairwell arched upwards to the second floor, while a dramatic fireplace dominated the room. Antique furnishings completed the picture and I was admiring the mantle work when a gruff voice called us into the room on the south side of the building. Two stone-faced men with hunting rifles met us and gave us hard stares until a voice called from the other room.

"In here!"

I smiled at Tommy and our bodyguards and went through a small doorway to a huge banquet room. Dark walnut paneling gave the room a gloomy look, even though light spilled through a south window. A large table was set up in the middle of the floor, while a couple of couches kept vigil against the north wall. Large bookcases lined the back wall and I could see a large collection of Louis L'Amour books, confirming my suspicions about this man's nature and mannerisms.

The man himself sat at the head of the table, with two men situated behind him. The men looked uncomfortable in their roles, but I suspected they were ordered to be there as a show of force. The head guy was unremarkable physically, but his eyes were another matter. They were fiercely blue and intense enough to make you uncomfortable. I got the impression this was a man used to getting his own way, lording it over his people like a feudal baron. In all honesty, I didn't care what he did. But to his point of view, I was trespassing and needed his permission to continue on his land.

I started the ball, taking control of the conversation like I used to do when I was an administrator in another life, keeping an unruly parent off balance. "Name's John Talon. I have a crew with me on the other side of this island. We had a run in with a group of men who are intent on destroying the Constitution and Bill of Rights. They're led by a murderer named Thorton, travelling like military, even though they're not. We're on our way to D.C. to stop them and take the documents to a safe place."

Those blue eyes stared at me for a minute. "I'm Ed Mulvaney. When the shit went down I took what was mine and made a run for this island. Took several people with me and we spent the first year fighting off the zombies and other riffraff. Spent the next year getting this place where we could actually live without the danger of killing a zombie for breakfast every day.

"We watched Parkersburg turn into a dead zone, but managed to keep ourselves safe. We don't need anyone or anything." His tone was belligerent and I couldn't figure out why, but managed it when he said. "I fought for this island and don't plan on giving it up without a fight!"

I saw where he was coming from. He probably figured someone would tell him he couldn't keep the place he fought for and wanted to make sure we knew he would fight.

I tried diplomacy. "Mr. Mulvaney, I'm not interested in your island. Fact is, if I was to tell you that you had no right to be here I'd be the worst kind of hypocrite. If you've made a life here you've certainly earned it. But I have to tell you one thing. When I secure the founding documents and make sure they're safe, we're putting together a new government, with new laws. As a citizen of this country, those laws will apply to you."

His response didn't surprise me. Ed banged the table and shouted, "I'm the law here! What I say goes or it doesn't go. That's it! You got that, Talon?"

I stayed calm. "I'm not interfering in how you run your affairs. If the people around you are interested in staying with you and are willing to conform to your rules, fine. But," I said, hardening my tone, "You will abide by the laws that will be set forth by the convention we will be having shortly. This country will not fall into a bunch of feudal lands ruled by miniature kings. Once we finish our work out here, we will be gearing up to wage war on the zombies. You will be expected to comply." I never broke eye contact and it was clear he didn't like being spoken to in that manner. But I meant every word and he knew it.

Ed grumped mightily. "How are you going to enforce your laws? I could gun you down right now and no one would do anything about it." He was playing a bluff hand, but he was game.

I put the radio on the table. "Once these guys are done with you, I imagine there wouldn't be much left. Right, Duncan?"

Duncan's voice crackled through loud and clear. "Say the word and we'll clean house right now, boss."

Ed jumped as the voice sounded loudly in the hall. He probably thought Tommy and I were just drifters. I finished his argument for him.

"Mr. Mulvaney, right now we are facing over two hundred and fifty million zombies, give or take a million. I need every hand I can get to start the fight to wipe them clean off the map and make this country run again. I need independent men like you to help put things in order. With so many dead, there's land to spare. Why the hell should I care about your little island when I can claim millions of acres elsewhere? If you want a fight, fine, I can get two hundred men here in three weeks and we'll shove your island up your ass. But I'd rather have your help."

Ed looked shocked, then deflated. He was up against it and his bluster was not going to cut it this time. He glared at me. "I can keep this land and house, long as I follow your laws?"

I knew when to be gracious. "I never wanted them. You earned them. But I could use your help with the coming fight. Can I count on you and yours to lend a hand?"

Ed nodded. "Done. You need supplies or anything?"

I shook my head. "We're good, thanks." I was grateful not to have to fight this old bird or his brood. They looked capable, although how much actual fighting they have done staying on this island was anyone's guess. I did have a question, though.

"Ed, there might be some men who are following us and they are not to be trusted. They look like military, but they're not. Are you able to handle a serious assault?"

Ed looked at me funny and said, "I think you're a little late, son. We saw what looked like a military convoy pass by earlier this morning. They barely got away from the dead at Parkersburg, driving across the railroad bridge."

Inwardly, I cursed. I was hoping we were much further ahead of Thorton than a few hours. This was going to make things harder to say the least.

"That was them. Glad they passed you by. We need to get going then, it was a pleasure to meet all of you." I stood up, ending the conversation.

Ed stood and spoke up. "Where's your convention going to be and who can go?" he asked, hooking his big hands into his belt.

I turned to the door. "Leport, in Illinois. We'll be meeting in the fall, if we finish this business first. You're welcome, or one of your folks here."

Ed nodded. "That'll do. We'll get a say on the laws?"

It was my turn to nod. "We'll vote on the big ones, majority rules." I actually hadn't thought that far ahead, but it made sense.

"Good enough. We'll be there." Ed came around the table and held out his hand.

I shook it, appreciating the gesture. "Ask for Nate. He'll set you up. Now, we need to get going. Thanks for your hospitality."

"Anytime." Mulvaney seemed genuinely pleased by the outcome of the meeting and I figured he would. There wasn't a need to fight, he keeps his land and can help rebuild a country. A win all around.

Stepping out on the lawn, Tommy pointed to a thin column of smoke rising from the east. From this distance, it looked to be small, but the roiling of the smoke at the base told me it was a decent fire and was far enough away to look small.

"Thorton, you think?" Tommy asked.

"No idea," I said, but inside I had a feeling we were on a collision course.

As we headed back onto the roads that would take us to the RV, my radio suddenly spoke up.

"Hey John?" It was Duncan.

"Yeah, what's up?"

"We got company. Watch yourselves if you're coming back now."

"Live?"

"Nope."

"Everyone okay? How many?" I got concerned, since Nate had gone to the river virtually unarmed.

Duncan laughed. "About fifteen. Yeah, we're fine, but Nate's pissed."

"Why?"

Duncan was cryptic. "You'll see. I'm going to head up top and...dammit!" I heard a loud banging and awful groaning in the background.

"Duncan? Duncan?" I shouted into the radio.

A full minute passed and Tommy and I exchanged some concerned looks. The radio popped again.

"All right, we're good. Sucker just surprised me. I may not be going up top. Good luck. See you. Duncan out."

I exhaled slowly and Tommy and I both started walking quickly back towards the RV. I felt very underpowered, having left my heavy weapons back in the RV. But, I had faced hordes before with just my pick, so I needed to see the situation before I got depressed about it. Besides, I was curious as hell over why Nate was pissed.

As we jogged along the service road, throwing a wave to the curious cows, I said to Tommy, "Frozen zombies."

Tommy nearly stumbled as my words registered. "W-What?"

"Frozen zombies. Living things, even slightly living, shouldn't be able to freeze solid in the winter then reanimate when they warm up. Throws your theory out the window," I said smugly.

"Ever heard of carpenter ants?" Tommy said.

"Yeah, used to kill a dozen or so after every rainfall. So?"

Tommy smiled. "They have a natural antifreeze that keeps them from freezing and dying. Virus could do the same for vital systems. Extremities could be allowed to freeze, but the brain and heart could still be active."

I hated to say it made sense, but then walking corpses defied logic so here we are in Ohio. Whatever sense *that* made.

We passed the tilled fields and made our way into the woods. After a couple hundred feet I could hear the telltale sign of zombies. The groaning was loud and persistent, like they had treed their prey and were frustrated it wouldn't politely come down and be eaten.

We approached the small glade of trees that surrounded the RV and I wasn't looking forward to a fight in the woods. Trees and branches had an irritating habit of tangling up your weapons, getting in your line of sight and making you trip when you least could afford to. I inched forward with my SIG out and Tommy was about fifteen feet to my left, moving slowly with his Glock.

As we got closer, I could finally see the situation clearly. There were about ten zombies milling about the RV, while over by the side of the river I could see five more standing, shifting from side to side, groaning their heads off and raising their arms up and down in an attempt to get at what was in the river.

When I saw Nate I burst out laughing. Tommy looked at me like I was nuts, but when he saw Nate he started to laugh, too. Nate was standing in the river, with the empty gallon jugs around his waist, cursing and fuming at the Z's waiting for him on the side of the water. The jugs made it look like he was wearing a big plastic tutu and any minute I expected him to pirouette out of the water to bust on some undead ass.

Our humor was short-lived. The second I made a sound, three of the zombies turned and spotted me. As soon as they made eye contact they moaned loudly and started for me. The movement made the rest turn and they started for me as well. Well, it was bound to happen sooner or later.

I waved Tommy to the woods on his side and stepped back into the woods on my side. I pulled the radio and got hold of Duncan.

"Duncan?"

"Yeah, John?"

"Tommy and I will deal with ones by the RV, when we get them clear, take care of the ones by Nate. You probably won't be able to shoot from the roof, so you and Janna will have to get out there and take them down," I said, stepping back deeper into the brush.

"Will do. Watch yourself." Duncan signed off.

"You too." This was going to be hard. We couldn't use guns because we wouldn't be sure of where any of the crew was so we couldn't risk a shot. It was old fashioned hand-to-hand with the undead. Strangely, I was clam about it, just accepting it as a job to do and nothing more. Once upon a time it was hard for me to kill them because I would think about who they might have been, where they might have come from, whether or not they might have loved ones holding out hope they might see them alive again. Now I didn't care. They were the enemy and I had a job to do.

I backed deeper into the woods, hoping I could draw most of them in, letting Tommy take a few out from the rear. But it didn't last long when a fresh chorus of groans signaled that Tommy had been spotted. That was good news and bad news. Bad news was my plan for a rear attack just fell apart. The good news was some of the ones following me were now after Tommy and the odds just got better.

I'll take what I could get. I shifted my grip on my pickaxe and made sure I had swinging room as the first zombie stumbled into view. They had a rough time of it, since the woods had gotten somewhat overgrown and tangled their legs up somewhat. I'm sure they'd complain to Mulvaney if they could

The Z, a guy who looked to be roughly my age, came bouncing off a small tree on my right. I swung hard and brought the semi-pointed end down right on the top of his head. The metal cracked through the skull without much resistance and scrambled his eggs but good. He dropped with an exaggerated sigh and I readied for the next zombie, a fat guy with no shirt on and large open wounds on his big stomach. The wounds leaked a nasty black fluid which I was sure was all bad news. I brought the pick around in a baseball swing and cracked a home run on his temple. He spun around and I was treated to a view of his back, which was missing so much flesh I could see his stretched rib cage. I guess when he bought it he was face down and revived after the zombies had chewed him for a bit. It was still gross.

I turned around and walked twenty feet deeper into the woods, then turned at a right angle and moved ten more feet away. Two more zombies were crashing towards me and I wanted to make things more difficult.

The first one was a young blonde woman, who looked like she might have turned fairly recently. Her skin was not yet fully grey and her eyes were clear. She opened her mouth and moaned as she grasped at air, trying to reach me. Her companion, a gent probably in his sixties, dressed like a businessman except without shoes, came from completely the opposite side.

They were coming at me at the same time, so I couldn't get one without the other getting to me. I couldn't back up any more, because the underbrush had gotten thick enough that even I couldn't push through it. Nothing to be done then. My timing was going to have to be perfect. The woman was slightly faster, so I had a second to deal with the man.

I raised the pickaxe high and the second she was in range, brought it crashing down on her head. I left it in her skull as she tumbled to the side and spun around to face the other zombie. My right hand was pulling my knife as I turned and I brought up the blade from my waist. The zombie arms were inches from my shoulders when I lunged, slamming the knife up under the chin and puncturing the brain pan. The zombie's arms stayed outstretched for a long second, frozen as the brain stopped sending signals to them. Slowly the man fell back, my blade sliding out of his chin with a wet sound. He fell straight like a tree, landing on a rock and looking for all the world like he was sleeping.

I wiped my blade off on his coat sleeve and went to get my pick. The woman had died less peacefully, her features were frozen in a mix of hate and hunger. It was pitiful to look at, but she was in a better place now, anyway. I put my foot on her head and braced it, taking the top of the handle in one hand and knocking the blade out of her skull with the other. It reminded me of removing an axe from a stubborn tree. The things you think of these days.

No more threats were nearby, so I started to venture out of the woods. As I moved to less undergrowth, a tree trunk suddenly exploded in front of me, just as I heard a shot coming from Tommy's neck of the woods. I ducked instinctively, cursing and ran forward to get out of the line of fire. The last thing I needed was to get shot by one of my own crew members.

As I stumbled out of the woods, I ran right into another zombie. I hit it so hard I knocked it over, sending in back onto its butt while its arms flailed in the air. The momentum laid it out completely and I used the opportunity to stand on its chest and spike its head. The arms grasping at my legs fell away and I looked to see three more coming at me from the water where Nate was starting to come out of the river.

They were bunched together, making it difficult to single them out for destruction, but I had a plan for that. Grabbing the zombie I had knocked over by the collar of his shirt, I waited until they were in range, then swung the body like a dead cat. I hurled the corpse at the other three and managed to knock down two of them. The third came at a rush and I spun away, letting it pass by. I swung my pickaxe around and buried the flat end in the back of its skull. It fell with a croak and I faced the other two that were starting to get up.

Not wasting an opportunity, I walked over to one and kicked it over, stepping away from the hands that tried to grab my ankles. I stabbed the zombie that was on its hands and knees in the back of its neck, shutting it down, then swung my pick at the Z that was starting to sit up. My spike went into the temple and buried itself to the shaft. Glazed eyes rolled up as the zombie fell over.

I scanned the area and watched as Nate dealt with the last zombie. Dripping water, he simply walked up to it, kicked it in the chest, knocking it to the ground. When it sat up he kicked it in the head, putting it back down. While it was down he stomped on its neck, snapping it like a twig.

When it was over, he walked back to the river and collected his water jugs like nothing had happened. I chuckled and looked back to where Tommy was supposed to be and he stumbled out of the woods, dragging a zombie that had a grip on his leg. Tommy was dragging it along and the zombie was getting a full face plant in the dirt as it kept its mouth open to try and bite.

"Little help?" Tommy asked.

"Shoot it, doofus," I said, laughing at the scene.

"Can't, my gun's jammed and I can't stop to clear it," Tommy said apologetically.

"Oh. Hold on."

I walked over, picking up a small log on the ground. When I got close enough I swung the log with a heave and slammed it down onto the zombie's head. The log, which was rotten, promptly disintegrated and did no more damage than had I used a pillow.

"Are you kidding me?" Tommy asked as he continued to drag the zombie along.

"You could do this yourself, you know." I replied tartly as I brought up my pick and crushed the Z's skull. It released Tommy's ankle and lay face down in the grass.

"Do you see a weapon on me?" He replied, turning and walking back to the woods. I did see then that he was without his knife or melee weapon.

"Whose shot nearly took my head off?" I called over my shoulder as I surveyed the area around the RV. I didn't see any more zombies, but there may be more coming because of the noise.

I went over to the river to help Nate pick up the jugs of water. "We should probably get moving," I said, grabbing a handful of water.

"Why's that?" Nate asked, stringing a rope through the handles and heaving the jugs onto his shoulder.

"Guy I spoke to said he saw what was probably Thorton heading by a few hours ago," I said.

"Dammit! Thought we left that fool behind." Nate paused. "Wait, what guy?"

I spent the remainder of the walk to the RV explaining about Ed Mulvaney and what we talked about. When I finished, Nate simply shrugged his shoulders.

"He's got a nice setup; can't fault him for wanting to keep it. But if there's a dead town right across the river, he should want to start clearing it out. But if he falls in line, he'll probably make a good ally. This would be a good spot as a jumping off point for an eastern campaign," Nate said while he looked around. Tommy was emerging from the woods as we spoke.

"You volunteering for general work?" I teased, knowing Nate was as keen to get home as I was.

"Leave it for the young bucks," Nate said. "Speaking of which…" Nate climbed into the RV and I could hear Duncan squawk and Janna laugh as Nate dumped forty pounds of water jugs on him.

I went to the back of the RV and grabbed the spray bottle, using it to clean off my weapons. Tommy joined me as I was finishing and began spraying and burning his own.

"We headed out soon?" He asked.

"Yeah, we need to keep moving," I said, looking at the sky. "Hopefully, we'll find a place as nice as this before dark." The sun was well past the high mark and we had probably four hours of daylight left. It was enough to get rolling and find a place to hole up.

Inside the RV, I was going to ask Duncan why he didn't get up to the roof and lend a hand, but when I saw the pile of disassembled guns, I figured I knew what the answer was. Nate got up in the driver's seat and I waved him to get moving. Tommy and I got out of our gear and stowed it where it belonged.

As I sat heavily at the table, Janna spoke.

"Where to now?" she wanted to know.

I sat back and closed my eyes. "We need to move quickly. I was hoping to stay ahead of Thorton, but he was closer than we thought and actually managed to get ahead of us." I blew a long sigh at the ceiling. "We can't survive another ambush. Hopefully, he thinks we're still ahead of him."

Janna was quiet for a minute. "I saw you out there fighting. You're pretty good." Duncan looked up briefly from a gun but said nothing.

I shrugged. "These days, it's what I do."

"Well, you do pretty well."

I looked at her. "After the way you took out that Milovich guy, I'd say you do well enough by yourself."

Janna beamed and began reassembling a rifle.

CHAPTER 3

We rumbled out through the gate, pausing briefly to reattach the gate with some zip ties. There were some more zombies on the bridge and I figured Mulvaney didn't need surprises like that. We followed Route 50 and rolled past some suburbs that looked normal on the surface, but a closer inspection showed a lot of zombie activity. Route 50 was joined by 68 and we had to navigate around a few abandoned cars, but nothing too difficult.

When we reached Nemesis Park, the two roads split and 68 went through Parkersburg while 50 went east. Across the river I could see hundreds of zombies lurking about and every once in a while one with better vision would follow our progress on the road. I contemplated setting a fire just to make the job easier in the future, but Thorton would know we were behind him then. Given the terrain of trees and hills, I didn't want snipers around every turn.

We crossed the river again and rolled past some subdivisions and strip malls. Everything was a mess. This area looked like it had been hit hard, then hit again. I doubted there would have been anything of value and doubted even more that we might have found anyone alive.

We travelled under the I-77 interstate bridge and moved past rusting cars and trucks. There were huge scorch marks on the bridge, suggesting at one time there was a serious fire which blocked the way. Heck of a choice. Get burned alive or eaten alive.

"John, you want to see this." Nate's voice from the front of the RV interrupted my thoughts.

I pulled myself to the passenger seat and looked out. I could see the column of smoke very clearly; whatever was causing it was still burning well. It was very close, as a matter of fact. We could find the source fairly quickly. I nodded to Nate.

"Let's see what it is, doesn't look like we'll be too off base if we investigate," I said.

Nate nodded and began looking for roads that would take us closer. A side road looked promising, so we turned down Red Hill Road. A few hundred feet took us to another turn, which seemed likely to take us right to the source of the fire.

We rounded the bend and drove up what looked like the entrance to a subdivision. There were large homes on either side of a center lane and a gate had been placed across the road. Forest surrounded the homes and in the trees ropes or cables had been used to create an effective barrier to any wandering zombies. Whoever lived here had kept an eye on the long haul. The thing that was odd was there didn't seem to be any guards and the gate was wide open.

Nate looked at me and I shrugged, figuring we might be able to puzzle it out by looking around a bit. One of the houses was ablaze, the source of the fire, but the homes were far enough apart that no other dwellings were in danger. I put my gear back on, loading up more on ammo than before and bringing my heavy rifle with me. Tommy, Duncan, and Nate all suited up as well and Janna belted on a pistol, too.

The minute I stepped outside, I could feel it. I looked back and could see the others sensed it as well. It wasn't a feeling of immediate danger, but it was an overall oppressive feeling. I got the sense that once we crossed the mountains the feeling was going to get worse.

We spread out and approached the open gate and Tommy was the first one to speak. "Anybody else feel that?"

Duncan replied, "Like we just walked into a graveyard?"

"Exactly," Janna said.

It was then I realized what it was. We did just walk into a graveyard, only it was the entire east coast. This land was dead. It was owned by the dead and they were its masters. Everything felt like a threat. The hairs on the back of my neck stood out so much I was amazed they didn't fly off and imbed themselves into the nearby trees.

"Tommy and Duncan, check the tree line. Janna and Nate, check the houses. I'm going to look over the fire. I'll see you in a minute."

A chorus of 'Roger that' hit my ears and they were off. Duncan and Tommy split up to take either side and in seconds they had disappeared. Janna and Nate went to the first house across the street from the burning one and went inside. I approached the burning building and looked it over, trying to see what might have caused the fire.

I didn't see anything out of the ordinary until I worked my way around to the other side of the house. There, in the grass was a man lying face down, badly burned.

I rushed over to him and saw that he had been shot as well. This was a bad sign. I began to turn him over when he cried out in pain. I was so startled I nearly fell over.

"Hang on. I'm going to try to get you away from the flames." I tried to grab unburned parts of his arms and managed to pull him further away from the fire. His face was contorted in pain and tears streamed down his cheeks. I turned him over and tried to give him some water. He pushed my hand away and tried to speak.

"Kids…kids…" he whispered.

"Were there kids in there?" I asked, looking back at the flame-engulfed house. I didn't have any hope of rescuing anyone from there.

He shook his head slightly. "Last…last… house."

I had no idea what he was talking about. I stayed with him until I saw Nate and called him over. Nate came running and when he saw the man he cursed.

"He says there's kids in the last house, I think," I said. "Check fast, there may be trouble."

Nate nodded and waved Janna over and together they ran up the street. I looked back down and saw the man was trying to speak again.

"Killed… all of… got… them… back." He spasmed in pain and it seemed like he passed out. I thought he might have passed away, but he opened his eyes and in a fit of strength grasped my hand. "Save them! Save… us…" His eyes closed and his hand fell away. A second later a rattling breath escaped his burned lips as his head turned away.

I had seen death enough to know when a soul was gone. I gently laid him down and looked back at the burning building. The flames were dying down and through the broken windows I could see several blackened forms scattered about in the rooms.

The fire had not been kind and I stopped counting after I reached twenty. I walked away from the man and the fire, silently saying a prayer for the dead. I wasn't much of a man for religion, but after what these people went through, I hoped they had some peace somewhere.

I walked out to the street and tried to figure out what the man had been talking about. 'Got them back' made no sense, how might he have gotten revenge on his killers? Deep down, I knew who was responsible for this and I hoped one day soon there would be a reckoning.

"Holy Jesus." I looked up the street and the strangest procession was coming back at me. Janna was holding a baby and Nate was cradling two small children. Behind them a procession of seven kids followed, trailed by Duncan and Tommy. All four of my crew had on the most hardened expressions I had ever seen. If a zombie horde walked out of the woods at that moment I might have given them the option to run away before facing those four.

Before they reached me I could smell the gasoline and I suddenly understood what should have happened but by some miracle didn't. Inside I was filled with rage and despair. Right before they reached me, a small girl in the back, about eleven or twelve years old, suddenly bolted for the flaming house, screaming for her mother.

"No!" I yelled, trying to intercept her, but she slipped past and ran into that inferno. Her gas-soaked clothing burst into flame and in seconds she was a spinning, screaming ball of fire. She didn't last long and crumpled quickly to the ground, the flames turning her small body black and red.

I hung my head and tried to hold back the rage I was feeling. I couldn't let the killer loose. Not yet. I snarled and thought *Another debt to pay, Thorton. Even if this wasn't about the documents, I would hunt you down for what you've done!*

"We found them in the last house," Nate said, putting down the two little ones. They ran to a couple of older girls in the group who picked them up. "It looks like someone started a fire, but the kids managed to free themselves and put it out without getting hurt."

"Guess the parents weren't so lucky," I said. I pointed to the man on the ground. "Seems like he tried to make a break for the kids and was shot for his trouble. He died a few minutes ago. Said something about getting back at them, but I have no idea what that might mean.

"Let's get the kids cleaned up and see what they can tell us," I said, walking over to the children. I squatted down and looked at them. They all looked back with big frightened eyes. "My name is John. My friends and I are going to try and help you. You don't need to be scared anymore. I promise you no one will hurt you."

A little girl maybe four years old, detached herself and came over to me. She looked at my rifle and then turned big blue eyes on me. "Will the bad men stay away?" she asked, her eyes brimming with tears.

I put my rifle down and reached out to her. She came into my arms and I hugged her tight, ignoring the gas on her. "Sweetheart, bad men are afraid of me. *And if they're not, by God they will be.* You're safe." I looked up at all of the kids. "You're all safe now."

We spent a good deal of time getting clothes for the kids and getting them cleaned up. We searched each house for usable items and food and came away with a good supply of essentials. Janna took care of the baby and although I had a whole lot of experience in that arena, I didn't argue.

What we gathered from the older kids was a group of military looking men came to the subdivision and tricked everyone into letting them in. Once they were in, they shot the leader and herded all the kids into a house. They poured gas on the kids and around the house, telling the adults if they fought the kids would burn. The children had no idea what happened after that, although they heard a lot of screaming, yelling and laughing. The little girl who ran into the fire was brought to the house after the leader had been with her for a while, but they didn't know what had happened to her. She cried the whole time, they said and held her stomach like it hurt.

Someone started a fire but the older kids managed to free themselves and put it out. They were afraid to leave because the military men had said if anyone left they'd be shot.

"Sounds like Thorton, all right, ain't no way it could be anyone else," Tommy said in the little powwow we held at a house.

"I agree, it's his style," Nate growled. "Can't wait to kill those sons of bitches."

"One thing at a time. Question now is, what do we do about the kids?" Duncan asked, looking over at Janna who was feeding the baby. We had found the infant's house and supplies, so we were good to go for the little guy. Just seeing him reminded me of Jake and once again I quietly prayed my family was safe.

"We can't take them with us and we can't leave them here," I said. "We need to get them back to one of the communities where they will be taken care of."

Tommy thought that one over. "Okay, makes sense. How and who?"

I thought a minute. "A road trip is too dangerous and would take far too long. We need fast and safe."

"Like what?" Duncan asked.

"Well, the easiest way I can see is to send them on the river. Get a good boat, load it with supplies and gas and hope to hell they make it," I said.

The rest of the men thought a minute and the nods I received told me they figured it was the best and safest route. It was going to be a long haul, but I had a feeling they would make it. The trouble would be deciding who would go. I put the question out there, but before we even had a chance to discuss, Janna spoke up.

"I'll do it," she said quietly, bringing the baby up to her shoulder and patting its back.

I nodded. "Thank you. I appreciate it."

The baby gave a good belch then settled down to sleep. Janna rocked him gently and said, "I need to do this. I've done some not-so nice things and I want to contribute to the new country. If saving these kids and seeing them to safety does it, I'm happy."

I knew she would be safe and I knew Duncan would be sorry to see her go, but I understood where she was coming from. I stood up and went over to her. "Thanks," I said, offering my hand as an equal. She looked up at me and smiled, firmly shaking back.

"All right," I said. "We know what we're doing tomorrow. Let's get some rest."

It took us nearly half a day to get the supplies and boat we wanted for the trip. Nate found a nice Bayliner and bass boat and we took them down to the river and got them set up at a boat launch.

Duncan spent some time with Janna going over maps and routes and I used my time looking for gas cans. The idea was for Janna to travel as far as she could every day and night without having to stop anywhere to refuel or even look for supplies. The bass boat was intended to be pulled along and it would hold the spare gas cans. In case of a fire or something, at least the gas wouldn't blow everyone up.

We set the kids on the boat, after getting some hugs from all of them. Janna had one of the spare ARs, her pistol, and plenty of ammo. Below decks was crammed with foodstuffs and baby supplies.

Janna gave each of us a hug and none of us was surprised when she gave Duncan a huge goodbye kiss. The rest of us found other interesting things to look at while they were so engaged. I thought the milkweeds were particularly fascinating. When she finished with Duncan, she hopped aboard the boat and fired up the motor. Nate had instructed her on how to operate it, so it was time for departure.

"Good luck!" I called. "If you see anyone at Starved Rock, tell them we're okay and will be back soon." My heart ached and I desperately wanted to go home with her, but I had a duty to take care of and a man to kill.

Janna waved and pulled the boat around. The kids waved to us and we waved back. We hadn't fully won this one, but I guess you could call it a tie. As we boarded the RV and started down Route 50 again, my mind went back to the burned home and murdered people. I hoped that wasn't what I was going to find when I returned to Starved Rock.

Tommy must have been reading my mind when he said, "Charlie won't let it happen. Our families are safe. You'll see."

"I wish I had your faith, my friend," I said soberly.

"Only thing that keeps me from losing my mind." Tommy replied. "Did I tell you Angela is pregnant?"

I smiled. "Congratulations. That's good news."

"We have to win this," Tommy said. "We have to."

I sighed. "God only knows."

"Well, I keep praying He watches over Starved Rock real particular-like," Tommy said.

"Me, too, brother. Me, too."

Chapter 4

Captain Tamikara was pissed. They had spent over eight days traveling to this middle of nowhere state park, staking out the resort, fighting a few zombies that had been lost in the woods, only to finally realize they were in the wrong place.

The ten men had arrived at a resort, thinking it was the correct one. It looked like a wilderness resort and it was in the right area. They stormed the lodge and the guest houses, breaking into the indoor amusement park and trashing the miniature golf facility.

It wasn't until a private noticed the local attraction brochure stand by the check-in desk and saw a Starved Rock brochure. After looking through the literature, Tamikara realized they were at the wrong lodge.

Consulting several tiny maps, Captain Tamikara realized he was closer than he thought and given where he was, could tactically maneuver men from three different directions to attack the right place.

Gathering his men around some tables in the lodge's Häagen-Dazs café, Tamikara outlined his plan.

"We're here, thanks to the ineptitude of our map reader." The Captain said, pointing to a spot on a brochure map. One of the privates scowled but wisely said nothing. "Where we *want* to be is about five miles to the east of here." He pointed to a second spot on the map. "What we will do is divide into three teams and attack from three different points. Team Alpha will proceed along this road and come in through the main gate." Tamikara pointed to another part of the map. Team Bravo will backtrack and take this secondary road which looks like it leads directly to the main lodge here." The captain looked around at the faces. "Team Charlie will go the farthest, making their way to the river and coming in through the trails, here." There were looks around the table. That part of plan looked like it involved some serious hiking.

Tamikara continued. "The main objective is to come in from three points and to engage as many targets as possible, keeping them from concentrating their defense after the initial surprise wears off. I am hoping that they can be picked off one by one and since they aren't expecting us, this should be easy." The men around the table grinned and anticipated some overdue fun.

"Just to keep things interesting, there should be four women here and only two men. One of the men might give us some trouble, but I doubt any of you should have trouble dealing with the women." The captain's voice fairly dripped with innuendo and a couple of the men leered.

One of the privates raised his hand.

Tamikara raised an eyebrow. "Yes?"

"What's the plan for the residents?" he asked.

Tamikara snorted. "Kill them, idiot. Now, if there aren't any other stupid questions, Corporal August will give you your team assignments."

Corporal Will August stood to his full height and looked down on the men. "Team Alpha will consist of myself, Hernandez and Showers. Team Bravo will be Sergeant Dent, Private Lapinski, and Private Ness. Team Charlie will be Privates Cruz, Inglis and Corpin. Captain Tamikara will be leading Team Charlie. Any questions?"

The men looked at each other and shook their heads. They had done this sort of thing before and it didn't bother them at all.

Ted spoke again. "All right. We want to move in as close to tandem as possible. Team Charlie will take the truck, Team Alpha and Bravo will go overland. Get your gear and check your weapons. We'll move out first thing in the morning."

The men headed to their rooms and the captain watched them go. He walked up to the balcony and looked out over the lodge lobby. *Might be nice to settle down here*, he thought as he stretched out on a couch. *Hopefully Talon's men will be able to thin the herd considerably before they're killed. Then I can cash the rest and be free of Thorton once and for all.*

With these thoughts Tamikara drifted off to sleep.

On a hill to the north, a pair of eyes watched through binoculars the lights flicker off at Grizzly Jack's Hotel and Water Park. Those same eyes had watched the progression of the men through the lodge and it was immediately clear who they were and what they were doing. The silent watcher had been briefed thoroughly on the men he was observing and it took only a moment to identify the main target. The way they attacked the lodge, it was also clear they had no clue what they were doing and if there had been any number of zombies in the place, the job would have gotten easier.

As it was, Charlie back-crawled out of his observation post and hurried down the trail. He was going to try and be as prepared as possible for an assault and sell his life as dearly as he could for his family and for John's if need be.

As he silently made his way back to his home at Starved Rock Lodge, he was reminded of his home in Missouri and the strange path that took him to where he currently was. Charlie James grew up poor and spent much of his life outdoors. His father was a backwoodsman, claiming ancestry to the Jesse James clan, although no one really believed that. Charlie learned to stalk and hunt at an early age and many times the supper table had meat he himself had taken. Charlie had not expected much out of life, figuring to do pretty much what his father had done, but surprised everyone, including himself by getting a scholarship to college. He did well, eventually earning a degree in forestry, intending to become a conservation officer. But during a weekend trip to St. Louis, he met a girl going to school there and like many turns of fate, took Charlie out of the woods and brought him to civilization. A quick romance turned to love and Charlie followed the young woman out of Missouri and up to Springfield, Illinois. They married, Charlie found a job and they settled into what he considered the good life. In short order they had a baby girl and friends and family thought it was funny to see the huge country boy turn into a pile of mush when he was holding his daughter.

When the Upheaval hit, Charlie was away from home. He returned to find his wife fighting off three attackers, trying desperately to save her baby. Charlie killed the three with his bare hands, but it was too late. His wife had been bitten and the baby had gotten infected fluids in her mouth, causing them both to perish. Charlie buried them together in his back yard, then turned his back on civilization, intending to die avenging his loved ones.

His overland travels took him north, where he met a fellow survivor. John Talon was the first man he had met who hadn't given up on the notion of life after the zombies and made him believe it was possible to live again. Charlie owed him more than he would admit and when John entrusted Charlie to watch over the baby Julia, Charlie forged a bond with the other man that was stronger than brotherhood.

John and Charlie had a bond of honor and Charlie was humbled and proud to be asked to care for John's family, his reason for living. Charlie would not let him down and now called on all the reserves of his upbringing to keep his oath.

Living in the state park had re-honed the woodcraft that had dulled over the years and Charlie was as deadly a predator that had ever stalked prey. Tomorrow, he was going hunting and the men he went after would quickly realize you never chase a dangerous animal into his own lair.

Charlie entered the lodge and hurried to the main room. He called down the rest of the families and outlined the situation and the plan.

"Well, they're here. They took longer than I had dared hope, but at least they hadn't arrived before Winters could warn us." Charlie still resented having Dan Winters around, but couldn't refuse the fact that without Dan's warning, things could be much worse.

"They attacked Grizzly Jack's, thinking it was the right lodge, but they probably have figured out their mistake by now. I expect them to attack in the morning, so we need to be ready tonight." Charlie looked around at the grim faces before him. Sarah was holding a sleepy Jake and Rebecca was settling Julia down. Angela looked worried and passed a hand over her stomach. Sarah saw the motion and reached out to grasp Angela's hand in a comforting squeeze. Angela smiled and offered to take Jake, who reached out for his aunt. Mike was standing over Nicole, holding her shoulders, his face a mask of grim determination.

"I don't know how they are going to attack, but I will know more in the morning. As soon as they move out, I'll radio back and we can do one of two things." Charlie laid out a map of the park on the table. "If they all come down the main road here, Mike and I will ambush them on the way, taking stragglers out as we need to. If they split up and I hope they do, we'll be able to take them out piecemeal." Charlie indicated three points on the map. "Sarah, the lodge is yours. You and Angela keep an eye on the roads, I don't expect these guys to go overland. Mike, you head towards the back entrance and keep an eye on the back door. Rebecca, I need you to stay with Winters. He might need some attention and you're all we've got."

Charlie turned to Nicole. "I need you to take the kids and bring them to Wild Cat Cave. They'll be safe there and if the worst should happen and we all don't make it or are captured, you need to get out, get to the boats and get the kids to Ottowa. They'll be able to help you there." Nicole bit her lip but stayed steady.

Charlie looked around the group. "From what we heard from Simon and from Winters, this group is nothing more than renegades, sent on a mission to punish. John has his job and he gave me mine. I'll see this through. Get some rest and I'll be radioing in the morning what our plan is."

Everyone nodded and drifted off to their rooms. Sarah took a now sleeping Jake back and headed to his bedroom. As she passed Charlie, she stopped for a second.

"Do you think he's all right?" she asked, looking up into Charlie's eyes.

Charlie nodded. "If he were dead, we'd know it somehow, you and I. I think he's okay."

Sarah smiled. "Thanks, Charlie." She walked away and patted Jake's back, settling him into a deeper sleep.

Charlie watched them go and turned to Rebecca. "I don't know what's going to happen tomorrow. But I wanted you to know that while John showed me how to live, you and Julia make it worth living." Charlie reached out and pulled Rebecca close, taking a free hand and gently placing it on Julia's little head.

Rebecca fought back tears as she turned into Charlie's embrace. She knew her husband and had every confidence in him, but there was always a doubt something could go wrong. She had to trust him, however, as they all needed him to survive.

Rebecca turned her face up to Charlie. "I believe in you. You'll get us through this."

Charlie kissed her gently, then kissed Julia. He disengaged himself and watched as Rebecca and Julia walked off to their room. Rebecca turned around when she reached the stairs and said. "John knew what he was doing when he asked you to take care of us. You're the best there is." She turned out of sight, leaving Charlie by himself.

He thought about that for a second, then smiled grimly. *Time to get ready*, he thought. He walked over to the supply room and picked up a couple granola bars. He refilled his water and grabbed an extra knife. His tomahawks were waiting for him and he strapped them on carefully, testing the blades to make sure they were sharp. Three extra magazines for his Glock were placed within easy reach and he pulled down an extra blanket.

Satisfied with his equipment, he headed out the front door and made his way to his observation post. He needed to make sure he was able to communicate how the enemy was attacking and needed to be watching when they made their move.

Settling into his spot, he idly wondered if he should just walk over and set the building on fire. But he dismissed the thought, feeling pretty sure there likely was a guard who'd shoot at the first flicker of a match. Charlie unrolled his blanket and eased himself onto the ground and settled into a light, dreamless sleep.

The sound of a car door closing woke Charlie in the early light, where the sun had not yet fully risen and the moon was still very clear in the sky. The river at his back had mist rising off the gently moving surface and the forest was slowly waking to a new day. Animals were shaking the sleep out of their eyes and here and there he could see movement in the corners of his vision. For some reason he noted the squirrels were particularly numerous this year. Must be all the squirrel he ate when he was a kid. It was greasy, but satisfying.

Charlie shifted and brought up his binoculars, studying the scene before him. Six men were moving away from the lodge across the parking lot and the truck they arrived in was pulling away, moving towards Route 71, a road that went behind the state park. *Four in the truck*, Charlie thought as he watched the men reach the road and spilt again, this time into teams of three. One group followed the truck and the other turned down Route 178, the main road leading to the main gate. Charlie nodded. *So it begins*, he thought. He pulled out the radio and sent a quick message to Mike. "They split up. Get everyone moving to their spots, you have probably fifteen minutes. Go."

Charlie slithered out of his post and rolled up his blanket, slipping it into his pack. He had a plan for it but it required the three men he was chasing to play along and he got the impression they weren't here to play.

He followed the high trail for a quarter mile, then slipped through the underbrush as silent as a ghost. He had the advantage of the high ground and knowing roughly where his enemies were going to be. Hopefully, they would appear without trying to do anything too clever. Charlie worked his way down the cliffs and hills, making as much noise as a field mouse. When he could see the parking lot, he stayed up in the brush, content to wait for the men to come to him. Given the rate they were moving, he should be seeing them in just a few minutes.

CHAPTER 5

Corporal August moved as quickly as he dared down Route 178. When he crossed a hill, he could see the river valley stretch before him and the bridge to Utica. Even in his hardened mind he thought it was a very nice place. He walked faster than his companions and was constantly looking over his shoulder to make sure they were keeping up. Private Hernandez was a former drug dealer and hated taking orders from anyone. He made the mistake of mouthing off to Corporal August once and had gotten a serious beating for it. Private Showers was an older, balding man, and was quiet, but August knew he was always calculating, looking for an angle or some advantage. Simply put, he didn't trust either of the two men with him, but since Captain Tamikara made the lists, he had little choice.

"Come on, let's pick up the pace." Corporal August growled over his shoulder. He didn't see the scowls on their faces or the way Private Hernandez half raised his rifle menacingly to the muted snicker of Private Showers.

The three men half-jogged down the large hill and turned into the park at the faded wood sign. The road was bracketed by heavy brush on both sides and the tree canopies darkened the way through considerably, since the sun was just barely coming up.

Following the entrance, the trio wound their way towards the parking lot, skipping over a couple of switchbacks and standing at the edge of a large expanse of asphalt. In the distance, a big building could be seen at the edge of the lot. Grass was growing up in numerous places and in a few years this parking lot would be a field.

Walking along the southern edge of the lot, Corporal August outstripped the other squad members quickly, as the two other men walked slowly, taking in the scenery. Corporal August turned around and saw that his two men were fifty yards behind him.

"Dammit!" he whispered. He couldn't yell at the men to move, because they were close enough to the buildings to alert the occupants. "Screw it! They can catch up in a minute." He turned his back on the men and stalked over to the building, which he could see was a visitor center by the large sign on the wall. He began to reconnoiter it, looking for less than obvious openings. His search took him around the corner of the building and out of sight of the two other men.

Private Ray Showers grinned and watched Corporal August get pissed and turn his back on them. He couldn't care less about this mission, he was just looking to get some female action as soon as possible. He said as much to his companion who responded by snorting.

"Shit, man. That ain't nothin'. We finish this, we can set up here and live like kings. Raid the water towns, man. Easy livin'." Private Hernandez reached down and scratched himself, something he did on a nearly continual basis.

"Right. We can be pirates and… did you hear that?" Private Showers cocked his head and listened hard. "Sounded like someone slapped somebody. You hear it, Damien?"

Damien didn't answer, he simply took a hesitant step, then fell forward onto his side.

"Jesus, Hernandez, you okay man?" Ray knelt down next to his friend and turned him over. "What happen…Oh, Christ!"

Private Showers fell back as he stared at the tomahawk handle sticking out at a right angle to Private Hernandez's face. The blade was buried deep in the soldier's skull, having crashed through his temple.

"Shit! Shit! Where's fucking August, God dammit!" Private Showers' face was full of fear as he grabbed at his weapon, stood up and scanned the woods for a threat. He caught something glittering out of the corner of his eye and as he turned, another blade hit him full in the throat, severing his windpipe and pouring blood into his lungs. He fell back, gurgling, his feet scraping at the grass, while his hands feebly tried to pull out the axe that had killed him.

As his vision began to go dark and his struggles slowed, Private Showers saw a large man emerge from the woods. He walked over to the two men and removed the first axe from Private Hernandez's head, wiping the blade off on the soldier's uniform. The man then turned his attention to Private Showers, who raised a weak hand for help. The man bent down and removed the tomahawk, causing more blood to flow into Showers' lungs. The last thing Private Ray Showers saw in this world was the man standing over him for a second, then disappearing silently into the woods.

Corporal August circled the building and hoped to find his men standing at the doorway. Instead, when he looked out on the parking lot, he saw two inert forms.

"Son of a *bitch!*" August ran over to the two men and surveyed the damage. He was concentrating on the men and didn't see a dark form flitting through the trees in the opposite direction.

He knelt and looked over the two and shook his head. *I knew this wasn't going to be easy,* he thought gloomily as he quickly stripped the men of weapons and ammo, placing the items in his pack and slinging the rifles across his back. *Shit.*

For a brief second, he considered just heading out the way he came, crossing the river and never coming back. He had enough weapons to survive and the thought was tempting. But he knew Thorton would eventually find him, so he'd better to see this through and hope for a win as opposed to certain death later.

Corporal August left the dead men and trotted out away from the trees. If anyone threw anything at him, he'd at least reduced the effectiveness with distance and might actually see it first and avoid it. He walked carefully back to the Visitor Center, his rifle at the ready, his nerves on edge.

Those same nerves got a healthy jolt when August looked down at the sidewalk in front of the building and lying there in the sun, was a bloody tomahawk. The blood was fresh enough that it was still bright red, not yet turning brown, soaking into the sidewalk.

"Mother *fucker!*" cursed Corporal August as he stared at the building. That certainly wasn't there before and he had to decide what it was. A challenge? Or a warning?

A sound form inside the building decided the issue for him. Someone cried out and August heard someone else trying to shush whoever had made the noise.

So something is worth protecting in here, hey? He thought, pulling open the door. *It won't be after I'm done with them.* Corporal August eased through the door, his rifle up and ready. He could hear strained breathing, like someone was in pain.

Moving cautiously through the little information center, he scanned the museum desk and book center. Nothing seemed out of the ordinary, so he moved to the double doors in the back end.

Corporal August peered through the tall, thin windows and could see what might have been a gift shop. There were some booths and tables, which indicated a possible snack shop as well. Someone cried out again and again came the sound of someone trying to quiet whoever was hurting. A woman's voice could be heard trying to sooth whoever was in there.

Corporal August smiled and burst into the room, slamming the door back and rushing in. "Nobody fucking move!" he screamed, pointing his gun at a woman who sat next to a still form in a bed.

The woman looked up at him and August was surprised to see she didn't look in the least afraid of him. That was weird. Usually women were afraid, or if they weren't, they learned to be.

"Who the hell are you? Who's in the bed?" Corporal August kept his rifle on the woman and looked closely at the inert form. When he saw the face, he had to hide his shock. "Well, I'll be damned. The little shit actually lived. I wondered if he did." August shifted his rifle. "Guess he managed to warn you all after selling you out."

Rebecca said nothing, placing a hand on Dan Winters' hand. He had cried out a couple of times, just like he was supposed to. She looked back at Corporal August and shook her free hand at August. "Go away, please. You're bleeding on the floor."

August looked at her like she was nuts. "I'm not bleeding, you stupid bitch. Now back up while I kill this little shit. I'll get to you in a second." August raised his rifle and aimed at Dan's head.

Right before he pulled the trigger, Rebecca said, "You're right, you're not bleeding. Yet."

August scowled. "Just shut up, you…"

Whatever Corporal August was going to say was lost in the crashing echo of his rifle's report as he pulled the trigger. But the bullet blasted through the roof, not Winters' head. That was because Corporal August was suddenly pulled off his feet and his shot went wild. August felt himself being lifted off the floor and then he was slamming into the wall, crumpling down dazed. His rifle skittered away on the floor, to be coolly picked up by the woman.

August shook his head and tried to get up, but a large hand grabbed a bundle of his shirt, hauled him off his feet again and threw him through the door. He fell to the floor in a heap and as he got to his hands and knees, he felt his sidearm being pulled out of its holster, then the rifles on his back were lifted off and tossed aside. August cleared his senses and leapt forward, rolling on his shoulder and coming off the floor in a jump. He whipped out his knife, a six-inch double-bladed model he had found on a raid. He snarled and waved it in front of him as he got a good look at his adversary.

"I'll kill you slowly for what you did to my men." August bared his teeth and readied for his attack. The man in front of him, while slightly shorter, was heavier built with a good fifteen pounds on Corporal August's six foot three lean frame. He looked at August and said nothing, reaching behind his neck and pulling out a gleaming tomahawk. Even in the dimly lit interior of the visitor center, August could see the edge shine wickedly.

August watched with interest as the man slid the tomahawk through the snack shop doors, where it was scooped up by the woman in there. The woman was holding his rifle like she knew how to use it and August realized he wasn't going to go back in there. But right now he cared about killing this man in front of him. He owed him that much. The man pulled a knife from a sheath at his hip and August grinned as he realized what this was going to be.

"Time to die, cocksucker." August stepped forward and lunged at the man, hoping his longer reach would be an advantage. He hoped for a quick kill, then he would deal with the woman.

Charlie stepped aside from the lunge and brought up his knife to slash at August's forearm. It was such a casual move it almost seemed like it was in slow motion. Charlie followed the cut with a sharp blow to the back of the corporal's hand, knocking the knife out of his grasp.

Corporal August hissed and brought his injured arm to his chest, holding the wound with his other hand. He stared hard at a man who looked like he had barely moved, yet managed to both cut and disarm him.

Charlie kept his eyes on the man and kicked the knife back over to him. He flexed his shoulders and held the knife loosely at his side. This was not like fighting John. With Talon, Charlie had to be alert all the time, looking for strikes within strikes within strikes. He and John had honed their skill over the last year, mostly for lack of anything else to do. Charlie liked to explode into action, having plotted three courses of action in the split second it takes for another person to react. He waited for the corporal to pick up the knife.

Corporal August was wary. He picked up the knife and held it tightly, trying to draw comfort from its grip. He had never faced a man like this before, someone who practically dared him to attack. But he knew if he ran, the man would simply hunt him down with that fucking tomahawk of his. Better to die on his feet.

Corporal August advanced slowly, keeping his feet on the floor while Charlie waited, looking almost bored. When he came within striking distance, August suddenly reversed his grip on the knife and raised it by his ear to slash at Charlie's head.

Charlie had no intention of waiting. When August raised his arm, Charlie struck, slipping his knife to his left hand while diving forward and burying the thin blade to the hilt in August's solar plexus. As August bent forward, Charlie pulled the blade out and stepped completely behind the other man. When the corporal straightened and tried to turn around, Charlie grabbed him by the shoulder and stabbed the knife into the base of his skull. The blade penetrated easily, piercing the spine and entering the brain.

Corporal August stiffened, then his eyes rolled up as he died on his way to the floor. Charlie watched him fall, then turned back to the double doors. Rebecca lowered her rifle when she saw it was her husband. She ran over to him and held him tightly, grateful her man was all right.

"You okay?" Charlie asked, kissing her lightly on the head.

"I'm fine." Rebecca smiled up at him. "Dan's doing better, but he's still unconscious."

Charlie frowned. "I heard him cry out. How did that happen.?"

Rebecca grinned. I knew you needed a distraction so I was pinching him for all I was worth."

Charlie laughed. "Some nurse. Remind me not to get sick." He held her again. "I need to go see if I can help everybody else."

Rebecca let him go. "I know. Be careful. Go find the kids."

Charlie nodded. "I will. I'll be back soon," he promised. He retrieved his tomahawks and trotted out the door. He hoped he would be able to lend a hand at the lodge, but when he went outside, he heard shots coming from near the building. He cursed as he ran for the stairs that went up the cliff face, praying he wasn't too late.

CHAPTER 6

Sarah and Angela had become very close in the previous year, nearly sisters in their outlook on things in general and life in particular. Sarah was singularly thrilled when Angela confided in her that she was pregnant. Angela and Tommy hadn't gotten married yet, but they were planning on a trip upriver to get the job done. Sarah was holding out a secret hope that perhaps she and John might be expecting, but it was too early to tell. Sarah was concerned as she was reaching the age where child bearing was going to be difficult, but as silly as it sounded, she wanted John to have another child. In her view, a man like that comes along once in a generation and one could probably trace his lineage to many great leaders throughout the history of the world. If John had heard any of this he would have laughed and said he just does what he does and things seem to work out, usually.

Sarah was sitting on a chair in a third floor room facing south when she saw movement in the trees. She called out to Angela, who was across the hall, looking out the back way. Both of them had heard a shot coming from the Visitor Center and knowing that Rebecca was there, shared a look of concern. But they would have to wait to check on their friend.

"We got movement," Sarah said.

"Coming over." Angela moved quickly to Sarah's side. "How many?" she wondered, trying to pierce the greenery.

"Not sure. Charlie said something about three of them, but I can only see two. Hold on, there's the third," Sarah said, picking up her little M1 carbine. It used to be John's but he gave it to her when she proved she was better with it than he was. It was the perfect size for her and since the recoil was very manageable, she had gotten very good with it.

"All right, little girl, let's get this done," Sarah joked with Angela.

"Yes, Mom," Angela joked back. She checked her Glock and Mini-14, making sure rounds were chambered and safeties were off. Seconds counted in fights and these guys wouldn't hesitate.

Sarah and Angela moved downstairs, preparing to meet the men on the ground floor. They reasoned that if things should go badly, they would be able to escape out a window and get into the woods a lot easier if they didn't have to worry about twisting an ankle from jumping out of a second or third story balcony.

Sarah and Angela went down to the front lobby and looked out the windows of the main door. The door was blocked with heavy planking, capable of stopping rifle fire if need be. Two sides had firing ports and Sarah peered out one of them, keeping her rifle barrel hidden so the men wouldn't know where to fire. They could see three men slowly making their way down the driveway and through the parking lot. The men climbed over the fallen trees and power line poles that John and Charlie had ringed the lodge with. The idea was to slow down any attacking zombie horde that had managed to breach the earthen wall and trench that enclosed the park.

As the trio stepped over the barricade, Sarah called out from the door.

"That's far enough. What do you want?"

The three men looked at each other for a second before answering. The sergeant, Carl Dent, spoke up. "United States military, ma'am. We're looking for survivors and offering assistance." One of the men giggled slightly.

Sarah wasn't about to be fooled. "Bullshit. You're Thorton's dogs. We've been expecting you."

Grins gave way to frowns as the men realized the one advantage they had was gone. Sergeant Dent cursed and spoke up. "If you know who we are, then you know what we're capable of. Why not surrender now and have a chance at living, rather than be shot down?"

Sarah laughed. "You're exposed with no cover except what you might find flat on your ass and you talk about me getting killed?" The men looked around and realized she had them dead to rights and they weren't sure where she even was. "Run along puppies, before I decide to spank your stupid asses." Sarah grinned at Angela, who just smiled and shook her head.

Sergeant Dent, a former welder who had spent much of his previous married life beating his two ex-wives, bristled at being spoken to this way by a female.

"Listen, bitch. If you want your brats to live, you'd better do as you're told and I mean right now. Put your weapons down and walk out here right now." Sergeant Dent's voice had lowered to an angry hiss and the man next to him, Private Drew Lapinski, spoke up.

"You know, lady. I prefer you fight. I'd rather John Talon come home to a dead son. Where is the little shit? I got dibs on cutting his throat." Lapinski turned to smile at his friend and when he turned back to the lodge, Sarah shot him through the mouth.

The bullet blew out the back of Lapinski's head, launching two teeth out of the newly formed hole. Lapinski teetered backwards and fell over a log, his feet sticking up in the air like a cartoon figure.

Sergeant Dent and Private Ron Ness dove for cover behind the logs, swearing the whole way. Private Ness was a small man, pudgy and whiny. He was useful to Thorton only in that he had an odd knack for finding supplies. If not for that and a complete lack of morals, he would have been working the fields long ago.

"She killed him! Jesus Christ! She killed him!" Ness kept repeating over and over. He had taken cover near the corpse and couldn't keep from staring at the ruined mess of blood and brains that oozed out of Private Lapinski's new orifice.

Sergeant Dent howled. "I'll kill you all for that. You hear me?" He steadied his rifle and fired at the door.

Sarah squinted out of the side portal as rifle rounds slammed into the barricade. Dent wasn't much of a shot and Sarah was waiting for him to lighten up so she could ventilate him as well.

Angela leaned against the receptionist's desk and noted sardonically, "I guess negotiations are over?"

Sarah sighted down the barrel of her carbine. "John liked to use a line from a movie in situations like this."

Angela cocked her head to the side. "What line?"

"When you have to shoot, shoot. Don't talk," Sarah said, firing suddenly. "When they threatened to kill Jakey I figured talk time was over."

She looked through the opening and smiled. Outside, the two women could hear cursing and squealing, like someone had been wounded.

Private Ness held a wounded ear and wheezed like a broken accordion. "She nearly killed me! Oh, God! An inch to the right and I'd have taken the shot in the eye!"

Sergeant Dent snorted. "Would have owed her a favor if she did. At least I would have been spared your bitching." He popped up suddenly and fired, ducking down as two rounds whipped through the air above him. "This is going nowhere. We need to get inside and take care of business. When I signal, you roll that way and I'll roll this way. I'll pop up shooting and you haul ass to that corner over there. I'll go this way and get in through a window. Get in yourself and we'll catch this bitch in a crossfire."

Private Ness blanched. He really didn't want to go anywhere but away from this crazy woman. But he was more afraid of the sergeant, who had proven on more than one occasion to be a bully and a bastard. Gripping his rifle, he rolled carefully to the right, trying to stay out of sight. When he had reached as far as he was able to go, he nodded at the Sergeant, who fired again at the door, receiving a round past his ear in reply.

Sergeant Dent quickly rolled to the left and when he reached the end of the barricade, he suddenly jumped up firing, blasting away at the spot where he thought he had seen the shots coming from. Ness wasted no time and bolted upright, running for all he was worth. He ran as hard as he could for the corner of the building, expecting at any second to feel a bullet slam into his back.

Sarah ducked as the bullets punched into the door and a couple managed to make it into the firing port. Sarah looked up just in time to see both men split and run away in opposite directions.

"Damn. This just got harder." She picked up her carbine and extra ammo. "Let's go, little girl. We've got work to do." Sarah turned around and looked at Angela, who had turned ashen all of a sudden.

"S-Sarah?" Angela pulled her hand from her side and it came away bloody. She gripped the counter as a wave of nausea struck her.

"Oh shit. Hold on, Angela!" Sarah ran over and grabbed the other woman, easing her to the floor behind the counter. The tactician inside her head figured this would be a good place for Angela to hide in case that animal outside got in.

Sarah gently eased Angela's hand away from the wound and lifted her shirt to survey the damage. The bullet looked like it came in on the right side, low on her rib cage. The round followed the bone and exited in an ugly wound. The exit wound was nasty and bled freely, but it didn't look like there was any internal damage. Sarah put her pack under Angela's head and pulled out an extra shirt which she folded and placed under the wound to control bleeding.

"Take it easy, honey, you're going to be fine. It's a nasty flesh wound, but it's a clean in and out, no damage to anything vital," Sarah said.

"Oh, God. The baby! Will the baby be okay?" Angela gripped Sarah's arm and winced in pain and fear.

Sarah patted her hand. "The baby will be fine. They're tougher than we are. Besides, that's Tommy's child and he's got hard core genes."

Angela relaxed a little, but was still worried. "Are the men gone?"

Sarah shook her head. "They're probably looking for a way in. I'm going to have to do something about that. Can you handle it from here, Momma Bear?"

Angela gritted her teeth and pulled her weapons closer, determined to fight dearly for her unborn child.

"Good girl. I'll be back with Rebecca. Just hang in there. If anyone besides us comes near…"

Angela interrupted. "They'll wish they hadn't."

Sarah nodded and switched out the magazine in her carbine for a fully loaded one. She wanted all the rounds she could use, because this was going to be a fight. She briefly thought about Jake, but pushed that out of her head. She needed to be clear to deal with this danger and like his father, Sarah had to trust Jake would be okay.

Thinking about John sent a pang of longing through Sarah and she desperately wished he was here now. But she was determined not to let him down and have everything normal when he returned. *And when he gets back, he's going nowhere without me ever again!* Sarah thought.

With a quick nod to Angela, Sarah swept into the hallway, looking for a man who was determined to kill her.

Chapter 7

Private Ness ran as fast as his fat legs would carry him. He ducked around the corner and leaned against the wall, gasping for air and clutching his rifle against his portly frame. He crossed a hand over his eyes, trying to wipe out the image of Lapinski with his brains blown out.

Jesus, Jesus, Jesus, what the fuck are we doing here? Ness thought as he steadied himself. He slowly brought his breathing back to normal and realized he needed to get moving and try and find a way in.

He held his rifle in shaking hands and moved around a small fenced area, past a couple of old soda machines and towards a path that might take him to the back of the lodge. He could see a large glassed-in area, presumably a restaurant or bar of some sort and he figured he could at least get in that way by breaking the glass. Private Ness found a little of his confidence returning, although he realized that he had had enough shocks to his system with the death of Lapinski.

Just as he reached the glass, he noticed movement on the flagstone patio. Whipping around the corner he jerked his rifle, only to be scolded by an irate squirrel who didn't appreciate intruders in her realm.

He calmed down and turned back to the glass, opened his mouth, and screamed for all he was worth. From behind a small storage shed, a huge man was silently charging at him, holding an enormous knife in one hand and a tomahawk in the other, looking for all the world like a ghost of the past coming for revenge. His face was stone cold save for his eyes, which were with fury. Ness completely forgot the rifle in his hands as he fell to his knees shrieking.

His screams were brutally cut off in a barking gasp as cold steel ended his life.

Charlie James cleaned his weapons quickly and darted for the other side of the lodge. He was still hunting and he knew there were others to feed his 'hawk.

Sergeant Dent heard the scream from the other side of the building. *I'll be damned.* he thought. *The fat little fuck might be useful after all. He'd better save some of that bitch for me.*

Dent circled around the far edge of the building, keeping out of sight and looking for a way in. The windows and doors of the first floor seemed to be sealed up, limiting his options. But as he looked around, he noticed some marking on the sidewalk by an access door. Trying his luck, he grasped the handle and pushed down on the latch, something no zombie would ever have been able to figure out. The door opened quietly and Sergeant Dent smiled as he slipped inside.

Outside, Charlie climbed the short ladder which allowed him to see over the wall blocking off the patio. He didn't see the door close, so he shrugged his shoulders and climbed down, heading to the stairs to try and get to the cave where Nicole and the kids were. At the very least he could help protect them from the men coming from the east if they got past Mike.

Sergeant Dent moved carefully through the building, letting his eyes adjust to the darkness. A little light filtered through the windows, enough to allow him to see where he was going and what was in the rooms he passed, but little else. He slipped past what appeared to be a conference room, but now it was filled with various free weights. The second room he passed gave him a glimpse of a sparring room, complete with punching bags and mats.

These guys used their time wisely, Dent thought as he passed a room which seemed filled with short term supplies. *Looks like they're prepared for a war or something.*

The hallway ahead turned to the right and Dent approached the area carefully. If he figured it right, he should be close to where that woman fired on him. Dent's lips curled back in anger at the memory of one of his men being killed by her. He hoped when he found her that Ness had already cracked her and had her bent over a table, just waiting for him. That thought made him smile as he crossed the lobby. A look behind the desk made him openly leer.

An attractive woman was lying on her back, clutching her side. Her eyes were closed, but when he approached, she gasped and tried to lift the rifle at her side. He moved quickly and kicked the rifle away, kneeling down next to her prone form. Dent shoved the barrel of his rifle under her chin and smiled evilly.

"Behave yourself, missy and you might live a little longer." Dent said. Angela's eyes burned hatred at the man next to her, but she remained silent. Dent ran a hand down her chest and onto her stomach, noting the hard bump there.

"Well, well. What have we here? Is Talon expecting another brat? Too bad he's probably dead and won't see this one." Dent continued his one handed groping of Angela who squirmed but refused to say anything.

Dent lifted her hand away and saw the wound. He grunted when he touched the wound and Angela sucked in air at the pain.

"Poor baby. Well, that's what you get when you shoot at my men. You're going to get something else, too." Dent shifted the rifle to fumble at his pants. When the barrel was out from under her chin, Angela seized her chance and pulled her legs back, kicking Dent hard in the head, knocking him flat on his back. Angela shrieked as a fresh wave of pain hit her and the piece of clothing that had staunched the flow of blood on her side, ripped away, causing fresh blood to seep out of the wound.

Angela fell back holding her side, gasping as wave after wave of pain shot through her. She tried to reach for her other gun, but Sergeant Dent had recovered and scrambling to his feet, grabbed a fistful of Angela's shirt and hauled her off the floor.

"Stupid little fuck!" Dent growled in her face. "I'll make you wish you never pulled that shit." He pulled a fist back and punched her brutally in the face, knocking her head back.

Angela's vision swam and she could barely remain conscious. The pain in her side was matched by the sudden pain in her head. She feebly raised a hand to try and defend herself and this excited Dent.

"Still some fight in you, huh?" the sergeant sneered. "I'll fix that." He pulled his big fist back to deliver another blow when a strange voice spoke next to him.

"Hey."

Dent turned to look and his head snapped back as his nose was smashed flat by the rifle stock which hit him like a baseball bat. He dropped Angela and fell back, grabbing at his ruined face. He didn't see the rifle stock swing again, cracking him on the side of the head, knocking him to his hands and knees. A third blow landed on his kidneys and he screamed in pain, launching himself forward and crawling away into the hallway.

Sarah knelt down next to Angela and surveyed her swelling face. "I'm so sorry, sweetheart. I never should have left you." Sarah gave Angela's hand a little squeeze and was relieved to get one in return. "Charlie got the other guy, I saw him through one of the windows."

Angela struggled with the fog in her head. "Ke..kuh…" she said numbly.

Sarah leaned closer. "What?" She was nervous, because she didn't want Dent to come back shooting and she couldn't spend too much time with Angela.

The wounded woman summoned her strength and cleared her head. "Kill him," she said to Sarah, gripping her hand and looking straight into Sarah's eyes.

Sarah smiled grimly. "Done." She gave Angela a reassuring pat on the hand and gathered up her carbine, noting the dings in the stock caused by Dent's head. *By the time I'm done with him, he'll wish he never left California,* Sarah thought as she headed out the door into the hallway.

Dent had fled into the main ballroom, pulling out his sidearm and taking refuge behind the rocks of the great central fireplace. He winced as he sat down, his back hurting something fierce and his nose was one mass of pain. The sad part was he hadn't even gotten a look at whoever had hit him. *As soon as I get a look now, that's all I need.* He thought as he eared the hammer back on his gun, a 1911 style pistol.

Sergeant Dent heard a step and peeked around the corner of the fireplace. His eyes grew wide when he saw a woman enter the room, carbine at the ready. She was a little bit older, but none the less attractive for it. Her green eyes scanned the room, the rifle held at the ready. Her aristocratic features were devoid of emotion, only her eyes shone with fury and determination. She was dressed for combat and moved like she knew what she was doing, but there was no doubt from the curves in all the right places she was all woman. Dent felt himself stir and he wanted this woman more than he wanted the other one. But this one had obviously been the one who hit him and needed to die.

As he readied his gun, Sarah approached unawares. She knew he had to be here somewhere, but finding him without getting hurt was going to be tough. She followed a blood trail and noted it went around the edge of the fireplace. Her eyes narrowed and her mouth curled up on one side and if her husband had been here, he would have advised all present to look out.

Sarah darted to the left, keeping the fireplace in front of her. As she moved, Dent suddenly sprang out, pointing his pistol at the spot where he thought he saw Sarah last. Her movement took her out of his line of sight and his perplexed look did nothing to improve his bloody features.

Sarah kept moving and when she was far enough, could see part of her enemy through the fireplace. She knelt and fired quickly at the part she could see, sending a bullet into Dent's ass.

Sergeant Dent screamed as the .30 caliber bullet punched through his buttocks, spinning him around and causing him to drop his pistol and grab his ruined rear with both hands. He overbalanced himself and crashed to the floor, squalling as his injured butt connected with the hardwood.

Sarah stepped around the fireplace and kept her rifle on the squirming, squealing soldier. He was trying to crawl forward and as she stepped closer, he suddenly spun around and fired at her!

Sarah ducked instinctively as the heavy bullet whipped past her head to bury itself in the heavy beams of the ceiling. She spun away to the other side of the fireplace, keeping it between her and Dent.

Dent howled in pain and rage and dragged himself to the side of the fireplace. "You were dead to begin with, but I'm gonna fucking hurt you for this! *You hear me?*" he screamed at Sarah.

"You talk too much," Sarah said as she slowly backed away from the fireplace. She had both sides covered, so Dent couldn't break cover without getting shot. *Trouble is,* Sarah thought. *I can't chase him down either.* It was a stalemate, at least until Dent either bled to death or made a mistake.

Sergeant Dent had turned himself around, cursing the entire time so he faced the fireplace. If the woman came to get him, he could send a few shots her way and maybe he could get lucky.

Suddenly there was a fusillade of shots, with bits of rock and wood splintering and flying about and Sarah ducked, looking for the source. She heard a choking gasp, then a deep rattling noise, like someone was breathing their last. Curious, Sarah looked over her shoulder and saw that the shots had not come from her side of the room and the windows were all intact.

Sarah slowly circled wide, keeping her carbine ready. She could see Dent's feet and they weren't moving. As she stepped closer, she could see the ruin that was the man's butt and Sarah winced at how much that must have hurt. When she finally could get a clear look at the man, Sarah's eyes grew wider at the bloody mess that used to be a man. Dent's back had been hit at least five times and his head had been hit twice. The right side of his face had literally been blown away.

Sarah looked back and saw Angela holding herself upright by the ramp railing, still pointing her gun at the fallen man. Her face was a study in anger, her one eye swollen and bruised and the only sound in the room was Angela's labored breathing.

Sarah quickly ran over to Angela and gently removed the gun from her hand.

"Good job, Momma Bear. Let's get you taken care of." Sarah held up the other woman and led her to a room with a spare bed to get her some much needed attention.

CHAPTER 8

Mike Talon sat on a ledge overlooking LaSalle canyon. He had heard a few shots coming from the West, but they died down after a few minutes, leaving him to wonder if everyone was all right. More than once he looked futilely towards the canyon where his children and John's were being hid, but they were beyond his sight. He wanted more than anything to go and protect his family, but Charlie had given him a duty and he would not let either Charlie or John down.

It had been quite an eye-opening experience for Mike since those early days when he was trying to save his family from the slavering hordes. The river had been hard enough, but trying to survive in the Visitor Center had been brutal. When John had showed up, Mike hadn't recognized him at all. Where his once easy-going brother had been, stood a combat-hardened veteran of the zombie war who showed no fear whatsoever of the undead. When Mike brought his family back to Leport, he was amazed at how many people spoke of John in terms of 'hero' and 'leader'. When Mike found out about all that John had been through, he looked at his brother with new eyes. Mike found himself respecting his older brother and slightly envying him, as well. It was nice for a while to be known as the brother of John Talon, but Mike had this feeling in the back of his head that people were making comparisons and he was coming up short.

That was a big part of the reason he wanted to bring his family back here. He wanted to prove he could contribute as well, that Mike Talon was as capable as his brother.

Mike learned in the first few practice sessions that John had far outstripped him in the combat area. But John had insisted that Mike continue to train and Mike found that he had grown in confidence as well as ability over the past year. Zombies no longer frightened him and he found himself eagerly anticipating battle when zombies were on the horizon. John laughed when he told him this, saying it must be something in Talon blood because he did the same thing too.

One thing Mike didn't have to practice was with his handgun. Even John admitted Mike was the best handgun shot he had ever seen and much to Mike's secret pleasure, John bragged about his brother every chance he got.

All these thoughts ran through Mike's head as he waited for something to happen. He figured he'd have to wait and then formulate his game plan, since he didn't know for sure where the enemy was going to come from. His big worry was they would stop somewhere in front of him and he'd wind up chasing them through the woods.

He checked his gun again, his beloved Beretta 92, making sure he had topped off all of his four magazines. The 9mm mags held twenty rounds each, which gave him eighty rounds to get the job done. He also had a ten inch field knife on his belt in case things got too close for comfort. Mike was good with the blade, not as good as Charlie or John, but could hold his own. He preferred the 9mm, though.

Mike was staring at a squirrel when suddenly the squirrel perked up and stared out towards the South. He turned around and listened for a moment and in a minute he could hear a truck working its way along Route 71. Taking his pack, Mike ran carefully to the berm, staying hidden as the vehicle moved close, then passed.

Mike popped his head up just as the truck moved away, noting the two men in the front seat and the two men riding in the back. Four was going to present a problem, but Mike hoped surprise would be enough of an advantage. He loped along the ditch, keeping the truck within earshot and when he heard the vehicle slow down, he left the relative safety of the berm and headed back for the trees.

Once he was in the trees, he moved until he cut the trail which led to the other parts of the park. In total, the park was over three miles long and slightly over half a mile at its widest point. It was a secure place, something that Mike had longed for; his family and he had a job to do today to make sure it stayed that way.

Mike followed the trail to the parking area where he was sure the truck was. It was the only logical place to make a back door assault and he smiled at how he was thinking so differently than he had been just a short time ago. *Next I'll be talking about staged assaults and pitched battles*, he thought.

Mike could hear voices as he approached the parking area and as he walked, a plan formed in his head. Tackling four men at once was suicide, but he figured he could whittle them down and take them out one at a time if he played things right.

Mike crouched just inside the tree line and could see the four men talking and one of them was giving orders, a shorter Asian man. After a few seconds, the men started down the trail towards the trees, with the leader bringing up the rear. The men carried their rifles at the low ready, able to bring them up and fire very quickly. The man in charge didn't have a rifle, just a nickel-plated firearm Mike couldn't identify.

Mike rolled his shoulders and flexed his fingers, then stepped out of the trees directly in front of the men. "Four of you, hey?" he called out.

The men stopped suddenly and the two on front raised their rifles. They hadn't expected resistance this soon, which was part of Charlie's plan. Always strike first and let the enemy react, rather than act.

Private Deez Corpin, a former California Penal System regular, sneered at the sudden apparition and called over his shoulder to his companions. "Ain't nothin'. Just one with a handgun and he's fifty yards out." Corpin adjusted his rifle and took aim at the stranger. "I got him."

Mike saw the rifle shift and swiftly drew his handgun, bringing it up to his vision, sighting quickly and pulling the trigger. Private Corpin's sneer froze on his face as the 9mm bullet cracked into his forehead, snapping his head back and toppling him to the ground.

"Jesus!" cried Captain Tamikara, ducking down behind the two men in front of him who had crouched as well at the sudden killing of their comrade. He aimed his weapon at the spot where the shot had come from, only to find that the man who fired on him was gone. From the trees a voice said plainly and clearly,

"Three's easier."

Tamikara swore and grabbed up the fallen soldier's weapon. "Son of a bitch!" he yelled. "Get him!" he cursed at his men, both of whom showed no real interest in pursuing a man who just made a killing shot with a handgun at over fifty yards.

The men, Privates Demitrius Inglis and Hector Cruz, shared a glance and shrugged. They couldn't resist the order with Tamikara at their backs, since he would just as likely shoot them as the man who was now stalking them. Figuring speed was the best option, Private Inglis bolted from his position and ran head on into the forest, followed closely by Private Cruz. In the space of ten seconds, they had gained the edge of the forest. Without stopping, they plunged in, following the clear trail.

Captain Tamikara was caught completely off guard. One minute he was behind two of his men, the next he was all by himself out in the open. He spent a minute cursing the two soldiers for abandoning him, but realized they did actually follow his orders. "Shit." he whispered to the corpse at his feet. Tamikara looked around and quickly ran after his vanishing soldiers.

Private Inglis moved down the trail, covering everything on his left while behind him, Private Cruz covered everything on his right. The two men worked well together, having been on the zombie cruise since the beginning. They didn't enjoy what they had to do at Major Thorton's or Captain Tamikara's orders, but they recognized a better chance at survival at the cost of some morals and ethics.

"When you gonna slow down, man?" Cruz said, whipping his rifle up to cover a rabbit that broke out from the trees on his side.

"Watch and learn, bro. You see Tamikara anywhere?" Inglis said.

"No, why?"

"Chance to get free, right?" Inglis cast a smile over his shoulder at his friend.

"Dude. That's awesome! What's the plan?" Cruz's heart quickened when he thought about being away from the craziness of Thorton.

Inglis swept his rifle around a large tree before answering. "Big river on the north has to have some boats somewhere. We get one, we get gone. No one find us ever again, just you and me."

Private Cruz smiled, suddenly having hope in his heart, when out of the corner of his eye he saw a small flash of light. Turning to see what it was, he was struck in the chest by a bullet, the hope in his heart replaced with a small caliber bullet. He took three steps and fell to the ground, wheezing out his last as he lay staring at the great canopy of leaves above his head.

Private Inglis skidded to a stop as his friend fell, thinking at first he had just tripped over a branch or something. But he heard the echoing sound of the shot and when he saw he blood seeping out of Cruz's chest, he knew exactly what happened.

"*Nooooo!*" Demitrius screamed. "*Hector, NO!*" Inglis fired wildly into the woods, spraying bullets in every direction. He kept pulling the trigger until the gun went dry, then he reloaded and started firing again, tears blurring his vision as he stood over his fallen friend. No one had known that Hector and Demitrius were lovers and now Inglis was all alone.

In the midst of his second round of firing, a second flash from the woods appeared and Demitrius felt something punch him in the chest. He looked down and saw dark blood pouring out of a small hole in his clothes. He immediately stopped firing and dropped his rifle from suddenly nerveless fingers. Falling to his knees, his head dropped down onto his chest. A snapping branch made him lift his head up and he could see a man approaching through blurred vision.

Demitrius realized he was done for and lay down next to his companion and took Hector's cold hand in his. As a tall man cautiously approached, Demetrius' vision went red, then completely black.

Mike Talon looked down at the two men he had killed, lying side by side. A small part of him felt remorse, but the practical side reasoned these men were here to kill him and his family.

Looking up the trail, Mike saw movement and ducked back into the brush. His backpedalling feet discovered a hidden tree root and Mike fell backwards, crashing to the ground and loosing his grip on his Beretta, which flipped away behind him.

The fourth man, the leader of the group came panting down the trail and Mike could hear him muttering and cursing as he came across the two corpses lying hand-in-hand on the trail. Mike dared not look up, because he was unarmed and had no idea where his weapon was at the moment. The ferns on the ground covered him and he knew he couldn't be seen easily, but if he made a noise he was as good as dead.

Captain Tamikara stared at the bodies of Cruz and Inglis, then crouched down, sweeping the forest with his rifle. He didn't see anything, but that didn't mean unseen eyes weren't watching him right now, waiting to take another shot. Tamikara decided it would be better to keep moving, than just stand there and be a target. He had heard the firing and saw the spent shells around the bodies. He wondered if perhaps one of the men had wounded their attacker, but Tamikara dismissed that thought. *Fucker wouldn't have come here and made these two hold hands. Sick bastard.* He thought.

Tamikara moved down the trail again, trying to keep low and hoping a bullet wasn't on its way to his back.

Behind him, Mike Talon waited until he couldn't hear his adversary's footsteps on the rocky trail, then he sat up quickly, spinning around and scrambling frantically for his fallen weapon. He had to find it fast and he ducked down under the fern ground cover hoping to catch a glimpse. He looked around and thought he saw something shiny about ten feet away, but when he got to the spot it was just a piece of quartz.

Damn, damn, damn, damn, damn! He was getting frantic, as the man he was supposed to keep away from his family was heading in that direction and if he didn't find his gun soon, he was going to have to confront him with nothing but his knife!

Scrambling back and forth, diving up and down, Mike finally located his Beretta. The gun had actually flown much further than he had thought, but he grabbed it and made a mad dash down the trail after the other man, hoping he would be able to see him long enough to get a shot.

Captain Tamikara bolted down the trail, nearly diving down the stairs that took him near the river. He righted himself just in time and pausing to catch his breath and wiped off his sweaty brow. *Haven't run this much in years,* He thought as he held onto the railing. *Gotta keep moving, no idea where the guy is who killed the other two.*

Tamikara followed the trail as it straightened out along the river. Dense forest was to his left and the lazy Illinois River babbled quietly against the shore to his right. Behind him, Mike Talon was racing for all he was worth.

At the bottom of the stairs, another pursuer paused at the railing, then slipped into the woods as a man came crashing into the bottom of the trail, skidding along the gravel and coming to a stop three feet from the edge of a small inlet. Mike Talon groaned more with embarrassment than injury. He had forgotten about the stairs and when he came upon them unexpectedly, he tried to correct his speed, but it was too late. He literally flew down the stairs, skidded along the bottom four steps and crashed to earth at the base. As luck would have it, he managed to slam his knee into a step at the bottom, causing him to wince as he hauled himself painfully to his feet. *At least I didn't drop the fucking gun.* he thought disgustedly. John would laugh his ass off if he knew. Mike had no intention of telling him, but this made the chase more desperate. Mike tried to move quickly, but his injured knee only allowed him a limping jog at best.

Mike gritted his teeth, ignoring the sting of his scraped hands and arms and moved as quickly as he could.

Ahead of him, Tamikara paused as he heard the crashing behind him. He didn't know what to make of it, except that he wanted to make sure he was ahead of it and out of sight. In front of him the trail forked west and south and Tamikara knew he needed nothing to the north. But in an attempt to deceive his pursuer, the captain stepped carefully in the mud along the side of the south trail, then backtracked to the west trail, moving in the woods for a bit before taking to the trail again. It wasn't much of a deception, but if it could delay for a minute, it would do. Tamikara was hoping to rendezvous with his other men at the lodge and make a finish of this matter once and for all.

As he hurried along, cold eyes watched him carefully before slipping back into the dark hollows of the woods.

Mike Talon cursed with every step. He was sweating from the pain of his fall and could feel his knee stiffening up on him. He tried bending it and keeping it loose, but he knew it was swelling and was going to slow him down even more. He couldn't give up, though, he had to get to his wife and kids and make sure they were okay. That was his only focus right now. If he ran into the last man, great, but it wasn't as big a priority anymore.

As he limped towards a fork in the trail, Mike Talon briefly glanced down the south trail and noted the footprints in the mud. He smiled as he saw the obvious attempt to backtrack and try to trick him into heading down that trail. Mike knew the trail was a loop and even if the man he pursued went down it, Mike would get ahead of him. As it was, he continued limping down the west trail, hoping he was gaining on his quarry.

As Captain Tamikara passed another set of stairs, he noticed the landscape was changing. The woods to his left were becoming more rocky and had more cliffs and overhangs. He could vaguely see something that looked like a small canyon through the trees. A small steam of water wound its way through the woods, spilling gently into the river. Further on he saw another canyon, this time it was marked by a sign that read "Basswood Canyon." The same sign indicated the lodge was straight ahead. He smiled and continued, hopeful that he would link up with his other men soon.

Approaching another fork in the trail, Tamikara was about to continue west when he heard something that made him pause. At first he wasn't sure he had heard correctly and was about to dismiss it when he heard it again. It was a child's voice, echoing off some hidden cliff. It puzzled the captain until his quick mind figured it out. *They moved the kids to a safe spot! I'll be dammed. And I found them.* Tamikara raised the rifle and started up the south trail, grinning. *Thorton will love to know I personally killed Talon's son*, he gloated.

He moved up the stairway and kept the rifle in front of him. Suddenly, something large moved through the trees, startling him and making him jerk his weapon around. The barrel knocked against a support hard enough to wrest the weapon from his grasp and Tamikara watched helplessly as his rifle fell down a small cliff to clatter against the rocks at the bottom and settle in the water of another creek. *You gotta be kidding me. Seriously?* Tamikara thought as he stared at his now useless rifle. He could go down and get it, but he didn't want to have his pursuer gain any ground on him, if he had indeed fallen for the false trail.

He shook his head and drew his nickled Browning and continued climbing the stairs, moving closer to the source of the kid sounds he was now hearing clearly.

CHAPTER 9

Nicole was worried. She had made it to Wild Cat Canyon with the four kids, but the boys were getting restless and Jake had just discovered that the canyon walls echoed. He alternated between bird calls and train whistles and Logan, his cousin, wasn't helping by laughing every time Jake did it. Julia kept wandering by the water and Anna was pouting something fierce and whining about wanting juice and not water.

"Jakey, shush, sweetie, we need to play the quiet game again," Nicole admonished as she kept Julia from wading into a deep pool. A small rivulet of water coursed its way down the canyon wall and a cave beckoned more than once to the boys. Logan was all for exploring, but Nicole knew he would rush ahead and get himself stuck if she let him look. She managed to hold him off by promising his father would explore the cave with him, but she saw him more than once looking at the cave and looking over in her direction, calculating whether or not she was actually paying attention.

"Whoo whoo!" Jake called, to the delight of Logan as the sound travelled down the cliff faces.

"Jakey, honey, you need to be quiet. Logan, would you please help mommy?" Nicole had decided to break out the snacks and handed a small bag of peanuts to Logan. She set Julia down and the toddler wandered over to Jake where she began tapping him on the head.

Jake giggled and moved away, heading over to the mouth of the canyon. He was on the trail, knowing enough to stay out of the woods, but his three year old mind would let him wander if sufficiently distracted.

With Nicole busying herself with the snacks and sulky kids, Jake found himself able to wander farther and farther without rebuke. He looked once over his shoulder and he moved cautiously down the path, his little feet unsure on the uneven surface, but he cheerfully pressed on.

Jake picked up a shiny rock, looked it over for a moment before flinging it ahead of him. He watched the rock bounce on the trail ahead of him, laughing as he moved to pick it up and throw it again, happy with his new game.

The rock bounced down the trail and a booted foot covered it. Jake scampered forward and looked up at a man staring down at him. "Throw rock?" Jake asked, looking around and not seeing his new toy.

Captain Tamikara stared at the little boy in front of him, stunned at his sudden appearance. He recovered quickly and realized this was one of the kids he had been looking for. "Hey little man. What's your name?" Ted asked.

The little boy looked up with big brown eyes and puffed out his little chest. "I'm Jake!" he said with all the pride of a toddler.

Tamikara smiled. He couldn't believe how his luck had changed. First he lost his squad, then his rifle and now the son of his adversary lands in his lap.

Jake hadn't noticed the smile on the man's face, he just squatted down and patted Tamikara's shoe. "Throw rock, peez?"

Captain Tamikara lifted his foot and saw what Jake wanted. "Oh! You want your rock! Sure, little buddy, go ahead and take it."

Jake reached down and picked up the rock, then cried out as Tamikara shoved Jake onto his back, stepping cruelly on his chest, pinning him to the ground. Jake yelled in fear and pain and Tamikara grinned as he leveled his gun at the little head.

"Get off of him!" screamed Nicole, as she aimed her rifle at Tamikara. When she had noticed Jake was gone, she hustled the kids down the adjacent path and came down this one.

Tamikara eased the pressure of the child but didn't let him up. Jake squalled and squirmed, trying to get free.

"I'll kill him right now if you don't drop that rifle," Ted said, staring at Nicole.

"Pull that trigger and I have no reason *not* to kill you," Nicole retorted. "But I'll do you one better. Hurt that boy and I'll just wound you and keep you alive until his father comes home and then let *him* have you."

Tamikara mulled that one over and decided he didn't like that scenario at all. If John Talon did somehow live, everything Ted knew about the man did not paint a picture of someone overburdened with restraint when it came to protecting or avenging his family.

Jacob yelled again, louder this time as he struggled to get out from under the man's boot. He had gone from scared to angry and Tamikara was amused at the boy's frustrated antics.

He faced the woman again, noting the steady barrel of the rifle she continued to point at him. "We have a problem. I let him go, you kill me. I kill him, you kill me . Seems like the only thing keeping me from being harmed is this boy being alive, but in my control. See where I'm going with this?" Ted cocked his head to the side, grinning nastily.

Nicole's eyes narrowed and her finger caressed the trigger of her rifle ever so gently. She had never wanted to kill anyone as badly as she wanted to right now. But she was afraid if she fired, the man holding Jacob would fire by reflex, wounding or killing Jacob. And she would never forgive herself if something happened to Jake. She had to stall and hope someone would show up. Charlie, Mike, anybody.

"You're not going anywhere with that boy." Nicole said firmly, readjusting her aim so her front sight was on Tamikara's face.

"You know, I was hoping you'd be more reasonable. As it is…what?" Captain Tamikara bent down slightly. The boy had said something very clearly and he was suddenly smiling.

Jake looked over Tamikara's shoulder and said loud enough for both Ted and Nicole to hear, "Kitty!"

Ted looked over his shoulder and screamed. He tried to bring his gun up but it was knocked out of his grasp by a tan-furred beast of fang and claw that leapt out of a tree on top of him. Tamikara was slammed to the ground and the big cougar quickly fastened its fangs on Ted's neck, immobilizing him except for his mouth, which continued to scream for help.

Jacob scrambled to his feet and went over to the big cat, rubbing his head on it's back. The cougar released Tamikara long enough to nuzzle Jake, who laughed as he was knocked down by the big head.

Nicole shouldered her rifle and went to retrieve Jacob, thanking the big cat for settling the situation. She hurried to get the other children in her charge, again hoping someone would come and tell her the coast was clear.

The cougar, excited by the prospect of fresh meat, again clamped its teeth on Tamikara's neck and dragged him down the trail. She was going to her den, a cave in Tonti Canyon. No one save Charlie knew where it was and he kept it to himself.

Mike Talon, cursing his leg, was making his way to the big set of stairs when the cougar came bounding down, dragging a still screaming Tamikara along with it. Mike blinked twice and after making sure he had seen what he thought he had seen, hurried up the stairs to reach his family and the other kids. When he reached the top, he met up with Charlie, who had come from the other direction. Between the two of them, they realized they had successfully accounted for all of the attackers. Charlie's eyes grew wide at the description of the cougar and Nicole later confirmed that the big cat had indeed saved Jake.

Marveling at fate, the group scooped up the kids and made their way back home, to stand vigil until their other loved ones made it back.

Back in the caves, Captain Tamikara was barely conscious when the cougar set him down. He realized he couldn't move, as the cat had punctured his spine when she bit him. His last thought before the dark claimed him was a futile wish to have just stayed at the other lodge.

The cougar, unaware of the man's passing, proceeded to shred his clothing, tearing it away so it could feast on the flesh beneath. Sending a growl into the darkness of the cave, she summoned three cubs who came bounding out to feast as well, justice taking the form of a cougar family in the forest of Starved Rock.

CHAPTER 10

"You better back up and get the hell out of here, Thorton, or we'll blow your ass to hell!"

The voice was full of fury, although still unseen. Major Thorton and his men had travelled early in the morning and it was a full day since they had torched that small community outside of Parkersburg. The going had been slow, there were several roadblocks that needed to be cleared, cars to be pulled out of the way, zombies to be eliminated.

Thorton and his men had discovered a network of roads in the hills to the north and south of Route 50 and buried in those hills were a number of communities and subdivisions that were still very much alive. But at their first contact, instead of the weepy welcome they were used to, two of the communities had opened fire at the first sign of the convoy and at the last one, one of Thorton's men had been shot dead by an unseen sniper when the man tried to sneak over the makeshift fences the people had erected.

Ken Thorton was outwardly calm, although he was raging inside with indignation and confusion. Several things were confusing him. *How did they know my purpose and more importantly, how in hell did they know my name? Unless they had a radio. Son of a bitch. These towns maintained communication and somehow one of the men from the town they torched got a warning out.*

Not to be turned away so easily, Thorton called out. "We're leaving, but sleep with one eye open, because we'll be back and when we find you, we'll burn your houses down around your ears. You hear me, you men with families? We're coming back and we'll remember you!"

"Here's something to remember us by, Thorton!" Another shot rang out and one of the men near Thorton suddenly threw his hands up and fell back. He lay on the ground with a neat smoking hole in his forehead. "Move on and don't come back!"

Major Thorton refused to be hurried, so he deliberately walked back to his trucks, his men cursing under their breaths at the loss of another of their number. Right now, they had a crew of seventeen men, when they had started with forty. None of them could have known that the men they sent to Starved Rock were dead. If they had, Thorton would probably have had a mutiny on his hands. As it was, several of the men cast sullen looks at their leader who just left their comrade to lie dead without retribution

Thorton had other things on his mind. If this community was informed against him, how many more would be the same? He was losing men too quickly to suit him and he would need as many hands as possible for the long trip back.

Rolling backwards, the convoy made its way back to Route 50 and rumbled east again. Thorton didn't really have a plan that went outside of getting to Washington. He wasn't entirely sure where the documents were that he wanted, but he had managed to convince himself that the Constitution and the Bill of Rights were in the Capitol Building, so that was where they would start.

Thorton brooded over the lack of understanding and cooperation and decided to change course and head south. South would allow him to travel more anonymously and this close to the goal, he couldn't afford any more setbacks.

"Turn here and follow this until I tell you differently," Ken said to his driver, as they approached the turn to 31. The plan, at the current time was to take the 31 until it ran into 16, then take that south until they found Interstate 33, which would take them to D.C.. Not as direct as route 50, but it was far enough south that it eliminated the chance of a broadcast from the survivor towns reaching anyone else.

The road signs pointed the way to a little town called Cairo and Thorton was as blind as anyone else when it came to seeing what the town was about. In the eastern part of the country, towns and communities tended to be buried within forests, with travelers coming upon them quite suddenly. The road itself looked like it made a couple of ninety degree turns through the town, so it would be impossible to see what resistance there might be. Major Thorton pulled his sidearm and held it in his lap, checking the loads. His driver glanced over and saw what Thorton had done, so he reached back and banged three times on the rear window.

There was a scuffling as men readied their weapons. They weren't going to be caught unawares again.

The convoy rounded the corner and crossed a small river. Immediately, Ken knew this town had nothing. The buildings were run down, windows had been smashed in, garbage was scattered about.

The trucks passed between two large brick buildings, but they had ground-level windows that had been smashed in, indicating that anyone forting up in those buildings had experienced unwelcome visitors.

Continuing on, Thorton looked to his right and saw a rickety bridge spanning the river. *Christ.* He thought. *Even without the zombies, this place was a shithole.* He shook his head at the places people had lived in, although he was tactician enough to appreciate the potential of this place. Surrounded on three sides by water and a forest to the east, people with some fortitude could have made this place a decent spot to wait out the zombies. Just block the bridges and set up a fence and voila! Zombie-free living.

Thorton chuckled. *Should make a brochure*, he thought. He chuckled again when they passed the second bridge and something caught his eye. "Wait," he ordered. The big vehicle came to a stop, causing a stir with the occupants and the following vehicles.

Thorton got out of the vehicle and stared hard at the second bridge that crossed the river. This one used to be a railroad bridge, judging by the beams on the sides, but when the rails were taken out, it became a footbridge. But that wasn't what had caught the Major's attention. He walked through the small gate that kept vehicles out and over to the bridge.

Lashed to the bridge was a fishing pole and by the looks of the string and pole, it had been tied recently. He looked down at the water and sure enough, he could see a bobber making lazy trails in the slow moving river. The water was shallow enough that he could see the lure had not yet caught anything.

Suddenly more alert, he walked back to the truck and looked around with more focused eyes. That was when he felt it. Someone was watching him and his men. He had no idea where they were or what their intentions were, but they were out there somewhere. Perhaps someone had realized this town could be made safe.

"Sir! In front! Quick!" the driver yelled.

The major, still outside the vehicle, spun around and saw something small and dark race across the road ahead of them and disappear between two homes at the point where the road turned its second ninety-degree angle. He stared hard at the homes and his eyes caught a ghost of movement within a house further up the hill. Scanning the tree tops, he could see several more homes tucked away in the hills.

"Should we investigate, sir?" The driver wanted to know.

Major Thorton climbed aboard the truck. "No point. If they wanted to talk they would have called out to us. As it is, I'm guessing its just some hand to mouth scavengers, probably kids, who could disappear into the woods without a trace if we tried to follow. Let them go. We'll round them all up later. Let's go."

The trucks continued on, with the soldiers breathing a sigh of relief. This place looked like trouble and there were a million ambushes waiting for them if they had tried to head up the hill.

Rounding the bend, the convoy moved past a dozen or so homes, some of which had their porches only a few feet from the road. All of the homes were in various states of disrepair, but Major Thorton couldn't tell if that was because of the Upheaval or that was just the way all the homes looked to begin with.

The trucks rounded a small bend and the lead driver suddenly whispered, "Jesus."

"What's the problem? Oh." Thorton saw what had elicited the blasphemy from his driver.

On the right side of the road, there was a large steel building. Thorton couldn't tell what it was used for, but that was only because his sight was blocked by zombies. Hundreds of zombies. They filled the parking lot and were scattered around the building and surrounding property. There were all kinds of zombies milling about, from dead men in suits to teenage girls in shorts. There were little zombies and big zombies and even a toddler roaming about.

That wasn't the disturbing part. The part that got Thorton nervous was when the trucks heaved into view, every single zombie swiveled its head to look at the source of the sound. When they saw the trucks, they throated a collective groan and surged forward, their hunger driving them towards the trucks, their arms uplifted and their mouths opening.

"Move it, get around them!" Ken yelled as he watched zombies move to try and cut off the road.

Thorton's driver gunned the engine and the truck leaped forward, causing a commotion in the back as soldiers were tossed around by the sudden acceleration. The trucks behind surged forward as well, trying to close the distance between the vehicles to keep the zombies from separating the trucks. With the number of zombies in the area, there was a real danger of them stopping the truck through sheer numbers. After that it was all over.

The last truck was in the worst danger, being far enough behind that it was going to have to try something different. While the first trucks moved forward, battering their way through the zombies that headed their way, the last truck swung wide, to circle around where the zombie numbers were thinner. This was a dangerous move as well, since there wasn't much room to get past them. The trucks couldn't go to the left, since there was heavy forest on that side and to the right was unknown territory.

Private Lansky, the driver of the last truck, swung wide of the assembling horde and roared down the small lane in front of the large building. As he passed the building, he saw it was the First Methodist Church of Christ, ironically. Given the number of zombies, the townspeople probably used this place as a makeshift hospital, but once the infection took hold, it devastated everyone.

Lansky hoped he could find a side street that would take him back to the highway and the safety of the other trucks, but his heart leaped to his throat when he saw the road ended. *Well, make your own.* He thought as he followed a small line of trees. He could see an opening to the west and headed in that direction, pursued by a couple dozen zombies. They stumbled along behind the truck and he smiled as he pulled away. He couldn't go too quickly, since recent rain had made the ground soft, but the big truck moved steadily forward.

Rounding the tree line, he pulled the truck through the field and stopped abruptly. Ahead of him was at least another fifty zombies and they were all turning to see the newcomer to their picnic. Across the meadow, Lansky could see the other trucks moving quickly down the road, pursued by at least a hundred zombies. They moved as one, effectively cuting off the road from him.

"Shit, shit, shit, shit." Lansky cursed as he looked around. He had nearly three hundred zombies in front of him, about thirty behind him and nowhere to go. In his side view mirrors he could see the ones from behind getting closer and he quickly rolled the windows up to give himself some extra protection.

"Keep moving, keep moving" Lansky repeated as he veered to the right and headed back to the open country. He could see a small building and what looked to be a road, so he gunned the engine and moved the big vehicle in that direction, hoping to find some more road where he could reconnect with the convoy and put some serious distance between his pursuers.

Lansky drove furiously to the northwest, then banked hard when he reached an access road. Heading south, he breathed a sigh of relief when he hit the road, figuring he was safe. That feeling lasted about ten seconds when he discovered his path was blocked by the zombies chasing the convoy. The ones that were after him were now spread out by the building and heading his way.

Lansky made a quick calculation, then shook his head. "Fuck you, Thorton." He figured his best chance of survival was to head back the way he came and to hell with this crazy adventure. The private turned the wheel hard to the left, veering away from the pursuing zombies and headed across the open field to go back to Cairo.

He slammed the gas pedal down and the truck lumbered across the field, bouncing a zombie off the bumper as he tried to thread the needle through the two groups. Lansky looked back for a second and at that moment, the truck fell forward heavily, slamming the private against the steering wheel. The truck's forward momentum carried it forward to where the front bounced high up, causing Lansky to hit his head on the roof of the cab. The truck came to a stop and Private Lansky, holding his head, took stock of the situation and realized he had hit a small creek that had run through the land. He hadn't seen it before and should have been able to see it, but with the field overgrown with weeds, it would have been impossible to avoid.

Settling himself back in the seat, Lansky tried the engine and was rewarded with it starting, but when he tried to put it into drive the wheels, settling in deep mud and water, just spun in place.

Grabbing his rifle and pack, Lansky leapt from the cab and landed on the far side of the creek. The weeds were tall enough to reach his knees and he used that as he ducked low and ran to the tree line to his east. It was backtracking, but it was the best he could do. If he could get to the forest across the street, he stood a chance. A slight one, but a chance.

He looked back and saw the zombies reach the truck and in a second they were all over it, crawling inside the cab, trying to figure out what had happened to the meat they had seen earlier. The creek wasn't deep enough to keep them from crossing and in a short amount of time there were about a hundred on the private's side of the water. Private Lansky ducked into the trees and moved southward towards the road and the forest.

As he moved, a dark shape rose up in front of him. It was a tall, white-haired zombie, dressed entirely in black. The long, thin arms reached out and a deep, guttural moan issued from dead lips. Lansky sidestepped the arms and shoved the zombie back, pulling his hand back as the creature snapped at him as it fell. Lansky could see an old bite on the left hand of the ghoul, probably how he bought it.

While it struggled to get up, the soldier recognized the outfit the zombie wore as that of a pastor. "So much for the afterlife. Right, preacher?" Lansky said ironically.

The ex-pastor lunged from a crouching position and the private stepped around a tree to avoid the long, sweeping arms. Not wasting any more time, Lansky ran as hard as he could for the road, knowing he could outrun this zombie quicker than he could kill it. He could shoot it, but he didn't want the convoy to know he was still alive.

Just inside the trees to the south, the convoy came to a stop. On the last vehicle, a soldier stood on top of the cab of the truck with binoculars. He had seen Private Lansky's escape and was watching when Lansky stood on the empty road and waved at the trucks before ducking into the forest.

The soldier climbed off the cabin and stood next to the driver's side. "The truck's stuck in a ditch, covered in zombies."

He hesitated before giving the rest of the news. He made a decision and hoped it was the right one. "No sign of Lansky, figure the zombies got him, considering how many there are." He looked pointedly to the east and to emphasize his statement, dozens of groans could be heard from the approaching swarm.

The driver, a newly promoted sergeant, cursed and shook his head. "Thorton's not going to be happy."

"About Lansky or the truck?"

"Watch it," said the sergeant as he picked up the radio. "Get in before you get your dumb ass eaten."

"Yes, sir." The soldier jogged back to the rear and climbed in. In short order the rest of the men knew Lansky was alive, at least for now. Every one of them wished him luck and in a small part, each one wished they could do the same.

CHAPTER 11

Ken Thorton took the news remarkably well, all things considered. A small crowd of zombies just ran him and his men from town and he had lost a man and a truck in the same day.

"Could be worse," he said to the reporting Sergeant. "Keep your eyes peeled and report if you see any more of those quick little things we saw back at the town. Thorton out."

Ken set the mouthpiece back and looked at his map. Route 31 went south and then turned east before it went north to link up with state road 16. The junction took place at a place called Harrisville. The map said there was a population of about three thousand, so Thorton got on the radio and called back to the other trucks that they may be in for a hard fight.

Just as he did that, he noticed something on his map. There were some small roads that worked their way through the hills and he could see a county road that connected to both 31 and 16 and allowed him to avoid the town altogether and gain about five miles in the process.

He showed the map to his driver. "See where this bend is? There should be a road working its way into the hills going in the opposite direction. Take the side road. If its labeled, it's a county road."

His driver squinted at the map, got his bearings and nodded. They should come up on it soon, since he didn't remember making any such turn like that.

Thorton considered bringing the men off alert, but since he didn't know what he might encounter, decided to let it go.

The trucks found the turn easily enough and began a slow trek through the hills. The road was nearly covered in grass and leaves and more than once the truck lurched a little as the tires slid and groped for purchase. Overhanging tree branches snapped off the roof and cargo area and surprised fauna dashed out of the way of these forgotten intruders.

As they moved slowly along, Thorton had a nagging doubt that resurfaced every once in a while. It especially surfaced when they were in remote, out of the way places such as this. America was such a huge place, with millions of places for zombies to hide. How was he going to deal with it all? Would he even bother? The more he thought about it, the more he realized that the best thing to do would be to find some central spot for himself, then parcel out land to his men, ordering them to find people and get them to deal with the zombies. Why should he dirty his hands?

Ken smiled as he dreamed big, watching the edge of the forest slowly move past. Even during pre-zombie years, this road was just gravel and dirt. With no one to maintain it, frequent washouts had carved big ruts in the path. Some were nearly big enough to swallow even a truck tire, so it was tough going.

About a half mile into the shortcut, they passed a home sitting on top of a hill. The opening in the trees was sudden and Ken could just catch a glimpse of a tilled garden and an outbuilding. *Makes sense,* He thought. *These people were pretty much on their own to begin with. What's a zombie to them? Probably more hospitable than their cousins.*

Thorton thought this particularly funny and told his driver who answered with a hearty laugh of his own. At the driver's suggestion to stop, Thorton shook his head. People in this part of the world were fiercely independent and notorious for their patriotism and woodcraft. If they tried anything funny, chances were the men would proclaim a feud and stalk and kill every one of them.

The forest became thicker and more hazardous and one of the rear trucks actually got stuck. It took men from both trucks pushing and another truck pulling to get it free. Thorton seethed at the delay, but since this shortcut was his idea, getting mad at someone else would mark him either a hypocrite or an imbecile.

Two hours later, they came to a fork in the road and crossing his fingers, Thorton ordered the trucks to go left. The convoy proceeded at the same pace and included a heart-stopping moment when the scenery dropped away to the right and there was about three inches of wiggle room for the trucks to pass a cliff. A switchback caused some concern, but got worked out once the rear trucks stopped trying to push the lead truck over the side of the road. Thorton had to get on the roof of the cab and pull his gun on the driver of the second truck to get him to back off.

They reached a small collection of homes about a quarter mile later and Thorton decided to call a halt. They pulled into the yard and the men gratefully got out of the trucks and stretched their cramped legs. Ken walked a little ways around and saw the two homes near the road were actually double wide trailers, sharing a large redwood deck which spanned the front of the trailers and the space in between. The third house, tucked away behind a small stand of trees, seemed to be a firmer building and looked like a small single story structure with a tall roof and large porch in the front. It looked exactly like one might expect a West Virginia cabin to look like.

As Thorton moved closer, a small boy looked around the corner of the building and stared at the Major with wide brown eyes. He didn't move as Ken walked around the trees, he just sat on a metal chair and waited.

Ken looked at the surroundings and saw two out buildings, one a garage and the other a kind of barn. A large field had been planted and there were chickens by the henhouse. A huge doghouse was near the chicken pen and Ken could hear goats on a small pasture up on the hill.

He stood before the cabin and the still-staring boy. "Hello, there!" He called out to the youngster, who looked to be a lean ten years old. The boy was dressed in simple work clothes, a clean t-shirt tucked into baggy jeans. Around his thin waist was a large belt and on that belt was a large hunting knife. The blade had to be ten inches long, which, given the slight size of the owner, nearly made it a short sword.

The boy just stared at him for a full minute before standing up. "Momma's sick. I got chores." He walked off the porch and headed to the chicken coop, uncovering a bucket of seeds and spreading the meal out to the clucking hens. A huge German shepherd pulled itself out of a shadow and with a meaningful glance at the newcomers, trotted up next to the boy's side.

Thorton's skin crawled at the mention of the word sick. He had a pretty good idea what might be ailing this boy's mother, so he stepped up onto the porch and unholstered his sidearm. He opened the door and noticed immediately the house was in immaculate order. Everything was neat and tidy; there wasn't dirt anywhere. Thorton didn't know what he was expecting, but it wasn't this. A simple living room with a lofted ceiling greeted him and over the fireplace he noticed a small caliber rifle. There was a small sofa, an easy chair and what appeared to be two children-sized wooden chairs.

He checked the kitchen and saw more of the same; the only thing out of place was a single plate and glass sitting on the table. Another plate and glass were in a drying rack next to the sink. In a small vase, some fresh flowers were adding a splash of color to a lonely scene.

There were two other doors in the house and Thorton opened the first and saw it was the boy's room. It was as neat as the other two, with a small bunk bed and dresser. A tiny bookcase was tucked into a corner along with a brightly painted toy chest. Thorton could see it was hand made and whoever had done it had made it a labor of love for his children.

In the next bedroom, Thorton met the boy's mother. She was lying on the bed, wearing a flowered house dress. Her hair was neatly combed and she looked to be resting peacefully. A tray of breakfast food was on the bedside table, untouched. For a moment, Thorton couldn't breathe and had to steady himself against the door frame. A flood of memories came back, memories of his own childhood and his own mother's sickness and eventual death. It was that death which propelled Thorton into the man he was today. How things might have turned out had his mother lived and he not gone into state custody he would never know. Ken took several deep breaths to shake the memories and steadied himself as he approached the supine woman. He saw the pill bottles and full glass of water and with a strangely heavy heart, knew this woman was dead. A quick check of her pulse confirmed it and in an uncharacteristically compassionate gesture, Thorton pulled the sheet over the dead mother's head.

"Why'd yuh do thet?" came a small voice from the doorway.

Thorton turned around and saw the boy had come back. He knew of no other response than to say. "Your mother's gone, son. She's passed away."

The little boy looked at Ken, then at his mother. His big eyes filled with tears as he approached the bed. He paid no heed to the huge man standing by him as he reached a small hand under the sheet and brought out his mother's hand. Gently taking her thin fingers, he brought it up to his face and squeezed out big tears onto the lifeless hand. Stepping back, he gently put it under the shroud and turned to the door.

"I got diggin' to do." was all he said.

Thorton followed the boy outside as he walked across the yard to the barn. He emerged with a shovel and went to the far side of the yard where Ken could now see two more graves. They both had simple crosses made with spare lumber. On one was written 'Dad' and the other 'Stevie'.

"Wait," Ken called out to the boy. "We'll help." Thorton signaled to his men and three came running over. He pointed them to the graves. "Dig a grave for this boy's mother. She's died recently."

"What do we care?" asked the nearest man, a corporal.

Ken reached out casually and took hold of the man's throat. "Do what I tell you or they'll dig two," he snarled in the man's bulging face before shoving him back into the other men who hastened to comply. Ken turned his back on the men and returned to the house. In a few moments he returned with a large bundle wrapped up in the sheet from the bed. The boy watched emotionless as the men quickly dug the grave, then turned as he saw Thorton approach with his mother.

"Hol' up, sir." The boy reached up and unwrapped his mother's face, stepping up on his tiptoes to give her one more kiss goodbye. "Bye, Momma. I loves you. Tell Dad 'n Stevie I'll see y'all in a bit."

Thorton wrapped the boy's mother's face again and gently placed her into the grave. The men covered her up with dirt while another man fashioned a cross.

Thorton faced the boy. "You going to be okay, here? You can come with us, you know."

The boy shook his head. "I got chores an' I got to care fer my fam'ly. Thanks jest the same." The boy turned and went into the house.

As he walked away, Thorton could hear the sound of soft sobs coming from the inside the cabin.

Ken reached the spot where the majority of his men were and addressed the group. "Take what might be useful from these two houses, but leave the cabin and the barn alone. We're moving out in ten minutes." Some of the men wondered at the major's sentimentality, but others dismissed it, figuring they would probably have done the same.

Fifteen minutes later, the trucks were moving out again and quickly came to the junction for Route 16. Route 16 was a much better road, being paved and maintained right up to the Upheaval. Travel was much faster and the road headed south, which suited Major Thorton just fine and after six miles through the hills they came across a collection of houses with the moniker of Mahone.

The houses themselves were up on a ridge overlooking the valley and the only thing that might have been a business once was a pair of pipes sticking out of the middle of a small parking lot which may have been a gas station once upon a long time ago.

The road banked upward and followed the ridge itself and Thorton could see valleys to the right and left. It was easy to get lost in the scenery, forgetting the events over the last two years and the total breakdown of civilization.

That breakdown happened faster than anyone could have prepared for and places that thought to insulate themselves against the rising of the infected found it already in their midst. No place was safe, no place was secure. Anyone who managed to survive the initial Upheaval, stood a chance. Anyone still alive after the waves of undead had swept the country, had half a chance more.

Thorton thought about the boy they had left behind and figured he was going to be okay. The cabin was isolated enough and the boy had that behemoth of a dog to protect him.

Ken's thought were interrupted by his driver. "Sir? We're coming up on another town, sir."

"All right, let's see where we are." Thorton checked his map and saw it was a town called Smithville. Route 16 connected with Route 41 and that worked for him. "Go slow and when you can take route 41 east, do it."

"Yes, sir." The driver, Private Redding, was a thin kid from San Diego who had managed to slip into the foothills and escape the carnage of the Upheaval. He had been recruited by another member of Thorton's army trying to live off the land and while at first he wasn't proud of the way he was treating other survivors, he figured it was better them than him.

Rounding two small curves, the road sloped downwards until it leveled out at the bottom of a small valley. A creek ran alongside the road while trees lined the edge of its banks. As the road emerged from the woods, Thorton and his driver could see a large agricultural building across the way and an abandoned gas station just up the road. On the left side of the road, several trucks and flatbeds sat where they had been left to rust and the most thriving business before the Upheaval, a bar, lay empty and vacant on the corner of the junction.

The convoy turned left and ran smack into a roadblock. Just before the bridge that spanned the small creek was a gate that blocked the road. It was a long cattle gate, anchored to metal poles set into the ground. Chain link fencing blocked access all the way to the water and Thorton could see that the creek was one of those deep alluvials, capable of trapping a zombie.

A teenager sat on top of a small watchtower was, waving frantically as the trucks came into view. He jumped off the tower and ran over to the side of the truck.

"Thank God! You're just in time! They're trying to break through the east road! You've got to hurry! Come on!" The teen leaped onto the running board and pointed at the road. Thorton looked over at Redding and shrugged 'Why not?' at him.

Redding said, "Yes, Sir," and moved the truck according to their new navigator. In a few minutes, it was easy to see what the excitement was all about.

About a hundred or so zombies had broken through a containment fence on the east end of the community's holdings and were now trying to spread out and feed on the survivors who were desperately trying to hold them back from causing any more damage. Already Thorton could see a few pockets of kneeling zombies, pausing in their rampage to feed on a hapless soul who was unfortunate enough to be taken down. Blood and screams filled the air as men fought with garden tools, improvised weapons and primitive bludgeons. The zombies outnumbered the survivors nearly two to one and Thorton could see this ending badly.

"Come on, you got to help!" The teen jumped off the truck as it rolled to a stop and ran forward into the fray.

Thorton climbed out more casually and took stock of the situation. There might be an opportunity here, he thought as an older man came running. He was about thirty-five years old and carried a gunk-covered shovel.

"Thank God! Start killing them sons of bitches!" He gestured frantically at the smaller pockets of fighting that was starting to occur. Thorton knew that in a short amount of time the survivors would be overwhelmed if he didn't step up.

"We will, but what's in it for us?" Major Thorton asked.

"What?" The man was incredulous. "What you mean?"

Ken folded his massive arms across his chest. "I mean my men have been on the road for a while now and could use some fresh food and supplies. As well as some new entertainment, you understand?"

The man's face was a torrent of emotions. He brought his weapon back a fraction as if he wanted to hit Thorton with it, but a fresh gurgling scream brought his attention back to the fight and he saw the teen who had guided the trucks to the battle get taken down with a zombie's teeth in his throat.

Thorton continued. "I can escape here pretty quickly, but you sure can't. Better make up your mind quickly." Ken smiled and raised an eyebrow in anticipation of the answer he knew was coming.

"All right, fine! Whatever, just hurry!" The man spat out the words then rushed to help his comrades. How he was going to break the news to the other townspeople he had no idea.

Ken signaled his men. "I want two squads, left and right, take point and create a firing wedge. Down the middle I want a three man firing team, with two teams in reserve. Try not to kill anyone living."

The men rushed off to fulfill their orders and Thorton watched them go. He looked over the area and saw some panicked faces in the windows of a small building. At least two of them looked to be of acceptable age to Ken's twisted eye. He smiled and waved at the faces, which vanished at the attention. *Better and better, he thought. Now let's hope that little bastard doesn't try to renege on the deal.*

Thorton's men spread out and the men in the front lines knelt down to make sure their shots went over people's heads on the other side. Rifles cracked and a dozen zombies dropped dead, quickly replaced by more. The rifles cracked again and another dozen dropped. By this time, the zombies noticed the additional prey and moved over to the attack. The outlying teams chose their targets and killed their ghouls accordingly.

Thorton watched the slaughter and was amused at how the townspeople fell to the ground and crawled back from the fight once the shots were fired. They regrouped a short distance away from Thorton and the major, sensing a shifting mood in regards to his deal, called back one of his squads to keep an eye on the townsfolk

After a short amount of time, the main horde was taken care of and Thorton called back his men.

"You four, reload your magazines and go with a couple of these nitwits and see what you can do about securing the east border. The rest of you, reload and keep your weapons handy. Don't go near any of these guys by yourselves until things are sorted out." Thorton looked back at the assembled group. Instead of looks of gratitude, he was receiving open looks of hostility. He didn't care, he had the upper hand and everyone knew it.

As he walked over to the group, a zombie that hadn't been properly killed unsteadily got to its feet. It swayed a bit before it got its bearings and the first thing it saw was the major. It was an average zombie, medium height with stooped shoulders and blood splatter along its mouth and neck. Its dead eyes locked on Thorton and it reached with a dead hand as it slouched forward.

Ken waved off the men who were raising their weapons and walked towards the zombie. At the sight of its prey getting closer, the ghoul bared its teeth and opened its mouth to groan again. Thorton never broke stride, he simply walked up to the zombie and in a single quick move, lopped its groaning head off of its shoulders. Thorton rarely used the blade at his belt, but he was as good with it as anyone he had ever seen. In his own mind, he was the best there was. It was a thick, curved blade with a sixteen inch cutting edge that was kept razor sharp. It was heavy enough and sharp enough to trim off limbs and Thorton kept it in reserve for special occasions.

Grasping the undead head by the greasy hair, he lifted it up and watched as the mouth snapped and snarled at him, the eyes never leaving his. Grinning, he tossed the head over at the group of men arguing and laughed as they scampered out of the way. Even without a body, the zombie head was as deadly as a pit viper.

"We kept our end of the bargain, now keep yours. We need food, supplies and women for the night. You figure out how." Major Thorton's face turned hard. "Anyone thinking about revenge or doing something stupid, may as well step up and get shot now and save me the trouble later."

The men glowered at the major and some were white-knuckled as they held their weapons, but to a man they knew that without the aid of the soldiers, they would have been wiped out.

"Go tell your women not to worry, none of them will be hurt or mistreated. Consider it part of the new currency and be grateful they have such valuable, ah, commodities." Thorton's men laughed out loud at that last and they broke out their tents and supplies in anticipation.

An hour later, after the gap had been fixed and no new zombies were within hearing distance, a group of fifteen women walked over to the men. One of them, a sharp-faced redhead, walked boldly up to Ken. "I got your word none of these gals will be hurt or treated bad? Your men just gettin' some and then we're done?"

Thorton liked the attitude of the woman and he spoke loud enough for his men to hear. "My word. No one gets hurt."

The redhead nodded. "Good. I'd kill you myself if anyone thought they could slap us around." She gestured to the assembled women. "Come on, ladies, let's get it done. Try and find yourself a cute one, at least."

The women reluctantly shuffled forward and for the next hour there were various noises coming from the tents and truck beds. Thorton did not participate in the festivities; he just stood and had a staring contest with the men who waited barely a hundred yards away. *Get used to the new currency, suckers.* Thorton thought as he cleaned and sharpened his blade.

When the last woman was released and the new supplies put away, Major Thorton ordered his men to pack up. There were a lot of grunts and groans, but the men did as they were told. They knew they were not welcome here and spending the night would have tempted too many angry husbands to try something stupid.

As they rolled out the east side of the survivor's territory, Ken took a look at the darkening sky and figured they could travel for another couple of hours and camp at the next road junction. It was going to be slow going, since they were going to be in the heart of the Smoky Mountains, but the road seemed fairly passable.

There weren't any settlements or survivors the rest of the way to US 33 and for Thorton, that was just fine. Things were probably going to get lively pretty soon, just when they left the protection of the mountains.

As the sun was setting over the western ridge of the Smokies, throwing sharp hues of red and orange into the air, Ken and his men rolled into a gas station at the junction of 47 and 33. They parked the trucks with the back ends facing the convenience store and men clambered out with cans and hoses and pumps to see if there was anything left in the tanks.

Several men checked out the convenience store for any supplies and they were pleasantly surprised to find a decent amount of junk food, drinks and other sundries. Thorton himself looked over a display of fireworks, pocketing several with the thought they might be useful in distracting the zombies or something.

With the light waning, the men settled in and one of the sergeants asked Thorton if he knew how much further they had to go. Thorton checked the map, checked it again and said, "About one hundred and fifty miles."

As the men digested that, Thorton climbed into the cab of the truck to stretch out and go to sleep. *One hundred and fifty miles.* He thought. *One hundred and fifty and then its all mine.*

Happy thoughts lulled Major Thorton to sleep.

CHAPTER 12

"On your left!"

"Move it, move it!"

"Watch where you're swinging that thing! Christ!"

"Where the hell did all these fuckers come from?"

"Didja see the one with the thong?"

"Focus, Duncan!"

"Can't hold this window! Back up!"

"They're busting through on this side!"

"Fall back, there's too many! Fall back, dammit! Regroup at the grass seed, make a barrier! Let's go! Tommy, find an exit! Duncan, back him up!"

Nate and I dropped the zombies we were currently killing and snatched up our backpacks as we bolted for the middle section of the landscaping store we had spent the last night in. We were on the border of West Virginia and Virginia and taking shelter in this store seemed like a good idea at the time. But I think we arrived too late and the local Z's were attracted to the headlights and noise of the RV. Add the sound of four snoring men and the ghouls were in a positive lather for our blood.

"Block the aisles as best as you can on that side, I got this side," I said as I began tossing thirty pound bags of fertilizer down the aisle to act as stumbling blocks. The more of them I could get to trip, the easier it would be to kill them. That was the theory anyway. As the undead began working their way into the store and coming down the aisles, I couldn't be blamed for lobbing a few at the nearest ones and knocking them over.

Tommy and Duncan disappeared into the back sections of the store, the wind chimes tinkling softly at their passage. The store wasn't the best place for defense, with its big windows and sliding doors for an opening. But it was the only place after a long drive through West Virginia that looked like it might not be infested with zombies. Man, were we wrong. The whole landscape was littered with drifters, some moving around, others just standing like they sometimes do when they haven't any stimulus to follow.

Nate and I kept throwing bags of fertilizer and grass seed, depleting one pile to make another. If we could bottle them up, make them come at us through choke points, we could whittle their numbers down without having to fire shots and attract even more of the stupid things.

One of the zombies got clever and was working its way around the crowd and came at me from an unblocked aisle. His diseased arms raised in triumph as he opened his blackened mouth to come at me.

"No you won't, either!" I said as I grabbed one of the last bags of fertilizer by the edge and swung it over my head and onto his. The heavy bag took the Z right on the noggin and jammed his head face down into his chest. Somehow his spine was still intact and his arms flailed about and he stumbled over another bag, losing the one that had replaced his head.

Nate looked over at the seemingly headless corpse and said, "How's he moving without a head?"

I laughed a little. "I knocked his head into his chest."

Nate rolled his eyes. "Just when I think I've seen everything you could do to a zombie…" he trailed off and piled another bag on top of his little fertilizer mountain. "You good on your side?" he asked.

"I'm good. Watch your left. If they get clever and come around we gotta bolt."

"Roger that. Watch your right, same reason," Nate said. He picked up a long handled tree pruner and slammed it down on the head of the nearest zombie he could reach. The high ceiling allowed for some serious swings. The Z dropped and another stepped into the same spot to be dropped by the same method.

I had a billhook with a slightly shorter handle, but it was devastating just the same. I could punch through their heads from above or swing from the side and lop off their noggins as quick as I could like. I only did that a couple of times, since a moving zombie head was still dangerous and when one of the ones still upright kicked the head back at me, I gave up the French Revolution thing. Besides, if I missed, I stood a good chance of taking Nate's head off. I'm guessing he'd save his serious cursing for that moment.

"Dammit!" Nate swore as his pruner got stuck in the frontal lobe of a withered Z. He pushed back on the pole and had the satisfaction of knocking over a couple more zombies angling to climb over the rising, putrid barricade. He twisted the pole and wedged in under a sack, creating another obstacle for the Z's to stumble over. He looked at my billhook and cocked his head. "Got another one of those?"

I slammed the point down on a teenager, perforating his hoodie and brain all in one shot. "Behind me, by the trimmer saws."

Nate hurried back there and with an exclamation of joy, he resumed his position with what had to be the biggest billhook I had ever seen. It had a twenty inch blade with a wicked curve to it, was about seven inches wide and the straight back was sharpened as well. With the four foot hickory handle, it was a medieval answer to a lot of zombie problems.

I watched in awe as Nate went full berserker on the zombies. Hands and heads went flying, chunks and cheeks were split, skulls were crushed and legs were chopped. After a full minute he had cleared his area and mine. The blade was black with zombie gore and the area was splattered pretty well, too.

"Holy shit," I said, wiping a bit of zombie off my arm while Nate wiped off the blade on a bag of seed and waited for more zombies. "Any more of those?" My own billhook, while an impressive ten inches, did not come near the awesomeness of Nate's.

Nate grinned and shoved a thumb back to the racks. I dropped my weapon and looked for myself, exclaiming aloud when I found not only another one, but three more as well. *We're sure taking these with us*, I thought as I propped the other two up on a counter.

Just when I started back to the fray Tommy came barreling around the corner.

"We got an exit, but we gotta go now! They're starting to congregate out back!" he said breathlessly. "Wow! What's that?" His eyes took in the heavy bladed brush remover.

"New toy. You should see it work," I said, hefting the big sucker.

"I will if you don't move your ass."

"Roger that. Nate!" I called. "We're gone. Move it!"

"Coming!"

I heard the meaty smack of metal striking flesh and I knew Nate was playing some more.

A second later, he was rushing past us, grabbing up the additional billhooks as Tommy led the way. We burst through a supply room and I took scant notice of the dead zombie lying facedown with a crowbar buried in the back of its skull. Nate took a moment to assess the shelves in the stockroom, then he jumped up onto one of them and braced his feet on the other.

With a heave, he managed to shove and entire shelving unit of paint cans onto the floor, creating a footing nightmare for the zombies that were sure to follow. The move bought us five to ten minutes if we needed it.

Just as I hit the back door, I could hear the crack of a rifle on the other side. I opened the door cautiously and saw Duncan standing his ground against about ten zombies that were advancing his way. A small zombie was at his feet, a neat bullet hole near the top of its forehead.

"'Bout time," Duncan said, trying to keep an eye on all the zombies headed his way.

"You'll thank us in a minute," I said. "Nate, would you care to take the left and I'll take the right?"

"That's so kind of you, thank you," Nate said, tightening his grip on his weapon.

"My pleasure." I stepped out into the lumberyard and approached a female zombie. She looked fairly rank, her grey skin contrasting with her dark, greasy hair. Her torso was uncovered and she looked like she must have had implants at some point. You could always tell on a zombie. I readied a two handed hold and when she came within striking distance, I struck with as much power as I could muster. The blade connected at the point where her shoulder met her neck and completely cut her in half. One part had the head and an arm, the other part held the rest. The two pieces landed about a foot from each other, with the head still snapping and the arm still reaching.

Duncan whistled. "Now that is a tool! I don't normally get excited about weapons of Z destruction, but I definitely felt something stir just now."

Tommy said nothing, he just edged a little further away from Duncan.

Nate and I went to work, hacking zombies from single pieces to several and the heavy blades made the job easy. I took a direct approach, lopping off heads to spiking the brain from the top, while Nate was more artistic in his approach. He would cut a zombie off at the knees, literally and then try to spear the head as the Z fell. The best was when we both swung at the same zombie. I was off target by a bit and caught the Z in the mouth, burying the blade into his skull to his ears, his teeth pinging off the metal. Nate came from the other side and crushed the ghouls spine with the straight edge.

We looked about our vanquished foes with what had to be the same sort of satisfaction knights felt when they had emerged from the battlefield victorious.

I wiped off the blade as best as I could and made a run for the side of the building. Angling out so as not to be caught by a Z close in, I saw the coast was clear. Signaling to the others, we rounded the corner just as the zombies from the inside of the building came crashing through the supply room door.

"Perfect," I said. "So much for the delay."

"Just keep moving," Nate said. "It wasn't supposed to keep them all day."

Peeking around the corner, I could see a clear path to the RV. That was the good news. The bad news was there were a lot of zombies milling about that were closer to the RV than we were and could easily cut us off if they saw us.

I held a quick conference. "I'm going to distract the ones near the RV. When the coast is clear, get aboard and come get me."

Nate nodded. "Duncan, you and Tommy get on the roof and give John cover. I'll get the beast moving."

Tommy and Duncan unlimbered their rifles and made sure they were ready to go. Nate pulled out the keys and made sure he had them ready as well. I wasn't sure what I was going to do to distract the Z's, but as with most of my plans, I'd make something up as I went along.

Running out onto the parking lot, I beheaded a nearby zombie and started yelling in a falsetto voice. "Oh, help me! Help me! The zombies are after me! Whatever shall I do? Wherever shall I go? Help me! Help me!" I'll admit most of this was for the benefit of my companions, who showed their appreciation by shaking their heads and rolling their eyes.

All of the zombies that were outside the garden center turned my way and gladly decided to offer some assistance. As a matter of fact, I was sure they would be most willing volunteers. I walked a little ways away, scanning the crowd for any fast-moving young bastards, then jogged easily away. The zombies, being of the staggeringly stupid variety, followed along, hoping I might trip and somehow break my legs and arms.

I ran down the street, passing a trailer sales yard and as I did, a large zombie stumbled out from between the sales office and display model. He was a little over six feet tall, but he looked larger because he was wearing a heavy winter coat. One of the arms was torn open and trailed some downy filler out of the tear. His vacant eyes locked onto me and he shuffled out with a purpose. I could see the RV pulling out of the Garden Center and it was amusing to see several zombies get knocked aside as the RV swept past.

But my immediate concern was the big son of a buck barreling down at me from the side. I hefted the billhook, then changed my mind. "You're too big to chance it, Frosty," I said as I pulled my SIG. One shot later and the big Z fell over like an axed sapling.

The RV pulled up and I hopped on board, taking Duncan's rifle as he handed it down to me from the roof. A minute later Tommy joined us and I went to sit in the front seat, only to stand up again as a pissed off cat snarled and tried to claw my ass.

"Jesus, Zeus!" I said, managing to blaspheme in two religions.

Nate laughed. "The little shit did the same thing to me. Ought to toss him overboard."

"Should have sent him home with Janna."

"Right. A cat on a boat. Great idea for cosmic harmony."

"Blow me. Where the hell are we?" I reached behind me and ignoring the kitten fangs in my hand, grabbed a handful of feline and shoved him into an overhead bin. I nursed a particularly long scratch and pawed through the maps until I found West Virginia. Following a line I had drawn earlier, I placed us…

"Virginia. We're in Virginia," Nate said from the driver's side.

"How do you know?" I said.

"Because the sign I passed said 'Welcome to Virginia'. You think they put those up as a ruse and we're really in New Jersey?" Nate said sarcastically.

"How would I know what they do out east? They're all nuts." I reflected for a minute. "At least, they were."

We drove on for a while, working our way slowly through the backcountry. Virginia is a different kind of state. It is liberally covered in pine forest and driving through it you start to feel constricted and claustrophobic. The trees grew right next to the road and many times we had to swerve out of the way of large branches that had the potential to crack the RV something fierce.

We passed a lot of zombies and a couple of places looked like they might have once held survivors, but were now overrun by the dead. One small building had dozens of bones scattered about, bleaching quietly in the warm sun. There was no indication of any violence, save the bones.

We passed through Winchester and had to resort to ghost driving once again. The big RV inched through the town, nudging Z's out of the way, travelling roughly one mile an hour. I was navigating from the darkness of the RV while Nate steered from the floor. I didn't see any signs of life, although I did see a large concentration of zombies near the airport, usually a sign that something might still be alive in there. We couldn't offer to help, since there were probably three thousand ghouls congregated there. Even in our little RV tank they had the numbers to really ruin our day. I made a small vow to do whatever I could later to help everyone who was surrounded by the dead, holding on to whatever small hope there was that someone, anyone, might be able to help.

Outside of Winchester, away from the main population centers, I called a halt and we pulled over under the protective canopy of a gas station. Nate and I checked for fuel while Tommy and Duncan checked for unwanted attendants and supplies. The gas station was tucked into a little clearing of trees and the forest was thick enough that we couldn't see into it very far, nor could we see the road any more than what was ahead of us.

Nate and I were both pleasantly surprised to find a decent amount of gas left over. Most places we checked actually had plenty of fuel. People in the Upheaval didn't want to waste time getting gas in their flight from the dead, they just wanted to get away. We managed to top off the tanks and fill three jerry cans as well.

As I put the cans away and checked the bungee cords on our outside supplies and weapons, I became aware of a noise coming from the road. I leaned over and spoke to Nate, who was checking our hoses and lines for leaks.

"You hear something?" I asked.

"No, you're imagining things." He paused. "Wait, I hear it, too. What is it?" Nate pulled himself out from under the RV and looked around.

Tommy and Duncan walked out of the convenience store carrying handfuls of beef jerky and bottled water. They looked at each other and then wandered over to where we were.

"What's that sound?" Duncan asked around a stick of beef jerky protruding from his mouth.

"I'm not sure," I said, helping myself to a piece of jerky. "Sounds like a lawn mower, but that can't be right. No one would be dumb enough to fire one of those up."

"Whatever it is, it's getting closer," Nate said. "I suggest we see what comes of it inside our little fortress?"

We all agreed and climbed back into the RV. Four faces looked out the front window as the sound came closer and closer. We quietly discussed what the sound was. I stuck with lawn mower, but Nate said it was too high pitched. Tommy said go-cart and Duncan was convinced it was some sort of six-wheeled contraption.

Whatever we thought did not prepare us for the sight that eventually showed up. Rounding the bend and coming into view was a John Deere riding mower. It was being driven by a stocky man chewing what might have been a cigar. He was going about two miles an hour and he was being chased by a horde of at least forty zombies. They lurched and stumbled along at roughly the same speed, neither gaining nor losing ground. The grim parade traversed our line of sight and then disappeared on the far side of the clearing. The man never once looked our way. The noise was the combination of the riding mower and the incessant moans of the zombies.

I looked at the empty space for a full minute, listening to the receding procession before turning to my companions.

Tommy spoke up first. "I got nothing," he said, still staring out the window.

Duncan shook his head. "Never saw a zombie pied piper before."

Nate frowned. "Shit, no one's gonna believe this."

I tended to agree with Nate. "Okay. Well, that's new. On to other business." I turned to my crew members and got serious. "I want to propose a side trip. I'm going to make it a vote, since we're getting close to D.C. and we've already had a stressful day."

Curious faces looked into mine as I continued. "Just up the way from here is a small town. It's not much, just a few small stores and a couple of subdivisions. Its probably ten miles out of the way, round trip."

"What's there?" Tommy asked.

I looked out the window at the road in front of me. "My parents' house."

I glanced back at the silent faces and wasn't surprised Nate was the first to speak up. "Hell, man. You sure you want to do that? You might have to put them down—could you do it?"

I shrugged. "If I had to. My point is we're this close and I couldn't go back to my brother and tell him I didn't have the heart to check on our parents. We're assuming they're dead. What if they're alive? I need to know one way or the other, but I am willing to leave it up to a vote."

Duncan shook his head. "Don't be stupid, bro. If it was us you'd make sure we knew, one way or the other. We owe you this at least, dude."

Tommy nodded. "Let's take a look. What could it hurt?"

I reminded myself again why I surrounded myself with such men and it was in times like these that I really knew what my friends were made of.

"Thanks, guys," I said.

"Shut up and tell me how to get there," Nate snarled kindly, tossing me a map.

I didn't need a map, having been here many times before. "Take 340 to Boyce, then head south on State Road 723. First right past Country Club Lane, that's their road."

"Will do."

I left the front of the RV and went to the supply cabinet. I unpacked my backpack and repacked it, making sure to take a couple sticks of the new jerky. I pulled out my M1A, checked the action, then loaded a couple of magazines. I pulled the magazines from my belt for my SIG and checked those as well, surprising myself when I found that two of them were only half full. I topped them off and then checked the action on my SIG, chambering a round and uncocking it before re-holstering it. I checked the edge of my knife and finding it less than what I wanted, I pulled a sharpener and gave it an edge I approved of.

I replaced the knife, checked my vest, and made sure I had matches, some paracord, my compass and a couple of flares.

Once everything was in place, I looked over at the table where Tommy and Duncan were cleaning their guns. Both of the men were staring at me.

"What?"

Tommy broke into a grin. "It's okay to be nervous, John. If I was going to check on my parents two years after the zombie apocalypse, I'd be nervous too. Are they alive, are they dead, are they even there? Too many 'what-ifs'. But I understand it. My parents were killed in the first few months. Duncan's caught the virus. We know. Maybe you'll be lucky."

I nodded. "Maybe. But I have to steel myself to the possibility that I may have to put them down. I cannot hesitate. I have to convince myself they aren't my parents anymore, that what made them my parents is gone forever, replaced by a man-eating fiend."

Duncan laughed. "Geez, when you put it that way…"

I joined the laughter and we all waited for Nate to tell us we were there. I was a mess of conflicting emotions. I wanted to know what happened to my parents, yet at the same time, there was comfort in not knowing, in nurturing the far-flung hope that somehow, someway, they were alive and surviving. It wasn't outside the realm of possibility. Dad was a former Marine, after all, and would have paid attention to the signs that the world was coming apart. He had enough friends and contacts from his days in the service that he might have actually stood a better chance than most.

Thinking about my father brought back a lot of memories, some of them not so great. I remembered the arguments we used to have about the Marines. He wanted me to join, I didn't want to, told him there were no more honorable wars to fight. He argued service itself was an honor and why didn't I love my country? In the end we agreed to disagree and he eventually came to realize that my becoming a teacher was serving the country as well, just in a different way.

The more I mulled over the situation, the more I began to convince myself that maybe they might still be alive. Dad was a crack shot and was more than prepared for an invasion. I used to kid him about his End of the World as We Know It preparations, but now it seemed like he was receiving signals well ahead of the rest of us.

"Heads up, kiddies!" Nate called from the front. "We're about a minute out."

I stood up and went to the front to guide Nate to the house. "The road ends in a circular cul-de-sac, my parents' house will be the farthest one on the left." I watched the familiar trees pass by, the one with the crooked branches and the one that grew through an old stock fence left to rust. Two seasons of uncleared brush and leaves covered the old road and Nate nearly drove off more than once. But we made it and Nate pulled up to my parent's home unopposed.

Tommy and Duncan swung out first, checking the area for roamers and unhelpful neighbors. The house sat in the midst of several trees, a small cabin-like home with a wrap-around porch. On the east side of the house was the garage door and on the west was a sun room my mom had my dad put on years ago. I remembered spending my summer nights sleeping "outdoors" in that sun room with my brother. We'd chat until the early hours, until our dad came down and slept with us to make sure we were quiet. Good memories. We'd moved to Illinois later, but returned to Virginia after Dad got fed up with the taxes. I wound up returning to Illinois for school and stayed when I met Ellie.

Nate, Tommy and Duncan all nodded and I stepped up to the porch. I could see the windows had been reinforced from the inside, indicating my father had taken the same precautions I had, once upon a time. I knocked on the door, feeling somewhat ridiculous, but it seemed like the thing to do.

Not getting an answer, I tried the handle and found it locked. I walked to the farthest window, reached above the frame, and retrieved a key my father kept there for emergencies. I opened the door and had my SIG at the ready, just in case.

The house was neat and tidy and besides a covering of dust, I couldn't see anything that would indicate what happened. There wasn't any sign of a hurried exit or any kind of violence. If I had to make a comparison, it was like returning to a summer cabin after a long winter away.

The only clue I got as to what may have happened was when I looked in on the office and saw a page of notes my father had made when he was doing some research. It was covered with bits of advice, like 'head shots only', 'watch sense of smell', etc. I had a flashback to my own research when I was holed up with Jake trying to figure out how to deal with the enemy.

When I went upstairs, I found several things out of place. My father's closet was open and looked like several pieces of clothing were missing. My mother's closet was untouched. I began to get a bad feeling and it was heightened by a grave I noticed when I looked out the window into the back yard.

I was on my way down to check it out when I passed by my brother's room. On the pillow on his bed was an envelope with Mike's name on it. I recognized my father's precise script and tucked the letter into my pack to give to my brother. I quickly checked my old room and found a similar letter addressed to me. My guess is our dad figured if we ever made it back, if things returned to normal, we'd at least understand what happened here if he could just let us know.

I opened the letter and was surprised to find my hand shaking. Inside was a single handwritten note:

Dear John,
If you're reading this, then I have the unfortunate duty to tell you that your mother is gone. She caught the virus trying to take care of one of her friends who got sick. She's buried in the backyard she loved so much. Stop by her grave if you can.

John, I have gone to help some friends and I don't know if I will ever be back at the homestead. It was a good place to live and to raise you boys, but without your mother, it isn't home anymore. If you want it, it's yours. If not, give it to Mike.

Son, I know we disagreed on a lot of things, but I want you to know that I was always proud of you. You and your brother made my life complete in ways I can't express in words and the greatest joy in my life was bringing you both into the world.

The honor I had at being a Marine cannot compare to the honor I have at being your father. I know you think I was disappointed because you chose not to serve in the Corps. That wasn't true. I was disappointed for the Corps, since they lost the chance to be led by a good man like yourself. As much as you deny it, you're a leader, John. I hope you have come to realize it as much as everyone else has.

I pray you and Jake and Ellie are all right and someday you might find me at your door.

Take care of your brother and remember I love you and am proud of you.

Semper Fi,

John Talon, Sr.

PS. I left supplies for you in the basement.

I read and re-read the note, trying my best to keep the tears from falling on the precious paper. I was sad my mother was gone, but at the same time relieved my father might still be alive. I suppose the best thing I could do would be to finish the mission and get back to my family, in the hopes that the old soldier would someday find his way to a place where someone could point him in the right direction.

I went downstairs and out the back door, heading to the grave I had seen from the second floor. Duncan was in the back yard, looking over some flower beds and he started when he saw me.

"Everything okay?" he asked, looking at the strain on my face.

I waved him off and went over to the grave. It was a simple affair, just two boards making a small cross over a mound of dirt covered with flagstones. I got down on one knee and spoke to my dead mother.

"I'm sorry I wasn't here, Mom. I hope you can forgive me. I know dad is gone somewhere and maybe I'll see him someday, but I have a job to do first. Jake is safe and so is Mike and his family, figured you would want to know that. Ellie died, but you and she are probably watching me make of fool of myself right now. I married again, her name is Sarah and she's a good mother to Jake. You'd like her. I gotta go, Mom, but we'll all be back someday, I promise." I kissed my hand and touched the cross and for a brief second I thought I felt a touch on my cheek. I knew it was my imagination, but I like to think that maybe she heard me and let me know it was all right.

I stood up and walked back to the house, trailed by Duncan, who understood enough to keep a respectful silence. The words of my father's letter burned in my brain and I added them to what Sarah had told me recently, although it seemed like a long time ago.

We re-entered the house and I led Duncan into the garage. Dad had mentioned the basement, although to be accurate, few houses in Western Virginia really had a basement. In the garage was a small door, about three feet high, hidden behind the workbench. It was a crawlspace that went under the house and my Dad had created a storage space in the crawlspace.

I pulled away the door and stepped down into the small trench my father had dug years ago. It ran the length of the house and allowed my dad to stand upright under the house. He placed several small shelving units under there and it gave him a lot more usable space than just a crawl space. Duncan looked around and was impressed with the simplicity of creating a useful area where most people just left it alone.

I followed the trench to the far end, passing the Christmas and Easter decorations. At the end I turned left and followed the trench to another end. At this point there was a small collection of bins and shelves. I opened three of the bins and looked inside. Satisfied, I handed the heavy bins to Duncan, who grunted under the weight. I opened a small safe sitting on the side and after looking in, pulled out two boxes. One was labeled "Mike" the other "John". I placed the boxes on top of two more bins then followed Duncan out of the "basement".

We carried our burdens back to the RV, where we were joined by Nate and Tommy.

Nate asked the obvious question. "Everything okay? I saw the grave out back."

I nodded. "My mother's. She got sick. Dad might still be alive, but he's left here for good."

"Sorry about your mom, John," Tommy said softly.

I looked up. "Thanks, Tommy. I feel better knowing for sure, but then I feel bad she's gone. Does that make sense?"

Tommy smiled. "Strangely enough, yes. What have you here?" he asked, changing the subject.

I opened three of the bins and pulled out dozens of boxes of ammunition. There was .223 ammo, .308 ammo, 9mm and .45ACP ammo. The three other men widened their eyes at the sudden resupply. I opened the other bins and showed them a quantity of reloading supplies, including a small single stage press.

Nate spoke first. "I like your dad more and more. He just have this stuff on hand?"

"Dad believed in being prepared and being self-reliant. I guess some of his stuff actually rubbed of on me," I said.

"What's in the labeled boxes?" Tommy asked.

"Good question," I said. "I've never seen those before." I took the box with my name on it and opened it. Inside was a brand new Springfield Armory 1911. It was a stainless Loaded model, with night sights. The wood grips had been replaced with ivory ones and it was beautiful weapon. A holster accompanied the weapon and I whistled with appreciation.

"Your dad knows his guns," Nate said, picking up the .45 and checking the sights. ".45 round would pop a Z's head like a melon."

"I know," I said. "But I'm going to stick with my SIG for now. I like the option of killing 13 zombies before a reload as opposed to eight."

Nate put the gun back. "That is true. What about your brother's?"

I shook my head. "That's his to open, as is this." I took out the letter from our father and placed it on the box, putting both up in a storage bin. "Hopefully I'll see him soon enough to give him both."

"Anything else we need here?" Nate asked.

I shook my head. Although this was the place I grew up, it wouldn't be home again for a long time. I just hoped that by the time all was said and done, it would still be here to come back to. Interestingly, I had no similar feelings about the place back in Illinois anymore, the home Ellie and I had shared. Maybe the uncertainty of life made thoughts of permanence a fantasy, something only fools thought to hope for.

I stashed those thoughts away as we pulled out. I looked back and I could see the home recede in the mirror. I could see the small grave in the back and I wondered how it might have been for my Dad. Not having to face that situation myself, I had to give Dad credit for having to put down the woman he'd been in love with for over thirty years. I don't know if I could have killed Ellie. I imagine a lot of people couldn't, they just locked their loved ones away in the hopes a cure might be found, or someone would be able to help. Probably a lot of people became infected that way, trying to do something, anything, for a son or daughter who got sick and came back.

We crossed a river on our way through Virginia and passed through what looked to be a state wilderness area or something. A small café was located on the side of the road and I asked Nate to pull over. We were supposedly in a town called Paris, but like a lot of towns, this one was just a small collection of homes situated near a highway.

The café was the Ashby Inn and Restaurant and looked like a hundred other places we had passed. I stepped out of the RV, looked over the rest of the town, and was reminded once again about what we had lost. It was dead silent and barely anything moved. I could see out of the corner of my eye the comings and goings of small animals as they went about their business.

I didn't see any zombie activity and it puzzled me for a minute. Since we crossed the Ohio River we had seen zombies everywhere, in fields and towns and everywhere in between. It was like this part of the country just gave up and joined the ranks of the dead willingly.

But things were quiet around here and it was a bit of a mystery until a voice spoke from behind me.

"Well, well. Looks like some gen-u-ine hard asses, that's fer sure."

I spun around, whipping my rifle to my shoulder. Whatever I was expecting to see certainly wasn't standing down the road from me. Down the barrel of my M1A I studied the speaker. He was a tall drink of water, probably six foot four or so, with lean muscular arms and legs. He was wearing a broad-brimmed hat which was pulled low onto his head, but even in the shadows his eyes were very bright. A thin cotton poncho covered his naked torso and a duffle bag of supplies lay at his feet. He wore a belt of sorts, about which hung flashlights, knives and what seemed to be a sharpener.

As eccentric as he seemed, his weapon really caught my attention. It was a pole as tall as he was, with a spike on one end and a two foot blade on the other. A handle jutted out at a ninety-degree angle about halfway up the blade and the really impressive thing was another weapon, identical to the first, was strapped to his bare back. With both hands filled with those killers, I imagined he could do some serious damage.

I lowered my rifle. "Name's John Talon. I'm traveling through to D.C.. Who might you be?"

The man stepped towards me and stopped as Tommy and Duncan came out of the RV and flanked me with their carbines at the ready.

"I used to be called James Carson, but it's been a while since anyone living called me that." He walked up to me and ignored the nervous fidgeting of my companions as he leaned in close. He studied me for a minute before exclaiming "You don't look crazy or stupid. Why in thunder would you want to go to D.C.? Fucking ghouls are all over the place over there."

I explained briefly what we were doing and why and at the end of my monologue, James was nodding his head.

"I can see the why and your reasons make sense. I just don't know how much of a chance you got, son." Carson said.

I shrugged. "If we want to become a country united again, we have to have our symbols on which we placed our faith. Otherwise, it's survival of the fittest and it will be centuries before we stand up again as a nation. I don't want do to that to my son."

At the mention of my son James' face darkened and he turned serious. "Good luck to you and maybe I'll see you again," he said as he turned away.

"Wait," I said. "Maybe you want to join us? Once this job is done, we've got a country to reclaim. We could use a good man."

Carson stared at me over his shoulder. "What makes you think I'm any good?"

I smiled. "You're alone in zombie infested territory, armed with medieval weapons against countless Z's. On a hunch, I'd say you're good enough."

James frowned. "No sir, I'm not good enough. At least I wasn't."

"What do you mean?" I asked, curious as to why he wasn't willing to join us.

Carson looked off into the hills for a minute before replying. "My son was torn from my grasp by the ghouls. They ripped him to pieces before my eyes. I couldn't save him."

"I'm sorry."

"Don't be. You ain't to blame." Carson shouldered his weapon and turned away. After a couple of steps he turned back. "They killed him, now I spend my life killing them. Eventually they'll get me, but I'll take out as many as I can before that day comes. I owe him that much at least."

"Good luck." I called to his retreating back. I regretted his leaving, but I understood why he was doing what he did. If I was in his shoes I'd want a reckoning as well.

We climbed back aboard the RV and started to look for a place to spend the night. A town called Middleburg was ahead on the map and I called Nate's attention to it.

Nate looked at the sky as we moved along. "Looks like rain," he said.

I glanced at the darkening sky. He was right. Hopefully it would be an uneventful evening.

CHAPTER 13

Lightning arced across the black sky, illuminating clouds thick with rain. Water fell from the heavens and trees bent in the howling winds, bowing under the weight of the falling rain. Deep rumblings followed the lightning and the hard concussion of strikes shook the foundations of the little buildings caught in this summer tempest.

The lightning exposed what walked at night, heedless of the rain and wind. In the brief flashes illuminating the landscape, the horror of the dark was revealed one slow step at a time. The dead were out in the storm and each strike of lightning showed them moving closer and closer.

I looked out of the hardware store window and surveyed the scene before me. Dead bodies were scattered around the road and store, forming small dams as the rain tried to wash their stain away. They were the losers in a running fight I had to get to this place, managing to separate myself from my team and getting cut off by the remaining ghouls which waited for me outside.

The lightning crashed again, revealing dark forms moving in my direction.

A sound from the back room caught my attention and I briefly cocked an ear that way. It was a small cough, small enough to belong to a child. I turned my head and caught the eye of the woman sitting back there. She looked at me fearfully, but relaxed when I shook my head. With the rain, wind and thunder, it was unlikely that the Z's would hear us. We couldn't shout to each other, but small sounds would probably go unnoticed. I wondered if the girl was infected. We'd know soon enough either way.

I found myself keeping a hand on my gun as I watched the zombies get closer. Not that the gun would be much help. I had used up my entire carbine and pistol ammo to get us to this place and all I had left was the mini pickaxe with a modified handle and my knife. If I was facing just one or two zombies, I wouldn't be so worried. But the lightning showed me ten times that number and that was something not any sane man would run willingly to.

Another sound from the back caused me to look again and this time I made eye contact with the man back there, husband to the woman. I shook my head again and he relaxed, although he continued to throw glances my way as if he expected me to attack him myself. I chuckled. In his shoes, I might have looked at me the same way too.

In the gloom outside, I watched the zombies milling about in the rain. They couldn't see, and they couldn't hear very well with the rain. The lightning flashes caused them to jerk one way, while the thunder caused them to jerk another. Some of them stumbled over fallen comrades, to be washed away briefly before regaining their unsteady forms.

But they steadily moved in this direction, one way or the other. As I watched them, an idea formed in the back of my head and the more I thought about it, the more it seemed plausible.

I carefully walked to the back of the store and hunkered down with the family of four that was sitting there. We had found them hiding out in the second story of a bank, taking refuge there when their car broke down. They were waiting for the ghouls in the area to move on before they made a break for it, but one of them happened to move past a window and was seen by a zombie. The Z pounded on the doors and windows so loudly it attracted the attention of every other zombie for a mile and the family was truly in trouble.

"What's going on?" the father asked me nervously. He was slightly built, but had intelligent eyes, which probably explained why he and his family were alive. His brow was creased with worry and he kept looking at his two children, a boy and a girl, both under seven years old.

I played it straight. "The rain is keeping the zombies from figuring out where we are right now and I'm going to use that to our advantage. We can't all break out of here because they'd be all over us in a second. But I can reduce the odds some; use the rain to *my* advantage."

The woman, a short, mousy-looking specimen, looked sharply at me. "You mean to go out there?"

I nodded. "Don't see much choice. As soon as the rain ends, their senses will be in high gear. They know we're around, but they aren't sure where."

"What do you plan on doing?" the man asked, reaching out and holding his son's hand. His son, Evan, hadn't said a word since meeting me. His father had mentioned something about Evan seeing his friend's family turn and go on a rampage, but I didn't need details. No one escaped unscathed from the Upheaval. No one.

"I'm going to arm myself with whatever I can and head out there, killing as many as I can. Hopefully I can do it without being swarmed," I said, looked around to see what I could use for weapons. The store had been fairly looted, but some things would serve.

"What if you are?" the woman asked, gently rocking her one year old baby girl. It was the baby that had coughed earlier. I was pretty sure the baby was sick, possibly fever, but I had nothing to help her with.

"I'll lead them away and you all can make a break for it. Behind this building is an alley, which if you take north, will put you on the edge of town. Head out across country and you should make it." I stood up and stretched my legs.

The man looked at me, then stood up. He offered his hand and I took it. "Good luck," he said.

"You too, if it comes to that," I replied.

"You could have left us to die," woman said suddenly. "Why did you help us?"

I considered that for a moment as I hunted among the shelves for usable weapons. I placed several hammers in my belt, some flat-bladed screwdrivers in my pockets and tucked a full-sized pickaxe handle within easy reach in my backpack. Every hardware store we hit we found hammers and screwdrivers. Made sense. What household didn't have a hammer? In another life, I owned three. I found a hunter's hat in the racks and put that on. With its two-inch brim, the rain should stay out of my eyes.

I went to the back door and listened carefully. I heard nothing but rain so I opened the door slightly, stepping back with pick raised to see if anything was out there. I pushed the door open further and waited again as rainwater began to pool inside the doorway. Nothing happened, so I spared a glance at the family and said, "It's what I do," and stepped out into the dark rain.

It was like stepping into a shower. I was instantly soaked with heavy drops. The hat kept the worst of it off my face and I was able to see through the rain a little bit better. I quickly checked the alley on both sides and was relieved when I saw it was empty. I moved as quietly as I could to the side of the building and looked slowly around.

I nearly jumped when the next flash of lightning revealed a zombie standing not five feet from me. His back was turned and he was slowly shuffling through the water that pooled around his bare feet. I could tell he was not alive, since there was a gaping hole in his right side, allowing me to see the rain hitting the ground on the other side. His long hair stuck closely to his skull and fat raindrops splattered on his dark skin. I looked around and saw another zombie several yards away and this one was facing slightly away from me as well.

I stepped quietly forward and silently pulled out a screwdriver. I waited for a flash of lightning and when the thunder came, I struck. Using an overhand grip, I punched the screwdriver through the top of the zombie's head. He stiffened momentarily, then dropped to the ground with a small splash.

As the flowing water ebbed around its newest obstacle, I looked over at the other zombie. It hadn't moved, so my tactics had been successful. I moved slowly, approaching it from the rear and I could see several pairs of glowing eyes in the gloom. They bobbed back and forth as their owners moved through the rain. The really creepy ones were the single glowing eyes. Get lost, Cyclops.

I moved slowly through the rain, having the crazy thought that the zombies couldn't see or hear or smell me, they might actually think I was one before it was too late. Sidling up to the next Z, I waited again for another crash of thunder and then I rammed the screwdriver through this walking corpse's skull, dropping it with a wet splash. I scanned the area and saw a pair of glowing eyes making for me in the dark. I didn't hear the telltale moan, which meant it wasn't sure what I was yet. I waited, looking around and assessing targets. The next flash of lightning allowed me to count the zombies nearby and the number was roughly ten. Under any other conditions, I would have avoided this at all costs, but since I had the advantage, I may as well use it.

The zombie sloshed closer, the glowing eyes fixed on me now, but still no sound. Its hands were still lowered, which was another sign it wasn't sure what I was. I moved the screwdriver around to my left side, crossing my right arm in front of me. As the zombie got close enough, I could see it was a female, possibly a nurse, judging by the stained scrubs it wore. I had a brief pang as I thought of my dead wife then steeled myself and when the Z got closer, I whipped my arm up and around, planting the screwdriver into the zombie's temple. The mouth opened briefly to protest, then the corpse fell permanently dead at my feet. I left the screwdriver in its head and pulled another.

I killed four more in a similar fashion, sliding through the rain, striking quickly and then disappearing before they knew what hit them. I left several zombies on the ground with screwdrivers stuck in their skulls and I was hefting two of my hammers when the worst thing happened.

The damn rain stopped.

I froze in place, while three zombies milled about in front of me. The wind was still blowing, but the drone of the rain had stopped and even I was able to make out other sounds besides the wind. I figured the darkness would help hide me, but they would be able to smell me out very quickly. In the blackness around me, I could see several more sets of glowing eyes and those were the ones that I *could* see. I knew there were several more out there whose eyes weren't glowing, who were a bigger threat because of it.

I felt completely exposed, more so because my gun was empty and the only thing I had standing between me and undead oblivion was some hardware store hammers and my battle-tested pickaxe.

As I considered my options, one of the trio in front of me happened to turn to the side and catch sight of me. I stood still, waiting to see what she would do next. I balanced myself on the balls of my feet, ready to spring into action, my hands gripping the handles of my hammers tightly.

She cocked her head to the side, leaned slightly forward and bellowed out the loudest, most mournful cry of the dead I had ever heard. It sounded like a cross between a calf and a bullfrog. The effect on the other two was shock and awe and they pivoted quickly to stare at the cause of the commotion. They looked at the yelling zombie, then over to me, then back to the yeller. They seemed to be confused as to what to do.

I didn't hesitate. I leapt forward and slammed the claw end of the hammer onto the top of the first zombie's head, spinning her away as she fell to the ground. I bolted at the other two zombies, then looked at them helplessly as I tripped over a submerged obstacle and hydroplaned past both of them. They gave chase and the closest one fell to its knees as it tried to grab me in closer for a juicy bite.

I wasn't about to be so accommodating. As it dropped down, I kicked it viciously in the face, knocking it back and giving me time to get to my feet. I had trained in ground fighting with Charlie and Tommy, but it was a losing proposition with two Z's after your ass.

The second one was on me as I got up and I barely got a hand up into its chest to stop it before it could knock me down. The zombie felt the contact and its head snapped down to try and bite the hand on its chest, missing my fingers by inches, but exposing the top of its head to a hammer blow. As I killed it, I pushed it back onto its friend, who was just getting to its feet. They both went down in a heap and I unslung my pick in the interim. I moved through the still-swirling water and over to the still-kicking Z. I rearranged its neurons, ending its dead career.

I hefted my pickaxe and looked around quickly for additional targets. I saw none close and decided to push the living shit out of my luck and get moving to try and rendezvous with my friends. We had gotten separated when we rescued the family. Running back to the hardware store I burst through the back door and stepped back as an axe cleaved the air where I had been standing. I moved forward and shoved the man back onto his rear end, taking my hat off in the process.

"Nice try, but axes are too heavy for extended work," I said, heading to the back room. The man scrambled to his feet and chased after me.

"Did you get them all?" he asked breathlessly, getting off the floor.

"Not even close," I said, crushing his hopes. "But I may have opened a corridor for us to move through, but we have to go *now*.

Get your stuff and let's get moving." I picked up my carbine from where I had stashed it and slung it over my shoulder.

The family was used to quick exits, bless them, and we were up and moving very quickly. I ushered them to the back door, after giving them specific instructions to wait for me and do exactly what I told them. The woman and her husband were both carrying a child, the woman holding the little girl. They stood at the door looking at each other while I replenished my screwdriver and hammer supply. Using the tools was okay, but it required me to get in closer than I liked. Couldn't be helped this evening.

I went to the back door and was just close enough to hear the husband apologize to his wife. She touched his cheek and told him to hush. He had done more than most men alive, so he was a hero to her. I hated to interrupt their moment, but we needed to move.

"Stay by me, let me know if any are getting too close. I'm going to go out and clear the alleyway and then I'm heading left to the center of town. We're going to move right down the center of the street. Stay away from cars and doorways and keep moving. No matter what happens, keep moving."

"Do you know where we're going?" the man asked.

"Down the block there is a bank we can hole up in if needed, but I'm hoping we can make it to the ball fields at the end of town."

"Why there?" the woman asked. "Won't we be exposed?"

I smiled. "Exposed on your own is bad. Exposed with backup is something else. That was the rendezvous point if we got separated. So I am hoping my friends will be waiting for us there."

"If they aren't?"

"I'll distract the zombies while you make a run for it."

"Oh, God."

I opened the door slightly and checked the alley. Water sloshed noisily around various piles of debris and dripped in a steady cadence from trees and rooftops. Gutters still spilled out onto the ground and the world had that fresh-washed smell. If it weren't for the fact a lot of zombies were out there looking to give me an unaffectionate nibble, I might have thought it was pleasant.

I stepped quickly through the door and moved to the edge of the building and peered around. I could see three zombies standing in the street, their tattered clothing sticking to their decaying skin. They were roughly six feet apart and directly in the way. I stooped quickly and grabbed an empty pop can and filled it with water. I stepped back into the alley, cocked my arm back and let fly, aiming the can to fall behind the zombies.

The second I let go I was moving. I went around the corner and headed for the zombies just as the can clanked back to earth from its flight. The zombies had their backs to me and were headed towards the can when I attacked. The first one, a small female, fell from my pickaxe without ever getting a look at me. The sound of her falling wetly to the road caused the other two to turn in my direction. I wasn't waiting for them to get set. As soon as I removed my weapon from the head of the first one I was advancing on the second. This one had to be an original, as it was nearly naked and black with decay. I swung hard at its head and was surprised at how little resistance there was as the metal sheared through the fragile skull. I faced the third and swung hard as he lunged for me, his outstretched hands ready to rend and tear. The pointed edge of the pick caught him near the back of the head by his torn off ear, while the heavy handle flattened the side of his skull. The full swing swept him off his feet and caused him to pinwheel into a heap on the ground.

I sluiced my weapon through the running water of a gutter and motioned the family to follow me. They sprinted towards me and spared no time to gawk at my handiwork.

We moved down the street, heads darting back and forth as sounds of pursuit in the darkness followed us. Cans fell over in alleyways and shadows moved where shadows should have stayed put. In the smashed-in windows of a small store, a shredded body was draped over a display table in the window, advertising a grim buffet for the ghouls inside. Another store had its windows boarded up, but a small severed hand wedged in the boards told the sad ending to that survivor's tale.

We reached the end of the street and I checked the situation. Across the street was the small central park of the town, which had a stage and several benches. I didn't see any zombies there, but the stage was useless as a defensive place. It was only three feet off the ground and, as stupid as they were, even zombies could climb that. To the right was another road, but that way was blocked by several zombies shuffling along in the dark. By the way they were acting, they knew something was going on somewhere, but weren't sure where.

That was about to change. I signaled the family to follow and we headed right, moving in the direction of the town center. I figured we would hit fewer zombies that way since there were more businesses and not as many houses.

Behind us, the zombies with clearer vision saw us dart out and move away and they dutifully gave mournful chase. If I had to say anything about the dumb bastards, they were focused. I didn't stop to count the numbers who were now chasing us, but I figured it would be more than I cared to handle at this time with empty guns. I was even out of ammo for my backup weapon, a Browning BDA in .380. I had given my PPK to Sarah when I found this one, as the BDA had the capacity for thirteen rounds as opposed to six. In all seriousness, it was a stupid choice for a backup gun, since it required additional ammo, but I liked the looks of it and it pointed well.

We moved up the street, keeping ahead of our undead pursuers when a fast zombie nearly caught me. We were moving past a small bar when the door flew open and a zombie child nearly flew at me. It was moving fast enough to overtake any walking adult and its vicious expression was fixated on one adult in particular: me. I quickly sidestepped and held out my pick to keep it away It flailed against the weapon and snarled and hissed its frustration at me. It was too fast to try and hit with a hammer or the pick, so I had to get it off its feet. I shoved back on the pick handle, knocking it over and into a small bush. It thrashed for a second and nearly bolted out of the greenery. Its dead eyes fell on the family behind me and the small terrified children being carried by their parents. Its little mouth drew back from its teeth and it rushed to the attack.

It only got one step in when my boot connected with its face, flipping it off its feet and dropping it on its back. I stepped in quickly and stood on its neck, while its little arms dug futilely at my leg. Drawing my knife, I bent down and shoved the blade through its eye and into its brain. A twist of the handle brought its struggles to an end.

The man stepped up to me. "What the hell was that? I thought they were supposed to be slow!"

I shook my head. "The little kids seem to be fast and some of them are very fast. God help us if we ever come across an infected school." Remembering a school in Indiana, I wiped my blade off and sheathed it, moving forward again into the dark town. The pursuing zombies had come a lot closer and their moans were pitiful.

Down the street I looked around another intersection. Across the street was the police station and I could see the signs of a last stand attempted at the building. Cars were parked to create a barrier and there were several uniformed skeletons laying about, indicating some officers tried to protect what was inside the station. The smashed in doors mocked the fallen with their failure and even in the gloom I could see it was a slaughterhouse inside.

I checked two of the fallen officers and was surprised to find a full magazine on one of them. The caliber was 40 S&W, so I quickly stripped the ammo from the Glock magazine and replenished my SIG. There were only ten rounds, but it was a great comfort to have my old friend ready for battle once again.

"Hey," the man called to me from the far car. I trotted over and saw what he was pointing at. This cruiser still had it's shotgun in the center holder. I opened the door and looked around, then took the standard issue Remington pump shotgun out. I checked the magazine tube and was happy to see it was full. I handed it to the man, who had a bit of a time holding his son and the shotgun, but I knew he would find a way to manage it.

Thinking our luck had turned, I started down the left street but stopped suddenly. In front of me were about twenty zombies, glowing eyes and all. They were right were I needed to be. Dammit. I looked back to the family and said, "Alternate route. Come on."

We turned around and went back towards the police station, arriving there just as the first group of zombies was approaching. They set up another undead chorus as we showed up, joined in harmony by the second group which was now giving chase. We veered left and ran down the street, passing what looked like a small museum. Why anyone thought a museum in a small town was a good idea was beyond me. After everyone locally had gone once, why would they come back?   Looking at the broken windows and blood-splattered doorway, apparently someone *had* come back.

"Come on," I urged to the family as we moved into a more residential part of town. I could see dirty white flags hanging limply from mailboxes, remnants from a time when people believed their government could save them. "It's not much more," I said.

"Can we rest?" The woman asked, panting. "My arms are killing me."

"I'd love to," I said. "But they might have other notions." I pointed to the approaching crowd of undead. They groups had joined together and we were being trailed by nearly thirty zombies. I had a profound sense of déjà vu.

"Give her to me. I'll carry her for a bit." I offered, shifting my pickaxe out of the way.

"No, I'll manage. We need you loose to fight if needed. Another little zombie might get you if you hands are full."

"Fair enough." I replied, re-shifting my weapon. "We have one block to go down this street and unless I miss my guess, one block to the south. Then we can pick up the main road again and get to the ball fields." One blessing of small towns is they were generally laid out in a grid pattern. If you knew your directions, you could navigate fairly quickly.

We sloshed down the dark street, passing under the canopy of several large trees. The rain dripping off the leaves made it sound as if the rain had started again. On both sides of us houses were dark and foreboding. I could see in several of them glowing eyes that peered at us from the gloom. Sounds drifted out to the street of dead things crashing into furniture and walls in their attempt to reach us. Behind us, mindless in their pursuit, was a small army of dead things, eager for the fresh meat that seemed so tantalizingly close.

I wasn't about to make it easy. As we rounded the corner, I jumped a small fence and ran up to a nice Victorian home. I grabbed the garden hose that was in the bushes and ducked as a decayed hand reached through the window to grab at me.

"Shit!" I said too loudly as a dead face plastered itself against the window and tried to gnaw through the glass. I considered shooting the thing, but realized it wasn't a threat stuck inside like it was. I had other things to do.

I ran back to the family and smiled at their quizzical looks. I was actually used to that look, having seen it many times from my friends. I tied one end of the hose to the corner post of the fence and ran the rest across the street. At about knee level I pulled it taut and tied the other end around the post of another home's fence. I threw a wave at the three zombies staring impotently from a bay window, then hustled the family back to moving. With luck, that little trick might slow down our pursuers enough to give us some more time.

Speaking of which, the group had gotten a lot closer and were within twenty yards. I pushed the family along and then ran to scout ahead. We had reached the main road I was looking for when the first wet sounds of Z's hitting the pavement reached our ears. I looked back and saw the hose had done the trick, tripping several zombies and causing them to trip up others as well. It was like watching dominos. Zombies in the back paid no attention that their brethren in front were hitting something and they hit it as well. If I was extremely lucky, they might bounce off that hose for a while. If I was lucky beyond reason, we might be able to make the ball fields and lose the group entirely, which would improve our chances of survival significantly.

We turned right on the main road and moved as quickly as we could through the town. We passed abandoned early-century-style homes, some with their windows broken, others intact but just as empty. Around us, the sounds of pursuit diminished as the trailing zombies dealt with the trap I had laid for them. Eventually they would get through, but not for a minute.

We passed side streets to neighborhoods and I could see plenty of townsfolk milling about, enjoying the night air after a cool summer rain. Trouble was, their eyeballs glowed and they wanted to eat me, so I didn't stay for their impromptu block party. We had to keep moving.

After passing three side streets, the town began to open up. I knew we were getting close to our rendezvous point, but we were far from safe. The houses at this end of town were closer to the street and it was easier to see which ones were home to the dead. Darkness shifted in many of them and will-o-the-wisp lamps promised something other than paradise. White flags hung on all of them.

We moved past the open and empty fire station and I looked at the empty bays with regret. Flashing lights attract the ghouls like junkies to crack and might have bought us some time. The fire station did have one thing in it that caught my attention. Actually, two things and they came running out at us as we passed.

Two little zombies, kids no older than six or seven, fairly hurtled out of the darkness, hissing fiercely. They raced at me and the couple and there was nothing I could do about it. The one that streaked towards me was a little boy, wearing only dirty blue pajama pants. His naked torso showed several bites and scratches and his mouth was ringed in dried blood. I jumped to the side to give myself room and waited with my pickaxe. When he came within reach I swung hard, intending to knock him down and finish him off. The pick connected right under his arms and I could hear ribs snap like twigs. He flew off his feet and skidded across the firehouse lawn, scrambling to regain his feet. I didn't give him the chance. Following his flight, I ran up and slammed the pick into his head, closing his eyes forever.

I quickly turned back, fully expecting to see one of the couple getting bit. But I was very pleasantly surprised to see that wasn't the case. The second little zombie was pinned to the ground by the man kneeling on its back, while its head thrashed to the sides, trying to bite anything within reach. The man drew a large knife I didn't know he had and with a practiced plunge and twist of the blade, the threat was over.

The man wiped his blade and stood up as I came over. "Anybody hurt?" I asked, placing an innocuous hand on my SIG.

The man saw my motion but ignored it. "We're good. Thanks. This one wasn't as fast as yours, so it was easier to deal with."

I looked at the man for a long second before replying. "Nice work, anyway." I wasn't fooled. I figured the man had some skills, otherwise he and his family would have been dead a long time ago. He was too steady for an amateur, too easily accepting of what I was doing. I had caught him watching me on occasion, not sizing me up for an attack, but looking for information that might be useful. "Let's keep moving," I said.

As we stepped up again, I heard the man give a long exhale, which told me he was relieved all went well. I couldn't blame him since I was doing the same thing.

Fifty yards later, we reached the park district building and I looked it over with a practiced eye. No first floor windows, one metal door to the parking lot, seemed to be okay. When I reached the other side, it was obvious it would never do. The ground sloped up and reached the second floor, which had many nice big windows and a big glass door. Hmm...no. We needed to get up, someplace off the ground.

We walked though the playground, trying our best to ignore the decaying remains of something small. There was an open pavilion at the other end that might work, provided we could get up on top. I looked back at the family and saw the woman was about done. Her arms were sagging and she kept shifting her child from one arm to the next. Pavilion it was. I went over and checked out the interior and didn't see anything. Pulling a picnic table over I made more noise than I wanted to but it couldn't be helped. The man had put his son down and was standing guard, holding the shotgun at the ready. I pulled another table over then a third. I hauled a fourth and managed to lever it on top of the other three. A fifth joined it, then I worked like a lunatic to get a sixth onto the fourth and fifth.

Finally finished and completely covered in sweat, I waved the family over. "I don't know how steady it is, but it's what we got." The man clapped me on the back and climbed up to the top. He waved his son up, who scrambled up and was quickly on the roof.

I motioned for the woman to go and she climbed up slowly. Just as she reached the top, a deep moan sounded from behind us. The zombie group had freed themselves from the hose trap and had found us again. Damn. Well, we would be safe on the roof. I climbed the picnic tables and found the woman still on top. Her husband was reaching out to her to pass the baby over, but she refused to move. I had left a six foot gap between the tables and the roof, the idea being that I couldn't push the tables over once I was on the roof, so I had better make sure we couldn't be followed. Right now, that plan was working against us.

"You need to jump over, right now," I said as calmly as I could. I could see the small army of undead working their way through the playground and it was a matter of minutes before they were on us.

"I can't!" She cried, holding her daughter tighter. "What if I miss and fall? We'll both be killed!"

"Pass your daughter to your husband. You can do it." I tried to be reassuring, but it was hard when the dead were closing in.

She stepped to the edge, then stepped back. "I can't" she whispered.

Her husband was getting desperate. "C'mon, honey, you can do it. It's just a little jump. You've jumped farther than this, you can do it. Please, honey, you have to get moving."

She stepped to the edge again as the first of the zombies reached our little pyramid. I felt the stack shift as they bumped into it, then I heard a creak as they began to slowly climb up.

I stood next to her. "They're coming. If you want to live, you have to jump now," I said in a forced whisper. I looked down, and figured we had fifteen seconds to live, as dead hands reached up for us and glowing eyes hungrily stared at us. More zombies had reached the tables and the moaning was awful. I never got used to it, no matter how many times I heard it.

She stepped to the edge again and again stepped back. "I'm so sorry, I can't. I can't!" She was hysterical now and screamed slightly at the sight of us being surrounded by ghouls.

"Dammit, Jesse! Do it now!" Her husband was furious and his outstretched hand grabbed at empty air.

"Fuck it," I said, not wanting to be dinner. I grabbed the little girl and tossed her into the waiting arms of her father as her mother screamed at me. Spinning back to Jesse, I grabbed her under the arms and threw her hysterically over the opening as dead hands reached up to grasp at my legs. I stepped back, ran the gauntlet of dead arms and leaped over the opening, managing to get tripped by a hand that caught a little too well on my foot. I fell into the opening, but my outstretched hands were able to grasp the edge of the roof as I went. My legs swung down and knocked over several zombies who watched my dive. I didn't wait to be chewed on, quickly used my backswing as momentum and swung my legs back up to the roof. I managed to get a foot over, levered myself up and rolled over onto the gravel surface as dead hands grasped the air where I was a second ago.

I looked over at the picnic tables and watched as the zombies walked towards the edge and promptly fall to the ground. One tallish specimen smacked his head sharply on the edge of the roof, leaving a black mark.

I glanced back at the family, where the wife was sobbing as her husband held her, saying she was sorry, over and over again. All three of them were crying, the only one not interested in the proceedings was the baby.

I took off my backpack and took out a bottle of water. I drank deeply, then passed it to the family. All of them drank and the husband looked at me.

"What now?" he asked.

"Now we try to call in the cavalry," I said. I pulled out my flashlight, took out the clear lens and put on a red one. I walked to the edge of the roof, away from the fountain of Z's and shined the light around three times. I waited five seconds, then did it again. I repeated this procedure twice, then went back to the family.

"Well?" the man asked.

"We'll have to wait and see. They may have had their own troubles getting back to the vehicle. We'll see," I said.

"So we're just going to wait here, then?" He sounded a little agitated.

"Jump off if you want to, but we're safe here. They can't get to us and in all likelihood my friends will be along shortly," I replied, probably more testily than I intended.

"What if they aren't coming? What if they're dead?" he asked, forcing me to acknowledge what might be true.

I looked hard into his eyes. "Then I won't leave until I kill every one of these bastards. You're free to do what you want," I replied.

He looked like he wanted to say something more, but at that moment, across the baseball fields, a flare suddenly sparked up. It hovered for a minute, then flew up into the sky, illuminating the fields and the Z's that were after us. The flare arced over the field and landed in the surrounding neighborhood, attracting the attention of the ghouls not on the picnic tables. We watched as many of them detached themselves from the group and head off towards the glowing light. I swung up my flashlight again and shined it on the dark shape I knew now was the recreational vehicle we had modified for our traveling purposes. I clicked it on several times and then put it away. I could hear a motor being fired up and when I looked up, the black shape had detached itself from the surrounding darkness and was making its way over to where we were.

In a minute, the large RV pulled up alongside the pavilion and the roofs were nearly level with each other. I quickly transferred the family to the RV and pounded on the top hatch. The truck pulled away from the pavilion and the hatch popped open. I looked down at the grinning face of my old friend, Duncan Fries.

"Hey, John. How's it hanging?" Duncan said with his usual penchant for trivializing the momentous.

"Great," I said. "Help me with these. The baby's sick, by the way."

Duncan recoiled. "Sick?" he said, his hand straying to his gun.

"Seems like a cold, had it for a couple hours," I said reassuringly.

Duncan visibly relaxed. "Send 'em down," he said, raising his arms to help.

I helped Jesse down first, followed by the baby, then the boy, then the father. All of them looked worn to hell and I had to admit a wave of exhaustion came over me as I swung down into the vehicle and closed the hatch.

The family was seated at the table and I threw a wave to Tommy, who was sitting in the back area and keeping an eye on our disgusting friends as we left them. He lifted a hand from his rifle and went back to guarding our rear. I passed through the kitchen area and up to the cab of the big vehicle, plopping down in the passenger seat.

"Nice work, bro." Nate worked the big vehicle around a couple of objects as he made his way out of town.

"Thanks," I said, closing my eyes. "Anything on your end?" Outside, the rain started up again, which would slow pursuit once they couldn't see us or hear us.

Nate laughed. "Nothing. You managed to have all the fun."

"You don't know half of it." I proceeded to tell Nate about the whole mess, from the hardware store to the pavilion. His eyes got wide at the mention of the zombie kids, but he'd seen them before, so it wasn't as big a deal. He thumped me on the chest when I told him about my near fall at the pavilion.

"You get yourself killed, slick, where would Jake be?" Nate asked severely. "You're taking some chances out here. Sarah would skin you alive if she knew."

I managed to look properly chastised. "I know, I know. I'm going to talk to our friends and see what they want to do," I said as I heaved my tired self out of my comfy chair. Zeus moved his head for a pet from his perch and I gave him one just for luck.

I sat at the table and spoke with the family for a few minutes. I gave the baby a dose of children's medicine, much to the thanks of her parents. After a while I went back to the front.

"What's up?" Nate asked.

"They're going to get a car and head west, get away from the population centers. I told them about the towns we had found and they're going to try and settle into one."

"Sounds good," Nate said. "Hey John?"

"Yeah?"

"Nice work."

"Thanks. Maybe this is a sign of things to come."

"Dreamer."

"Yeah."

CHAPTER 14

It was hard to fathom, in some ways, just how things turn out. Just a few months ago, Bodie California was the center of the world, a place to while away the time, not thinking too much about the future.

But sometimes, all it takes is an idea and through sheer will and determination, not to mention a forty man backup team, that idea can come to fruition. There is a certain amount of satisfaction in seeing something through, whether it be a sound idea or a crazy scheme.

Such was Major Thorton's state of mind as he looked out over the Potomac River at the Washington Mall. He was standing at the base of the Jefferson Memorial, having crossed the river late last night. The only bridge that was available to him was the one that crosses the Potomac at Alexandria. Thorton and his men had discovered that most of the bridges to D.C. had been destroyed by the military in an attempt to cut off the swarming zombies. The delay had cost a day of fighting and backtracking, but after some skillful maneuvering, they had managed to cross the river and make it north. The Jefferson Memorial was the first place Thorton saw that was related to D.C., so he declared that they should stay there for the evening.

One of the men discovered the small museum under the memorial and after the necessary precautions against the dead, they had managed to at least rest.

In the morning, Ken wanted to move on, but listened to his sergeants when they told him that the men could use a little more rest. They had been pushing hard for the last few days, doing little but ride in the trucks and there was less chance of desertion if they just took it easy for a day.

Reluctantly, Ken agreed and as he looked back he could see several men lounging on the steps of the memorial. It was a good idea and as he shifted his binoculars at the various monuments, he could see a great many things.

He saw stacks of corpses used as barricades and bodies strewn about where they had been run down by marauding zombies. The roads were choked with cars and dead people, both moving and not moving and nearly every one had a bad story to tell. He could see the remains of a woman who had been dragged from her car and eaten as she lay on the hood, her hands still gripping the windshield wipers as her legs were torn off. He could see dozens of small bands of roving zombies, shifting left and right as they looked for prey. The Lincoln Memorial was pristine white in the morning, save for hundreds of black splotches on the steps overlooking the reflecting pool. There was a glittering about the entrance that puzzled Ken until he realized it was the sun reflecting off thousands of spent casings. Apparently a last stand had been made there.

Through the trees to the West was another memorial, but Thorton didn't know what it was or if it had been a place of death as well. From his vantage point he could see a small house on a hill across the river, but it looked like it had been a last refuge as well. Scorch marks topped every window and the tan colored marble was black at the roofline. It stood about a huge graveyard and Ken was sure it was Arlington, although he had never been there. Fact was, Thorton knew very little about D.C. and had no real idea where the documents he wanted might be found. He knew there were some museums and figured they would be in one of them. He'd find it, of that he was sure.

The other thing he was sure of was he had made it to D.C. ahead of John Talon. The zombies he had seen were still wandering about aimlessly. If another group had arrived, the zombies would surely be agitated. But since they were docile, it indicated that they did not yet know that Thorton and his men were around and no one else was either. One of the things Thorton had noticed was there was no one left alive in the nation's capitol. Everyone had either left or succumbed to the plague. There was no in between.

One of the problems they had encountered was the trucks were too big and beat up to make it much further. They could easily push aside a swarm of zombies, but they couldn't keep pushing aside cars without taking some damage. After three thousand miles of hard travel, the trucks were on their last legs.

But since this was D.C. and there were several military installations around, Thorton figured he'd get new vehicles without too much trouble. As a matter of fact, Thorton had planned on such a visit to resupply and to see if he could get better weapons for his men. Something heavier in caliber was what he was thinking.

He put away his binoculars and turned back to the men on the steps. After looking at all the destruction around him and the sad state of his trucks, he reached a decision.

He stepped onto a small sidewall and looked down at his men. "I'm going to keep this brief. In the morning, we're going to finish our mission. We are going to procure the documents we came to get and then we are going to head back across country. We are going to have a new mission as we go. Each of you will be responsible for securing a state we leave you in. We will recruit new members, then you are in charge to secure your territory. You will still answer to me, but you will rule your own land." Several heads nodded in agreement with this statement. "Furthermore, the mission will change. Find survivors, kill the zombies. We will remake this country as we see fit. You will answer only to me, no one else. I can think of no better reward for your loyalty."

The men quietly clapped, and one man raised his hand. "How will you decide who gets which state?"

Thorton smiled. "Since I am a fair man, we'll choose fairly. Come with me."

The group went down into the museum and gathered around a large map of the United States. It was a map with the Louisiana Purchase depicted on it, but the current states were labeled as well. Thorton stood about ten feet away and pulled his large knife. Pointing to the nearest man, he said, "You're first." The major hurled his knife at the wall, burying the tip in Montana. "That's your state. Good luck."

The selection proceeded, with fate determining the outcome. It got harder as more states were chosen and the smaller ones had to be chosen at random as opposed to the tip of a knife. Since there weren't fifty men, some of the men received two states to make up for some of the larger states like Texas. Thorton chose Nebraska as his own state, citing the fact that it was in the center of the country and therefore the best place for keeping control over the rest.

"I'm glad that's settled. Now let's get moving. The bad news is our trucks are done. They got us here but they aren't getting us any closer. We're going to have to hoof it the rest of the way. The good news is there doesn't seem to be as much zombie activity as I expected. But watch your backs and don't fire unless you absolutely have to. The less attention we attract, the better. Sergeants, form your men, we're moving out."

The group, led by Thorton, walked along the Potomac tidal basin towards the Franklin Delano Roosevelt memorial. There weren't any zombies along the walkway, although they could see dozens on the road on the other side of the trees. Since they were hidden by overgrowth and close to the water, the zombies didn't see them.

Passing through a small opening in the trees, the men entered the FDR Memorial. The memorial was spread out over a few acres, utilizing stone and water to represent the years of the Roosevelt administration, through the Depression and World War II. Bronze figures focused the visitor on particular aspects of the president's years in office and various plaques described events relating to the memorial. In its day, the memorial was an interesting departure from the usual stone column, single figure memorial. This memorial documented a time period as well as a person.

At least it used to. Stagnant water and overgrown weeds greeted the soldiers and rounding a corner, the men were surprised by a bread line of bronze men. They were more surprised when two of the men detached themselves from the end of the line and headed over to the fresh meat line.

The two zombies, obviously attracted to the human-sized statues, had been frustrated to find their meals resisted their teeth most effectively. But when they saw the living humans come around the corner, their limited prayers had been answered. The first one advanced with arms outstretched, its blank eyes focusing on the prey at hand while its mouth slacked open. The other zombie, a smaller individual with deep claw marks across its skull and back advanced in a crouch, a single arm held forward to try and grab at a soldier.

Major Thorton held a hand up to stop his men and walked right up to the first zombie. Batting aside the arms, Thorton pushed it down on its face, then stood on its back while the other advanced. Grabbing the hand offered by the zombie, Thorton jerked it off its feet, tripping it over the zombie already on the ground. While it fell, Thorton stomped on the neck of the first one, breaking its spine and ceasing its jerky movements. The second zombie started to get up and the Major gave a mighty kick, connecting with the zombie's neck, snapping its head back and cracking its neck as well.

Ken stepped off the two inert ghouls and motioned for his men to continue to follow. The men circled around the zombies, whose mouths still opened and closed and whose eyes still followed the men as they sidled past.

Thorton eschewed the main road, deciding it would be best to continue to follow the basin. The walkway circled around the basin and since it was shielded by trees, the group could advance to their objective without attracting too much attention. Once they reached the open ground, it was going to be much harder, but there was no point in fighting hard now if it could be avoided.

The group quietly made their way to a bridge and Thorton cursed when he saw the path went up over the street and not under it. Dozens of zombies were milling about the abandoned cars and if they knew there was a buffet of live prey under the trees, they'd be down just as fast as their decaying legs could get them. He decided to try the water, directing one of his men to slip into the muddy basin and see if they could just walk in the shallows under the bridge.

The man walked over to the water's edge and stepping confidently into the basin, immediately sank like a stone. Two of his comrades rushed to the edge and grabbed him as he bobbed up for air. The men dragged the spluttering private over to the Major, and shook their heads at their dumbass friend.

The soaking wet soldier looked up at his commander and whispered, "Deeper than I thought, sir!" The man got to his feet, pouring water out of his rifle and wringing out his bulging pockets.

"Thanks." Thorton just shook his head and figured they'd have to try something else. Ken picked up a rock and hurled it at the zombies on the bridge. The stone cracked off a side window on a car and immediately every zombie on the bridge zeroed in on the sound, rushing over as quickly as they could.

This gave Thorton an idea and he had his men quickly gather up stones. Breaking the men into groups of four, he had them get as close to the road as possible, then wait for a barrage of stones. Major Thorton tossed four stones in quick succession, drawing the majority of the zombies away from the edge of the bridge. As the third stone was in the air, the men were signaled to run and they practically dove over the road, scrambling down the other side and ducking into the trees. Thorton waited until he could see rifles peeking out of the leaves, then began throwing the rocks again, this time a little farther away.

The second and third groups made it just fine, then they had to wait nearly an hour for a second band of zombies to clear the area before sending over the fourth and last group. This one included Thorton, who had to throw really far to get even a couple of rocks to hit and distract the zombies.

After reaching the other side, Ken decided to take a small break and let his men rest a bit. They lay down under the trees and bushes and Thorton himself sat under a small overhang which didn't allow him to be seen from above. As he looked over the lounging men, one of them suddenly slid under the bushes as if he had been dragged from the other side.

A shriek of pain accompanied the sudden movement and men were scrambling to their feet, grabbing weapons and packs. Thorton risked a look around the edge of the trees and saw six zombies had pinned his man down and were tearing him to shreds. The soldier's legs kicked wildly and one bloody hand, minus two fingers, slapped the back of a feeding zombie.

Major Thorton looked back at the bridge and saw at least fifty zombies peering over the edge, seeing the commotion and men. Thorton could almost do a countdown and then there it was: an ear splitting groan which waxed out over the Potomac Tide Basin, bounced off the Jefferson Memorial and echoed back again.

"Well, shit," Thorton said. "Time to go. No point in being quiet. Kill 'em if they get close, save your ammo if you can." Ken raced along the sidewalk, grateful the trees still screened him from the rest of the zombies. The men followed quickly behind, not one of them sparing a glance at their comrade, whose intestines were being shared among his killers. None of them saw the futile hand raise towards them, begging for a bullet to end the pain and eventual reawakening.

Thorton bolted across the road, skirting two cars that still had grisly occupants and raced into a grove of trees. There were several walkways in this area, so there were no cars to worry about, but there was no safety as they were surrounded by thousands of hungry dead people.

Major Thorton faced his men. "We've got about a half-mile run to anything that looks like a defensible building. We're going to head for the trees across the way, then we're going to move into the first building we can get to. If you fall behind, you're on your own." The Major drew his weapon and checked the loads. "Let's go."

The men burst from cover and ran as hard as they could, trying to get as much movement going before they got spotted by too many zombies. Trouble was, there were too many zombies to begin with. On the grounds of the Washington Monument, hundreds of zombies watched as the men raced across the lawn, their dead eyes widening and their mouths opening as they gave chase. During the Upheaval, these people had made an early stand against the ravenous hordes, figuring the higher ground might be of value. But they were quickly overcome and joined the ranks of the ghouls. Now they were pursuing food, something they hadn't seen in a long time and the need to feed was achingly powerful.

Crossing 14th Street was interesting, as Thorton leaped onto the hoods and roofs of abandoned and attacked cars. The men followed and only one slipped and fell. As he got up, a zombie head shot out from a vehicle and tore a chunk out of his shoulder. The man screamed and clutched his bloody wound, slinking down among the cars while the zombie that bit him chewed contentedly.

As Thorton looked back at the commotion, the soldier put his rifle barrel in his mouth and pulled the trigger, blowing his brains to the sky and slumping over. As the rest of the squad leaped over the inert form, each man hoped he would be brave enough to do the same, should the worst happen and they become infected.

The men ran full tilt into a small horde of zombies and used their clubbing weapons to take them out. Thorton used his knife to end two of them and then they were running again. They stayed by the trees lining the mall, figuring to keep exposure to a minimum. There were still at least ten thousand zombies out there and they were all coming to the realization that food was on the table.

As Thorton looked down the mall, he realized they were going to be quickly overrun if they didn't find some kind of shelter quickly. He decided to make a run for the nearest building, which in this case happened to be the National Museum of Natural History. He had only fifteen men left and at the rate he was going, he was going to be alone in a sea of zombies if he didn't make the right moves. He needed to get to the Capitol Building, as that was where he thought the documents were, but he could distract the zombies if he could get them to attack the front while he and his men slipped out the side and no one would be the wiser.

He passed in between two buses full of zombie eighth graders and ran up to the building, glancing at the broken glass and realizing someone had already tried to make this a sanctuary and failed. Too late to worry now. Thorton ushered his men inside, then began hauling benches and debris to cover the hole. "I need heavy stuff, now!" he yelled, levering a heavy planter over to the glass.

The men attacked the information booth, shoving and pushing it over to the entrance. Thorton and two of his men heaved the booth onto its side, effectively blocking most of the entrance. Outside, zombies were edging closer and the men could see that they were coming from all directions, attracted to the noise and the movements of their brethren.

"I need more, come on, we got two minutes before they're on us!" Thorton yelled. He didn't care about the noise, he wanted to attract the zombies to the front of the building. He also didn't care about securing the door too much because it didn't need to be permanent. He just needed a delay.

Two men came over carrying a counter full of brochures and heaved it on top of the desk as three other men carrying heavy planters tossed them on the pile as well. One man carried a stuffed deer and when he threw it on top, it tumbled out of the building and lay on the sidewalk. Thorton wondered briefly if the zombies would give it a nibble before realizing it wasn't alive.

"All right, we need to find an exit. Watch yourselves, because with that hole there could be a lot of zombies in here right now who couldn't find the exit." Thorton reached into a display and yanked a spear off of a Neanderthal. The shaft was solid and the spearhead was metal painted to look like flint, but it was pointy enough to serve. It would keep zombies far enough away that he could use his knife if he needed, or if the situation called for it, he could use it to split a skull or two.

They headed the opposite way they had come in, passing the huge display of stuffed elephants, looking over the museum directory as they went. The door they wanted was on the opposite side of the building, Thorton wasn't interested in service doors or maintenance exits. Trying to get through to areas like that meant dark walks through tight quarters, something no one did if they were sane in a possible zombie infested building. If a group made a stand here, chances were they were still around, lurking in the dark corners.

Thorton led the way, his flashlight and spear held in front of him. The men crowded close behind, the memory of losing two of their number still extremely fresh in their minds. One of the men glanced over at a display of a Northwest Indian lodge, the dark timbers carved in deep relief of ancient gods and grimacing faces.

"What are those shiny spots?" he asked his closest companion as they made their way slowly past.

His comrade, displaying a remarkable amount of education, replied, "Those are bits of mother-of-pearl, set in the eyes to make it seem like the gods are watching when the light hits them."

The first soldier peered close. "Did they hang them from strings, because some of them are moving."

"What? Oh, shit." The educated soldier whipped up his rifle and fired a deafening shot at the crowd of zombies that was moving out of the shadows of the lodge. Every soldier turned and suddenly there were curses and shots fired as moans filled the air. For every zombie, it took at least two shots, as the jumpy soldiers weren't able to aim very well in the dark. The last zombie fell not ten feet from Major Thorton, who flashed his light over the group.

"You can bet your asses that won't be the last bunch in here. We need to—" Thorton was cut off by the echoing of dozens of groans from zombies all over the museum. The crashing reports of the rifles was as much a dinner bell to the ravenous ghouls and from every dark corner, every smashed display, every alcove of learning came decaying forms, shuffling, grasping, hungry.

"Oh, fuck." Major Thorton spun on his heel and ran full tilt for the front of the building. His only hope was to get his men away from the perceived source of the noise, the place the zombies would go to first. If he was fast enough, he might be able to get his men out before they were cut off by too many zombies.

They ran to the north entrance, but the easy exit was already cut off by several dark shapes that swayed ominously in the light filtering in through the glass. They could make it through, but there wouldn't be anyone left if they tried to stand.

"Back! Back!" shouted Thorton as he shoved his way through his men. He had caught a fleeting glimpse of a floor plan and was heading to what he hoped was a side entrance. He tried the doors to the parking garage, but they were blocked and barricaded and he didn't have time to try and bust through.

He ran past the Starlight Café and as the group was about to pass a horde of zombie teens slammed into the group from behind. Four men were taken down quickly without a shot being fired. Thorton watched as one of his men was reduced to shreds by a trio of teenage girls, one of them still had her sunglasses on her rotting head. The other three were struggling under groups of six or more, while the tour guide, an older zombie in a red Washington Nationals hat, ripped out a soldier's eyeball and contentedly munched on it while the man screamed.

"Go, go go!" Thorton was down to eleven men and he didn't want to lose any more. One of the men casually joked that now they had more states to control. Ken shook his head.

They ran past the Rose Gallery and turned right. Thorton abruptly stopped when he saw the stuffed elephants in the hall. "Son of a bitch." He muttered under his breath. They had come in a complete circle and this hallway was filling up with zombies that had gotten in from the outside.

Now Major Thorton was mad. He had not only just lost a quarter of his men, but he had managed to get himself lost, with the exits blocked by dozens of ghouls. "So be it." He snarled, pulling his huge knife and hefting his spear. He turned around and headed back the way he came, moving right at the zombies that fed on the remains of his fallen soldiers. One of the zombies saw him and stood up, shuffling closer to see what this fool looked like.

Thorton barely slowed down. He stalked up to the zombie teen and neatly decapitated it, the heavy blade easily shearing the decaying tissue and bone. Thorton used the spear to stab another in the eye, killing it, while the tour guide was dispatched with another head-lopping stroke. His blood up, Ken rammed the spear through three of the feeding zombies, who hadn't noticed the shaft in their guts until Thorton lifted them completely off the ground, then slammed them headfirst into the wall. He left the spear and faced down the last two zombies, both of whom hissed and started for him with blood stained mouths and hands.

Ken waited for them to get close enough, then swung the blade in a vicious arc, killing both zombies in a single blow. The bodies dropped away as the heads bounced down the hall and the major wiped his blade off with a napkin from the café. The men looked around in awe at the sudden devastation. They realized just how a man like their commander survived the Upheaval.

"Don't save your rounds, kill it if it gets close," the major said to his men as he went over to the parking garage entrance. He moved some of the debris piled up in front of the door, then tried the handle. The door swung easily open, revealing the darkened interior of the garage.

Ken used his flashlight to look around and surprisingly, the parking lot was empty. There weren't any cars nor were there any zombies. Thorton shrugged. He could use a little luck right about now. The men hurried over to the lighted entrance and Ken cautiously peeked out. He could see hundreds of zombies moving towards the entrance of the museum, attracted at first by the men, then attracted by the movement of the other zombies in this particular direction. Zombies weren't particularly bright and tended to follow the general mob plan.

Ken looked across the road and saw a large quantity of trees and large shrubs, enough to hide in and enough to give pursuing zombies trouble. He motioned to his men and they darted across the opening, not bothering to try and go in small groups anymore. The last attack crushed their confidence and they had no plans on losing any more men. Thorton mulled this one over as he ran and realized he was going to have to start recruiting again. Oh, well. At least he still had the men back in California and Tamikara's group.

The group worked their way through the circular grove of trees of the National Gallery of Art Sculpture Garden, although they had no idea what it was called. For the men it was "cover from the zombies" and they had no idea if it was art, but they liked it.

The next building over was the National Gallery of Art, but Thorton had no interest in going there. He was done with buildings until he got to the Capitol Building and only then would he venture in. Instead, he stuck close to the buildings and overgrown landscaping, trying to keep out of sight as much as possible. In between the buildings, Thorton could see hundreds, if not thousands, of zombies wandering about the Washington Mall and if they caught wind of the meat slinking in the shadows, they'd finish them off very quickly.

It wasn't until they got to 3rd Street that things got a little dicey. The road ran in front of the Capitol Building and there wasn't a lot of cover from here to the steps of the Capitol. There were few zombies in the area, but all it took was for one to groan and the rest would be on the hunt. Thorton mulled over his situation and realized he would have to draw away the zombies somehow. He looked at his men and he asked, "Who's the best runner?"

One of the men raised his hand, a skinny kid barely out of his teens. He thought the major was asking for a volunteer to run to the Capitol Building. He was about to learn differently.

"Good. Pass your supplies to your friends and come up here." Thorton said. The man did as he was told, then worked through the brush to the major's side.

"All right. I need you to distract the zombies so we can make a run for the building."

The young tough's heart sank as he realized what he had to do. Screwing up his courage, he asked, "Will somebody be covering for me when I get back?"

Thorton tried to keep his incredulousness off his face. "Sure, we'll wait on the steps for you, by the big doors," he promised.

The young man breathed quickly for a few seconds, then walked casually out onto the road. He was immediately spotted by a trio of zombies, who groaned and started after him. This started a chain reaction as the soldier casually strolled down the street, keeping ahead of the zombies and jogging around the ones ahead of him.

Thorton watched amazed as the lad cleared the way for the rest of the men to get moving. They decided to walk slowly so as not to attract too much attention and some of the men swayed a little from side to side. They tried to resist making any sudden movements and did not walk in groups.

Ken watched out of the corner of his eye as his picked man led hundreds of zombies on a wild goose chase. He had never felt so exposed in his life and he only prayed the zombies on the lawn were too busy to notice the coup happening on the Capitol steps.

When they got close enough, they had to climb over a sea of dead zombies, each one with a hole in their heads. Past that was a sandbag barricade that ran around the entire building and beyond, closer to the Capitol, there was a maze of razor wire strung from one end to the other. Machine gun placements sat silent and impotent and everywhere was the pall of violent death. Skeletons were strewn about, some missing arms or legs, some missing heads.

Thorton slipped once and when he looked down he realized he was standing on hundreds of thousands of spent shell casings. He shook his head at the sad last stand made here in the Capitol.

"Damn fools, but it made a way for me," he muttered as he began walking up the steps. The sheer size of the building impressed the hell out of him and changing his mind about his Capitol, he realized he wanted the Capitol Building to be his house, his residential palace. Why not? He'd earned it.

The men gathered at the side door and just as they were about to enter, their pied piper returned, running mightily up the steps in triumph. His mates welcomed him back and returned his gear to him. Ken himself gave the kid a thumbs up before drawing his big revolver and ducking in through the door.

An hour later, on the other side of the visitor center, Thorton was thoroughly confused. They had searched the main atrium and alcoves but not a sign of the founding documents. There wasn't even a display case that might have shown they were ever there in the first place.

Thorton was unsure of what to do when one of his men called him over.

"What is it, corporal?" Thorton asked.

"Sir, what about over there, at the Library of Congress? Makes sense that those documents would be in a library."

Ken thought about that for a second. "Okay, let's go get them. Follow me." The men jogged through another grove of trees, the area having been cleared of any close zombies by the run of the young soldier earlier. The men crossed the street and worked their way over to the Library of Congress.

But when they reached the building, they saw that the front entrance had been barricaded very well and there was no way they were going to be able to get in this way. Working their way along the side of the building, they saw there were no ground level windows and the ones higher up were curtained closed. At the back of the building, they got another surprise. Several semi-truck trailers had been placed on the grounds and street, effectively blocking off any attempt to get in to the back of the building.

Thorton looked the situation over and he began to harbor a suspicion that there might be people alive inside the Library of Congress. Looking over the window in the back section, he thought he saw movement, but he couldn't be sure. Making a mental note to check it later, he headed back to the front of the building. He rounded the corner, nearly running right into a zombie. The diseased husk lurched up at him and without thinking, Thorton grabbed the zombie by the throat, cutting off its groan. He slammed the zombie into the side of the building until its head cracked, ignoring the clawing hands on his arm and he let it slide down the marble, leaving a black trail in its wake.

Ken thought quickly and decided to head back to the Visitor Center at the Capitol Building. Somewhere in that tourist section, they had to have a map or something that explained where the Declaration of Independence and Constitution were located.

As the men jogged back the way they came, dozens of pairs of eyes looked out from the Library of Congress over the landscape and hungrily watched them go.

CHAPTER 15

Robert E. Lee left his house when he decided he could not fight against Virginia. When he departed, the government seized his property and in a twist of irony, turned the proud general's land into the resting place of America's fallen heroes. I often wondered how Lee must have felt, the power of his convictions that he would abandon his home, travel across the country and fight for a cause he wasn't sure would prevail.

As I stood on the veranda of the Lee House in Arlington, I looked out over the river towards D.C.. I could easily see the Washington Monument, the Lincoln Memorial, and the Capitol Building. It was a calm, clear morning and without the smog of thousands of cars for over two years, the air was very clean and sharp. The white markers which made up the majority or Arlington Cemetery peeked up through the tall grass which untended, wrapped itself protectively around the graves. In a way, I felt I had done something similar to Lee. I just hoped my venture wouldn't turn into defeat.

A voice behind me spoke. "Wonder if we'll have a place like this for the fallen of the zombie wars."

I turned slightly and saw Tommy walk out of the building. He looked a bit older to my eye, like this journey was wearing on him as well. I knew he was worrying more and more about Angela and lately he had been fretting more, telling me that he felt something was wrong. I understood his anxiety, as my own nearly consumed me not so long ago, but fortunately I managed to pull through.

The biggest frustration with the breakdown of society due to the Upheaval was the inability to communicate. We had gotten so used to being able to connect with anyone, anytime, that not knowing was the worst of all. Add to the fact that even if we finished the mission today, we were still weeks away from getting home to our families.

"I suppose we could," I replied, "as long as we could make sure the ones we put there would stay there."

Tommy chuckled. "That's true. I was thinking about something this morning as I tried not to shoot Nate for snoring."

"What's that?" I had to give him credit. Nate's snoring had actually awakened the dead and there had been mornings when the RV was surrounded by cranky ghouls.

"The kids who were under five years old when the Upheaval hit and the ones born after will have no memory of life without zombies." Tommy looked out over the city. "They won't have any memory of what this country was like, there aren't many people left with living memory of significant events. They just know the here and now and the struggle to survive every day."

I didn't say anything as the mission we were on suddenly came into sharp focus. We weren't just trying to preserve a heritage. We were recreating the country. The ones who would follow us had no idea of how things used to be. They would have no guidance outside of stories. We were doing this so the foundations could be laid once again for a country to follow. We were doing this so as a people, as a country, we would survive. It was the ultimate do-over. All the anxiety I had felt about what we were doing, all the introspection which came up short, all the selfish reasons why we shouldn't give a damn, fell off my shoulders like a sudden rain shower.

I had thought about only one child and not the rest of them. For all my rhetoric about saving the country and taking it back, I had lost my focus on who I should be doing this for. It came in a rush, so much so that Tommy even noticed the change.

"What's wrong?" he asked, narrowing his eyes at me like he wasn't sure what I was going to do.

"Not a thing, old friend," I said. "You just reminded me why we're doing this and it's for the best of reasons. We're saving our past and saving our future. Thanks."

Tommy shrugged. "Okay, I guess. What's the plan?"

Before I could answer, a voice growled down from the balcony above us. "The plan is to move our asses as quickly as possible."

I looked up to see Nate standing at the railing, looking out over the city with a pair of binoculars. "What's up?"

"There's a shitload of activity by one of the museums and a general drift happening on the mall. If I had to guess, I'd say

Thorton beat us here. That, or someone was holing up in one of the museums and their defenses just collapsed."

I grimaced as I digested the news. I had hoped we had made it here ahead of Thorton, but it seems like we were short a day and he had managed to stir up a hornet's nest that we were going to have to subsequently kick.

"All right," I said. "Snag Duncan and let's get moving. We're probably in for a long fight, so load heavy. Tommy, find a map and see if there are any back doors we can access to minimize our exposure. We may have to hoof it, so take your packs as well. If we get separated, our meeting place will be the Jefferson Memorial. At sundown, if you're alone, you're on your own. Follow the river and save your own ass."

"But—" Tommy tried to interrupt.

"No buts. This time it's orders. If you see any of Thorton's men, shoot on sight. I figure the odds are about four to one, so any way you can whittle that down, do it."

"What if we have a shot at Thorton himself? You said before he was yours to kill," Nate asked.

I called up to the balcony. "I'm realistic. Dead is dead. Would I like to carve him up into little bits and feed him to a zombie kid? Sure. But a bullet to the brain works for me, no matter who pulls the trigger."

"Good enough," Nate said as he turned away to get his gear. "Duncan! Wake up!"

I turned to Tommy and froze. He looked at me and then glanced over his shoulder. The stiffening of his back told me he saw the same thing I did. Coming up the path to the house was about fifty zombies. They were spread out in a long line, moving through the rose garden rotunda that dated back to the 1870s. They had heard our voices and converged through the old part of the cemetery, where families had been allowed to erect personal monuments. Our route to the RV was blocked and there was no way that Nate and Duncan were going to be able to get out unless the zombies decided to move on.

I yelled to the house. "Nate! We've got company! Tommy and I will try to draw them away. Get to the RV and pick us up at the by the Tomb of the Unknown!"

Nate didn't answer, but I knew he had heard me by the silence. Nate was too seasoned to yell out and attract attention to himself and cause Z's to investigate. Right now he and Duncan needed to get armed and quiet and make a break for the vehicle as soon as they could. I could shout my fool head off, since the zombies had already seen me.

I ran to the wall that separated the house from the graveyard, with Tommy right behind me. It was a small limestone wall, about three feet in height. Not enough to stop the zombies, but it wasn't this side of the wall that was useful. The other side of the wall was a sheer drop of eight feet, followed by a deeply sloping hill which overlooked the tomb of John F. Kennedy and family.

The zombies were right behind us, so without too much thought, I leapt the wall and sailed down the hill, tumbling like a four year old when my feet hit the slope. I smacked my head somewhat sharply on the granite slab that covered JFK, then rolled to my feet. I watched Tommy slide gracefully down the grade, easily coming to a stop in the proper, upright position. I checked my pockets to make sure that I hadn't let anything loose and made sure my SIG was still in its holster. My rifle and new favorite melee weapon were still in the RV, hopefully Nate and Duncan would be able to get to it.

I looked up the slope, studiously avoiding looking at Tommy who I knew desperately wanted to make a comment about my landing. About twenty zombies had reached the wall and when they did, I shouted "Hey!" to get their attention. Dead eyes looked down and dead mouths moaned when they saw us.

Tommy and I watched as a couple came tumbling over the wall, flopping unceremoniously onto the turf and skidding down the hill to where we were. I stepped up to one and planted a heavy foot on its chest, drawing my knife and plunging it into the empty eye socket of the ghoul. Tommy did the same with the one on his side, only he was on its back and stabbed it in the back of its neck, severing the spine.

A few more plops on the lawns and suddenly there was a deluge of death, with dozens of dead folk tumbling over the wall. Some broke brittle bones on their landing, others had to extricate themselves from the turf, causing large chunks of sod to cling to heads and shoulders.

"We gotta go, there's too many and we don't have the equipment for this," Tommy said, tugging at my sleeve as I killed another zombie.

I nodded and we hurried down the sidewalk, passing the stagnant reflecting pool and wall.

"Which way?" Tommy asked as a fusillade of moans headed our way.

"Straight south," I said, heading down the road. Sheridan Avenue ran north and south, so we followed it. We jogged a bit to gain some ground, then as we saw the zombies didn't have any fast ones to deal with, we slowed to a decent walk. The average person could easily out walk the average zombie and we wanted this group to chase us a little. We needed to give Nate and Duncan time to get to the RV and get to the Tomb of the Unknowns for our rendezvous. And in all seriousness, unless we were surrounded, we weren't in that much danger.

The road turned west and the fastest way to get to the Tomb was to head overland through the grave stones and trees. The grass was overgrown and tangled, reaching our waists in the taller parts. I was a little nervous about all the tall grass, but we couldn't help the situation we were in. I was a little surprised at how well the Z's were able to sneak up on us, but as I had seen before, they did seem capable of rudimentary learning and ambush behavior.

Tommy and I moved as quickly as we could through the headstones and I noted how they were starting to look a little darker than normal, probably because they weren't maintained like they used to be. Behind us, the mass of zombies were continuing their pursuit, occasionally moaning to mark the morning as a bad one.

We reached McClellen Drive and I waved Tommy to follow me. I reasoned it made more sense to stay on the roads when we could see things better than take a chance in the tall grass with a prone Z. We moved east for a bit then turned southward on Roosevelt. I knew the general direction of where we needed to go, having been here several times in the past with my dad, but I would feel better when I finally saw the big marble structure.

I was so intent on looking for the Tomb that they nearly got us. We were passing through a copse of trees when four kids burst from the side of the road and launched themselves at us. There was no warning whatsoever. I managed to kick one in the chest before the other one hit me and it was a struggle and a half to keep the little shit from biting me. I was holding it by the hair and its nasty face was inches from my stomach. It clawed at my sides and grabbed my vest, trying to pull me closer. My hands were slipping in its greasy hair and I realized I had a good grip, but the scalp was coming off the creature. In a second the skin was going to completely tear, snapping the teeth, which showed in the front and sides from holes in its face, right into me. On top of that, the one I kicked was getting up and I had no defense. I couldn't pull my knife or gun and Tommy couldn't help because he had two of his own to deal with.

"Son of a bitch!" I hissed, suddenly pulling the little Z close and hugging it's head tightly against my side. It struggled to turn its head, but I held on for dear life as the second little Z came at me again. This time I was better prepared and when I kicked it down again, I dragged the first kid with me as I stomped on the prone one's neck, snapping it like a twig. I reached under my arm and got a good grip on the neck of the little girl that was trying her best to bite me. I pulled her away, breaking her grip on my vest and held her at arm's length while I awkwardly pulled my knife with my left hand. I rammed the steel through the top of her head and gave it a twist, blowing her lamp out for good.

I turned to Tommy and saw he was having some trouble. He managed to keep the two off of him by grabbing their necks, but he couldn't do anything to finish either one off. He tried bonking their heads together, but it wasn't working. I ended the stalemate by knifing the left one in the temple and Tommy used his free hand to pull his own blade and kill the other one. We wiped our blades off as best as we could and Tommy produced a lighter to finish off what we missed.

Blackening my blade just a bit more, I looked around and saw the grass around us waving and bending in the breeze. I thought it was nice until I realized the trees weren't bending and bowing like they should. As a matter of fact, there wasn't any breeze at all.

I looked at Tommy just as he looked at me. He had noticed the same thing I had.

"Run."

I don't know if I said it or Tommy said it, but we both bolted into a dead run, tearing south on Roosevelt just as fast as we could. Behind us came a loud chorus of 'Heeee-heeeee' as dozens of zombie children, ranging in age from five to fifteen, burst from the long grass and gave chase. They couldn't run as fast as we could in the short sprint, but in the long haul they would run us down. We tired, they never did. We had no choice but to run for our lives, since we had no guns other than our sidearms and no weapons besides our knives. Everything that would have allowed us to make a decent stand was back at the RV, which I desperately hoped was working its way towards the Tomb of the Unknowns at this very moment.

We ran through the trees on Roosevelt Avenue and as we passed more zombies came out of the cemetery at us. They looked to be all about the same age, around thirteen and I realized they must have been eighth graders on their trip to D.C.. As I digested that tidbit, I realized the Upheaval happened around the time when about fifty thousand eighth graders had gone to D.C. for their trips. Bottom line, they were everywhere and out for our asses.

"Move, move, move!" I panted, running for all I was worth. We needed to make as much space between us and them as we could, if we had to stand, it would be easier to string them out and deny them attacking en masse.

"Trying!" Tommy puffed. We were both in good shape, but after fighting and falling and running, it tended to wear you out a bit.

"We're almost there!" I said, seeing the white outline between the trees. "Come on!" We ducked off the road and headed straight for the amphitheater. It was a neat collection of columns and bench seating, ideal for small, formal ceremonies. The East side had the main viewing area for the Tomb of the Unknowns and if we were lucky, there wouldn't be any zombies waiting for us.

We zipped around the corner and I nearly collapsed with relief. The viewing area was empty and we had an unobstructed view of the D.C. grounds. I scanned quickly around and realized we didn't have any place to safely hole up and the kids would be looking for their lunch very soon. Our trip through the brush had slowed them down, but it wouldn't be long before they were on us.

I glanced around for defense and saw there was only one place to go. "Let's move." I ran over to the tomb itself, noting the inscription "Here Rests in Honored Glory an American Soldier Known But to God." I figured whoever was in there wouldn't mind us using his spot as an escape from zombies. I jumped up and caught the edge, swinging my legs up. I reached down and hauled Tommy up behind me and we both lay down in the center of the slab. The usual tactic was to find a way to suddenly disappear. It confused the hell out of pursuing zombies and generally seemed to close down their pursuit response. When prey was gone and couldn't be seen, heard, or smelt, Z's usually resorted quickly back to their dormant behavior. The hard part was choosing a hidey-hole with an exit, in case you were found.

If we could get enough of them to start wandering off, we might get lucky enough to be able to hop off and get away when the RV arrived.

As we lay there we could hear the zombies arrive, shuffling and scraping along the pathway that Marines for generations had walked, guarding the Tomb. I idly wondered if they had guarded the tomb until the last, finally succumbing to overwhelming numbers of teeth and nails. Knowing what kind of men they were, I guessed they probably stayed at their posts.

The worst part of waiting like this was we had to rely on our sense of hearing. We could hear them moving around, coming closer than we ever wanted them to. If we were really lucky, we could even hear them sniffing for us, trying to catch a scent they could follow. As long as we stayed still and quiet, I knew they couldn't see us or smell us. Unless one of them got up on the top steps and looked back, we were pretty much invisible. And even if one did get up on the steps, zombie eyesight was usually bad and not something to worry too much about unless it was a fresh one.

As we lay there listening to the shuffling and sniffing going on all around us, I became aware of a strange sound coming from Tommy. It started out as a weird spluttering noise, then it would stop, start again, then stop again. I dared to look over at him and was shocked to see him red in the face, trying desperately to hold something back. I nudged him slightly and that's when he let loose the fart of the century. It reverberated across the plaza, ricocheted off the amphitheater walls and echoed out towards the river. I swear I felt the marble slab vibrate. In another second, I expected the soldier in the tomb to pound on the ceiling and say, "C'mon, really?"

As I listened to the renewed moans and sniffing going on, trying to locate the source of the flatulence, I began to feel the beginnings of a deadly sensation. The absolute seriousness of the situation contradicted by the cosmic cutting of the cheese gave me the most dire case of the giggles.

Believe me, I tried to hold them back, but they kept working their way out through my fingers and nose. By myself it wouldn't have been so bad, but Tommy managed to get them as well and it must have been a strange sight to see two men giggling like schoolgirls, lying on the Tomb of the Unknown Soldier, surrounded by teenage ghouls.

The more I tried to hold them back, the worse it got. Tommy was no better off and every time he contained a giggle he let loose another fart.

Finally, I had had enough. "Screw this," I said, rising to my knees. At the sight of me, the dozen or so Z's that were lounging about groaned loudly and rushed the tomb. We were safe from attack, since they couldn't climb up here, but we were going to be surrounded by hundreds if we didn't do something quickly.

I pulled my handgun as Tommy got to his knees, letting a last one go into the wind. He pulled his gun as well and we went to work. Originally, I hadn't wanted to use our guns unless seriously needed, as I didn't want to advertise our whereabouts to the general dead populace. But I figured we could thin the herd out a little without too much worry about exposure. I lined up a snarling face on the outer edge of the crowd and fired, switching my aim quickly and fired again. Tommy was calmly plugging away on his side, working his way from the back to the front. Both of us had five magazines for our handguns, which gave us enough to take care of even this largish crowd.

"Save your last two, we're going to be moving soon," I said as I blew a hole in the forehead of a particularly nasty-looking individual. Half its face was ripped off and the other half was dangling down near its neck. Its eyes were still in their sockets, giving it a weird 'Tales from the Crypt' look.

I was on my third magazine when I finished with my side and Tommy fired his last shot nearly at the same time. We scrambled off our sanctuary and moved quickly down the steps to hang out between the huge hedges flanking the walkway. They were enormous and in bad need of a trimming, but that would have to wait.

As we got to the center of little hallway, three more zombies came into view on the far end. We froze, but they spotted us and started to limp in our direction. I pulled my knife and was about to charge when suddenly the zombies looked over to their left. I followed their gaze and saw the RV swung into view. It slammed into the three zombies, knocking them back before crushing them under the wheels of the big rig.

I slapped Tommy on the back as we ran for the vehicle and that big gas guzzling behemoth never looked so good. We boarded quickly and I handed my empty mags to Tommy for reloading. I worked my way up to the front and plopped down next to Nate.

"Was waiting for you on the other side, when we heard your gunshots. Figured you were making a stand so we came around to this end." Nate glanced sideways at me. "You might have saved a few."

I shook my head and told him about the eighth graders, Nate whistled appreciatively.

"Wow. That's why there are so many. Now we know. Do you think Thorton heard your shots?"

I gave the notion some serious thought. "I'd have to say no, probably not. But its all speculation. We're far enough away that pistol fire might go unnoticed whereas rifle fire would be heard all over. We'll see." I changed the subject. "If Thorton's in the area, I don't want to be getting sniper fire before we even get out of the RV. This thing isn't exactly subtle and since we're the only thing moving around here…"

"Got it," said Nate. "So what's the plan?"

"Well, the good news is the roads run along both the Mall side and the commercial side of the buildings, so we can park on the commercial side and be relatively unseen."

"Unseen except for the three million zombies wandering about."

"That was the bad news."

Nate just grunted. He moved the RV along the narrow road and I watched as several small groups of teens got bumped out of the way. They sprawled along in the tall grass, or bounced off a grave marker. I felt kind of bad for the markers, but there wasn't anything to be done for it.

Roosevelt took us to Eisenhower Drive, which in turn took us to Memorial Drive. The road had few cars, which made sense, who runs to a cemetery when the dead are walking? We encountered a few more vehicles when we crossed the bridge to Columbia Island and I saw the tell tale signs of past occupation by people desperate to get away from the zombies. The island would have made a good choice, but it had too many bridges to seal effectively and the in the first rush any defenders would have been swept away.

As we crossed the Potomac on Arlington Memorial Bridge, Tommy handed me my reloaded magazines. I thanked him and looked out across the water to the Teddy Roosevelt Island Memorial. I thought I saw a faint whisper of smoke coming from the forest and remarked on it to Nate.

"Looks like someone might be forted up on that island," I said.

Nate gave it a once over. If that bridge was blocked or barricaded, people could be living there."

"We'll check it out when we finish."

"Good." Nate was abrupt and didn't elaborate. I didn't press him, but I knew he was feeling the strain as much or more than anyone. This had been a rough trip and while Tommy, Duncan and myself were used to the threat of zombies, the constant stress had been an awakening for Nate. I was sure his heart was in the right place, but I began to get the feeling he was doubting himself.

On the other side of the river, traffic was a different story. Here the roads were jammed with cars and ghouls and Nate had to travel overland much of the time.

"Feels weird, even now," Nate commented as he wove the RV through a stand of trees, knocking down several zombies.

"What does?" I said, wincing as a Z bounced over the plow, smacking its head on the side of the windshield, leaving a dark greasy mark.

"Driving off the regular roads. Always feel like a cop is gonna nail me."

"Old habits," I said, leaving it at that. We all did things that made no sense in the world we lived in, but it was a comfort to still do them or think about them, as it was a reminder that this world wasn't all there ever was. When we found cell phones, even after a year and a half after the Upheaval, I'd check to see if there was any power, any signal. It was stupid, but I did it.

We passed by the Lincoln Memorial and judging by the rings of bodies, it looked like someone had fired their last on the steps. I saw the statues of the soldiers as they made their way through the simulated rice paddy while we worked our way past the Korean War Memorial. Their haunted faces matched the looks of the dozen zombies that roamed the same field.

I looked in the rear view mirror and saw we were being followed by dozens of zombies. They knew someone was driving the vehicle that kept knocking them out of the way and they could see Nate and myself as we plowed through throngs of them. I don't know why we didn't bother to try and conceal ourselves, but it probably had something to do with trying to get where we needed to be as quickly as possible. Tough as it was, this big rig was a target and the sooner we could get it stopped and get ourselves out, the sooner we could avoid an ambush. I just hoped that the zombies didn't stay too interested in it and we would be allowed to grab it and get back out of D.C..

"Hold on," Nate said suddenly. He swerved to avoid a huge crowd of zombies and the ones on the edge of the pack bounced off the plow and the sides of the rig with sickening smacks and thuds. The RV lurched one way and then the next as it bounced over prone bodies. Many of the ones we drove over were already dead and the crackle of brittle bones was easily heard above the din of the moaning Z's.

We swept down the street, hurling zombies left and right and Nate tried to thread the needle through a couple of trees on the side of the road. The fit was tight and I could hear the branches slam into the rooftop fences. There was a screech of tearing metal, a pause in our forward progress and then we sped forward suddenly.

I looked over at Nate just as Duncan called from the back.

"Shit, the whole roof fence got torn off!" he said.

"Damn," Nate said, looking over at me.

"Just get us to that red building over there," I said, pointing to the Smithsonian Castle.

"Trying," Nate said through gritted teeth. He wound around the World War Two memorial, plowed across the National Mall, and careened across the hill on which the Washington Monument stood.

I couldn't be too sure, but I thought I felt the wheels of the far side of the RV shift and leave the ground for an instant as we sped down the hill.

"Watch it!" I yelled, gripping the sides of the seat as we slammed into two cars, knocking them sideways and out of our way, splitting the weld that held the left side of the plow to the frame. I could see the one side dipping lower than the other. Another hit like that and we were going to lose the plow altogether. Curses from the back let me know that the hit had been unexpected by the other men.

"Anytime you want to drive, Daisy, you just let me know." Nate bared his teeth as he tried to steer us around a massive traffic jam of cars, limos and military vehicles.

"Maybe that road there." I pointed to the road that went around the Holocaust Museum.

"I'll try. Red Castle, right?" Nate asked about our destination.

"That's it," I said getting up and heading to the back. I motioned for Duncan and Tommy to come forward.

I spoke quietly as I opened the cabinet and retrieved my M1A and spare magazines. "Get the packs together and load up on ammo. Food and water will have to be abandoned. We can scrounge what we need later."

Tommy narrowed his eyes at me. "What gives?"

"We may have to abandon ship, we're crashing in deeper and I don't think we're driving out," I answered, grabbing extra boxes of ammo for my SIG and Nate's .45. I took the Springfield my dad left for me and put it in my pack. I wasn't familiar enough with it to trust it with my life and my SIG had become an extension of my arm.

Tommy looked out the front window and Duncan looked out the back as we all grabbed hold of a wall to steady ourselves as the

RV swung sharply around another obstacle. I saw the door buckle slightly as we hit another car.

The impact spurred Tommy and Duncan to furious action and they quickly and efficiently loaded packs with ammo and magazines. I noticed they kept a small supply of food and water with each pack, just to be safe. *New habits becoming old ones*, I thought as I went back to the front of the vehicle. *Wonder when we'll outgrow the new ones?*, I pondered as I steadied myself again as the RV moved to the opposite direction.

We pushed our way down the street between the Agricultural Department and the Bureau of Engraving. The two causeways that had connected the buildings had been blown apart and I wondered briefly why they had done that. A lot of these buildings were huge fortresses with no easy access from the street, so hundreds of people could have been saved had they forted themselves up properly. Of course, by the time the full nature of the threat had been realized, millions of people were infected and roaming the streets in search of a live meal.

Nate swerved the RV to the left as the Smithsonian Building came into view and we crashed through the garden in the front of the building. The last thing I heard before we came to a sudden stop was Nate cursing.

"Who the fuck put *that* there?"

CHAPTER 16

The rest was lost in a crunch of metal as we were thrown to the floor. Nate had his seatbelt on and I saw him slam forward and back.

"What the hell?" Tommy yelled from the back. He had fallen forward carrying loaded packs and was trying to climb off the floor.

I heard even worse cursing from Duncan and I realized he was in the bathroom when we hit. I pulled myself off the table and gave Zeus the cat a reassuring pat on the head, which earned me a nasty snarl. Zeus had flown across the entire kitchen and was hanging from the curtains.

"Holy hell," I said. "Nate, you okay? What'd we hit?" I asked, trying to see the damage.

Nate shook his head and unbuckled himself, straining to see the front of the vehicle. I joined him at the cracked windshield and looked down. The front of the RV was wrapped around a concrete planter that had overgrown and looked for all intents and purposes like an innocent shrubbery. Well, this bush had teeth and had bitten the shit out of us.

"We can't stay here, all the ghouls we pissed off are on their way. We gotta leave the RV," I said, grabbing my pack and slinging my rifle over my shoulder. I took one of the medieval billhooks from Tommy and started for the door.

"Why are we leaving?" asked Nate. "This place was designed to be a fortress." He looked back at me and crossed his arms over his chest.

"Sure, but not for as many zombies that are out there." I pointed to the garden and street. "There's enough of them to knock this rig over and in case you hadn't noticed, the last car you hit dented in the door. There's a big enough crack for a hand to get in and you know that's all they need."

Nate glanced over my shoulder and saw the dent. "Shit. Well, I need my pack."

Tommy threw a loaded pack to Nate.

Nate shrugged it on. "I need my weapons."

Duncan handed him a rifle and another billhook.

Nate blinked and then he laughed. "I need a big-titted blonde in love with me." Nate paused while Duncan just looked at him. "Well, all right then. Let's hope we can get inside."

I silently prayed we could while we exited the RV. The rig had stirred up a lot of attention, but it was all on this side of the museum. I was grateful we hadn't yet made our presence known to Thorton. Surprise needed to be on our side and when you wandered about at the head of a phalanx of walking dead, you tended to attract attention.

Fortunately, we were still alone in the garden as we got out of the RV and as we circled towards the building, we got a good look at all the damage our journey had inflicted on the vehicle. Looking at the mangled sides and paint that belonged on other cars, I was stunned we had made it as far as we had.

I moved to the back of the vehicle when a moan got my attention. A well-dressed zombie moved out of the bushes and stumbled at us. Nate hefted his billhook and with a single swing, crushed the Z's head and put him down.

Nate looked at his handiwork and commented, "You know, as useful as a gun is on these things, there's something oddly satisfying about taking them out with one of these babies."

I had to agree. It was like we were connecting with a more primitive part of ourselves to take out a primal threat. Would I wander into a nest of zombies with just my billhook or pickaxe? No. But I could appreciate the damage they did and the savings on bullets. Who knows? Maybe one day all we would have left were medieval weapons and warfare.

Duncan and Tommy had hurried to the main doorway and waved us over. The front gate did not look to be barred in any way, at least not from the outside. Inside might be a different story, but things looked relatively normal. The castle-like turrets jutted into the air, lending a distinctly somber attitude to the place. I liked it, although the red was a bit over the top.

"Something strange here, John," Tommy said, indicating the door. "When we first walked up, the door was locked. After Nate killed that Z, the door was open."

That was odd. "Are you sure you might not have jarred it loose when you tried it?" I reasoned.

"Could be, but it's pretty damn coincidental. I'm not sure I like what this might mean," Tommy said, hoisting his weapon and placing a hand on his gun.

"Speak plain, we're wasting time here," Nate said, looking around at the garden. It was hard not to feel very exposed where we were.

"If a ghoul was smart enough to realize we were here and unlocked the door so we could be ambushed, what else might be waiting for us?" Tommy asked.

I shook my head. "That's a little much. Chances are it wasn't locked very well to begin with and you knocked it loose," I said. "If it makes you feel better, I'll go in first."

"Nothing to do with scared, you know better than that." Tommy snapped, shooting me a dirty look.

"Ease up," I said reassuringly. "No one's doubting you. But we're outside in the middle of a shitload of zombies, so could we go where the odds might be a little better?"

Duncan snickered and that broke the tension. I nodded to Nate, who stood behind me with his rifle at the ready. I opened the door and quickly ducked to the side, allowing Nate a clear field of fire. He didn't shoot anything, so I stood up and led the way into the main foyer of the historic building. I walked past several display cases which to me seemed very close, until I realized they had been put there on purpose. Someone wanted to be able to funnel the intruders into a narrow corridor. As we walked, I noticed the display cases went straight through the building to the doors on the other side. I thought that was pretty clever. If someone was willing to act as a bit of bait, zombies who made it into the front would stroll on through and be none the wiser.

I stopped in the middle of the great hall and climbed over the display case there. The tall ceiling made the room seem colossal and I wished I had visited this place in another life. We walked slowly along the hall and I noted that the alcoves, which must have housed various displays, were now being used as rooms for occupation.

I didn't see anyone, but I was sure they were here. I'd seen enough hasty exits to know when someone is truly gone and when someone is hiding.

"Hello?" I called.

No answer. I thought I heard some twitterings in the shadows, but I wasn't sure. Nate and Tommy spread out to the other side of the hall, while Duncan and I looked this side over.

I peeked into an alcove and it was neatly arranged. A small sleeping area had a simple blanket and pillow, while a couple of crates served as a dresser. In the corner was a length of pipe and on a peg near the door was a belt with a large knife on it. The blade had to be at least ten inches. When I saw that I knew the people were in either one of two conditions: dead or hiding. No one leaves such a useful item behind. That would be like me leaving behind my SIG.

I tried again. "Hello? Anybody there?" I looked over at Duncan who shrugged. "We're not here to hurt anyone, we're just trying to pass through. We're glad to find living people here."

"Drop your weapons and put your hands up!" came a forceful reply. The speaker sounded young.

This was becoming tiresome. Couldn't anyone just talk to me without wanting me to disarm myself? Didn't anyone ever take into consideration how long it took to get this deadly in the morning? Seriously. I answered quickly.

"No."

I noticed Nate and Tommy were suddenly nowhere to be seen, taking cover. Duncan faded into the background, keeping his rifle handy.

"We have you covered! Drop your weapons!" The voice came again and this time I was used to the echoes and was able to pinpoint the general direction of the speaker.

"I don't like repeating myself. I'm not dropping my weapons and we're not staying any longer than to get our bearings and be on our way. We don't want anything from you, you can have your stuffed animals and archways and be dammed." I was getting a little irritated this went on as long as it had.

There was some kind of commotion at the stairs and I heard several voices in heated whispers. I waited patiently with my billhook resting on my shoulder.

Soon enough a small group of four young men and women came down the stairs and headed in my direction. One of the men was carrying a rifle and wearing a scowl. The others seemed pleasant enough. The leader, a blond man about twenty-eight or thirty, walked up to me with a smile and outstretched hand.

"Thank you for not making an issue out of things," he said. "My name is Jason Kenaten and this is Katie O'Donnell and Rita Sanchez." He motioned to the two women, a blonde and brunette, respectively. They were both young, probably near their thirties.

Jason continued. "The man with the gun is Mike Morten and he's a bit more stand-offish than we'd like."

I was about to introduce my crew when I was interrupted.

"Where's the rest of you?" Mike asked sharply, eyeing my gear.

I turned and focused my full attention on Mike, taking several seconds to answer. I saw him start to squirm under my gaze and decided to respond.

"The man called Duncan is behind you, pointing a gun at your head right now. My friends Nate and Tommy are likely training their rifles on you as well. Fair enough?" I asked, not really caring if he approved.

I turned back to Jason. "Thanks for unlocking the door. We'd have been in trouble out there had the zombies come in force. Name's John Talon."

"Not a problem. We did take risk on whether or not you were friendly, but it's been a very long time since we've seen anyone alive and to have two groups nearby in the same day has been uplifting to say the least," Jason said, smiling broadly.

Behind me, I heard Tommy whisper "I knew it!" I smiled to myself. But the comment by Jason gave me pause.

"Two groups?" I asked, figuring I knew the answer.

The one called Katie answered. "I was on watch when I saw a group of seventeen men moving through the landscape around the museums. They caused quite a stir at the Museum of Natural History and I saw most of the zombies on the mall move in that direction. Then I saw them go to the capitol building and haven't seen them since. Then you guys came." She dimpled at me and I nodded my thanks.

Several things occurred to me at once. First, Thorton didn't have as many men as I originally thought and the odds were getting better for a confrontation. Second, he probably didn't know where the documents were kept. That was a huge advantage for us and if we could get over to the Archives quickly, we could perhaps be out and on our way before he even knew we were there.

"How many people do you have here?" I asked Jason, indicating with my billhook the alcoves.

"We have thirty seven people here right now," Jason said and I could see behind the smiles that he was concerned about something.

"How did you guys get to be here?" I wondered aloud, as Tommy and Nate and Duncan left their respective cover and joined me in talking to the representatives.

Mike laughed, a harsh sound. "We were the chaperones for an eighth grade trip when the shit hit the fan. We were in here when the first big wave of zombies hit the capitol and watched as the military made a stand at the Lincoln Memorial and the capitol building. They thought if they made two points of contact that they could divide the zombies up and be able to take them out." He frowned. "Would have worked too, if there weren't so damn many of them. We watched the fall of the Lincoln Memorial and the fall of the capitol." Mike looked down.

Rita picked up the story. "We had to protect the kids. They were scared to death and had no one to turn to. Everything happened so fast!" She lowered her voice. "The screaming went on for days. People were hunted down by packs of zombies and torn to pieces. Office workers tried to run or fort up, but there were too many!"

I nodded. It was a similar story nearly everywhere. I was about to speak when Nate chimed in.

"Wait, you were here in this building during the last days?" Nate did some quick calculations. "You've been here for over a year and a half?"

Jason nodded. "It's been interesting, to say the least. We managed to fort up the building and when we discovered a tunnel to the building next door, we used it raid nearby buildings for supplies. We have a garden growing under the skylights over there and have been able to keep ourselves alive."

He continued his story and I had to say I was impressed with what they had done. In the middle of madness they had kept their heads and were able to at least stay alive. I felt bad for the kids because they had to realize their world was finished and everyone they knew back home either was dead or thought they were. I looked around and thought this was a tough place to grow up. I had to hand it to the adults too. They had families back wherever they were from and had no way to contact them, no way of knowing if they were alive or dead anymore. This virus took so much from so many it was a wonder we weren't all insane.

When he was done I related to him who we were and why we were here and what our plans were. I told him about Thorton and what kind of person he was and Jason said he was very grateful he had opened the door for us and not Thorton. The four of them were grateful to know there were thriving communities still and they weren't the only ones left in the country. They did wonder why we would risk our lives for a document that could be found in any history book, but I reminded them that the originals were about who we were as a people and as a country and we needed the symbolism to regain what we had lost. We needed a rallying point.

"You said there is a tunnel from this building to the one next door. Are there any other tunnels you know about?" I asked Jason.

"There is a utility tunnel access, but we've never opened it," Jason said. "I figured to leave well enough alone in case there was any possibility of leaving access for the zombies. In the madness people tried to hide wherever they could and it's possible some made it to the tunnels."

I mulled it over and figured it was worth the risk if only to get us across the mall. There was no way we were going to be able to make it to the Archives above ground without our RV and that worthy died an inglorious death on the steps of the red castle. Our only option at this point was to head underground.

"Where's the access door?" I asked.

Jason looked ashen. "You're not thinking of going in there?"

I shrugged. "Not much choice and not much time. We need to get across the mall and do it now. We don't have our vehicle and we don't have an army. We're limited."

Katie chimed up. "But what if you open the door and the tunnel is full of those creatures?" She bit her bottom lip in worry.

Duncan smiled and winked at her. "Then I'm sure John will shut the door."

I said nothing and followed Jason over to the stairs. We went down two floors, then made our way past a boiler room and what looked to be a maintenance storage room. Next to the massive electrical panels was a steel door marked 'Utility – Restricted Access' I walked over to it and saw it had a deadbolt lock. I tried the door and while the knob turned, the deadbolt was locked.

"We need the key. See if you can find anything," I said to the rest of the crew. Nate and Tommy and Duncan immediately began searching while Mike and Jason looked uncomfortable. After about ten minutes, Nate called out.

"Got a ring of keys here, might be one of them." He brought the keys over and I began the tedious task of trying to find one that fit. There was nearly a solid ring of keys and it took a while, but on what seemed to be the third to last key, the deadbolt turned. I took the key off the ring and held onto it, the hope being that the other access doors were all keyed the same. Dead ends tended to make me twitchy.

"Okay," I said, gently moving Jason and Mike out of the way, "I don't know what's on the other side of that door or who might be lurking in the dark, so let's get as much space cleared as possible. Duncan, you're on the left. Nate, you're on the right. Tommy, you're behind me." The men took their positions with practiced efficiency, making sure they had spare magazines within easy reach. I was in the most vulnerable spot, but I did not plan on getting shot. I was going to fling open the door, crouching low while Tommy flashed both his light and mine to give Nate and Duncan the best chance to see the Z's before the zombies realized the new situation.

I held the handle of the door and waited. When I heard, "Ready," from three people, I turned the knob slowly, hoping it wouldn't creak from inactivity. When it turned all the way, I jerked the door open and dropped into a crouch, leveling my SIG at the opening while holding the door open with my extended right foot.

When no shots were fired, I exhaled the breath I was holding and stood up. I holstered my SIG and pulled out my pickaxe, deciding to leave the billhook behind. It was a tactical decision, since the utility corridor was too narrow for effectively using the big weapon. The corridor was tall enough to get a good overhand swing with the pick if I choked up on the handle a bit and it was such a familiar weapon to me that I didn't feel like I was settling for second best.

Mike was the first to speak, coming from around the boiler. "You guys sure look like you've done this before."

"Once or twice," I said.

Rita spoke next. "What happens after you get the documents, what then?"

"We'll see if we can't find a vehicle, make a break for the water, head upriver, start heading home. Why?" I asked, checking my vest for magazines and making sure my knife was where it was supposed to be.

"Since you seem to know what you're doing and have a plan, could you take us with you?"

I expected the question, but I was hoping to have a chance to figure out a plan, first.

I looked at four faces and saw they had some semblance of hope for the first time in over a year. I imagined there were thirty-three other faces that were holding that same hope as well. Oh, well. This is what I do.

"Get your stuff together. Take only what you can carry. Station someone by this door. When we come back, we may be moving fast and you may have to move fast as well." I looked down the dark corridor and felt a strange primordial chill go up my back. I couldn't shake the feeling that this was a bad move.

There was an excited conference and suddenly Katie said, "What about the people at the Library?"

Jason looked sheepish. "Forgot about them. Can they come, too?"

"Library?" asked Tommy tentatively.

"The Library of Congress." Jason said quickly. There's a bunch of people holed up there as well."

"How many?" I was afraid to ask, but had to.

Katie answered. "There's about thirty of them."

Jesus. "We'll have to see about transportation. As it is, unless we can find a bus, we're in for a wild time."

Mike smiled. "Pal, you're in D.C.. There's buses everywhere."

I leveled a look at him. "Find one that works and get it back here before I return and I just might start to like you," I said as I ducked into the corridor. I didn't really want to find out if there was another hundred people living in the Space Museum that needed a rescue.

Tommy was right behind me and Nate followed with Duncan. Before the door closed I could hear Mike ask the others why I wouldn't like him.

CHAPTER 17

We moved quickly down the hallway, heading away from the Smithsonian. The way was dark as hell and we kept our light to one flashlight. Tommy, Nate and Duncan all had weapon lights, but wouldn't use them unless we hit a group of Z's. The nice thing about the corridor was it had been sealed against the elements, so there weren't any animals or bugs down here. The air was somewhat stale, but didn't have the sickly sweet odor of decay one usually found with dead people.

We moved over to a ladder and I was curious to see where it led, so Duncan volunteered to scramble up and take a look. He handed his rifle to me and drew his sidearm as he reached the top of the stairs. He opened the hatch and sunlight flooded down, momentarily blinding me. Duncan looked around and came back down.

"Well?" I asked.

"It's an access hatch, right in the middle of the mall. It opens with a key from the outside, since there was only a handle up there from here."

"Any friends upside?"

"Oh sure. Thousands. Want a look?"

"Um, no. Let's keep moving."

We seemed to be heading in the right direction and passed by a couple more ladders to the world above. When we reached a junction, I called a halt.

"I think we're across the mall, but I have no way to be sure," I said to the huddled group. "Since we need to head East, let's go right and at the first ladder find out where the hell we are." My voice carried in the dark corridors, which was fine with me. The sooner a Z heard me, the sooner he responded and I would have time to get ready to nail his ass.

"Hey, John?" Tommy spoke up.

"What?"

"How the hell are we going to move sixty seven people out of a zombie-filled city?"

"Not a clue. You know I just make this shit up as I go along."

"Just checking."

We moved eastward and that's when we heard it. There was a dragging sound, followed by a thud, followed by a deep moan. The problem was we didn't know if it was in front or behind us. The acoustics of the tunnels made it hard to tell. But we did know we needed to keep moving. I shined my light ahead and the corridor showed clear, but it stretched far enough ahead that I could only see a hundred feet or so. The moans continued and didn't seem to be getting closer or louder, but it sure as hell was creepy, knowing it was down here somewhere with us. Another concern was if we had to move through the tunnels quickly heading back, I didn't want a smelly corpse waiting for us.

After moving along about three hundred feet, we encountered another ladder. Duncan handed his rifle to me without a sound and clambered up. At the top he opened the hatch slowly, looked around, then scrambled through, opening it entirely.

I was looking up when the moan sounded again, this time much closer.

"Same one or different?" Nate asked.

"Not sure," I said. "Stay here, I'll go check." I walked down the hallway, keeping one eye on the floor and one on the distance in front of me. I didn't want to be watching for standing ghouls when a crawler nailed me in the knees.

About thirty yards down the corridor I found the source of the moan. It was a crawler, one of his legs was halved at the knee while his hands, torn by rough surfaces, were literally down to the bone. He raised his head and leered at me with black teeth. I gave him a nice smile, then crushed his skull with my pick.

As he slumped down, I heard shuffling in the darkness, like leaves being disrupted by the wind. I shined my light down the hall and sure enough, another one was moving in. This one was a little faster, being upright, but she was dragging a broken foot. When the light shined on her face, she bared her teeth and tried to increase her speed. Her arms raised and her hands clawed, looking to rend and tear with wildly colored fingernails. The things you notice.

I reached down and dragged the now-dead crawler across the hall, creating a tripping point. I figured to kill the walker when she fell. As she approached the obstacle, she surprised the heck out of me by stepping over it. I was nearly caught off guard as the situation suddenly switched.

"Clever girl," I said as I swung hard from the right just as she came within reach. I could hear her starting her moan and as I connected, I noted her necklace had some interestingly colored beads on it. The zombie went down in a heap, falling back over the first. She had closed her eyes in death and in the dim light she almost looked like she was sleeping. Scratch that. She looked like she was at peace, which I supposed she finally was.

I heard a shot behind me and the echo of the report bounced off the walls and travelled like a freight train down the corridor. I spun around and hurried back, finding Nate standing over a small corpse, holding a still-smoking pistol.

"What happened? I thought we weren't using our guns until we absolutely had to." I asked of no one in particular.

Nate answered. "Little shit came out of nowhere. He was on me before I could see him."

"He get you?" I asked softly. I had no desire to put Nate down, but I would do what I had to.

"No, he managed to get his mouth on my neck, but I got him off, no bites. He just scared the holy living fuck outta me." Nate looked up at the ceiling and blew out a long breath.

"All right. Let's get moving then. That shot will probably cause every Z in the tunnels and sub levels to come looking, so the sooner we're out the better." I crawled up the ladder and with a quick look around, stepped out. I helped Tommy up and was going to help Nate when he waved me off.

"No need for that, I'm fine." Nate came through the hatch and stumbled a bit, catching himself on the ground.

We were in a maintenance shed, exactly where, I had no clue. Duncan was on one side, Tommy was on the other. Both were looking out the windows at the respective views. The good news was we were able to gather ourselves unseen in a shed. The bad news was I wasn't sure where we were. I went over to Duncan's side and carefully looked out. I could see a road and a big building and judging by the sun I was looking west. There were a lot of ghouls wandering about and they generally seemed to still be moving over to the west.

Not knowing anything of significance on this side, I went over to Tommy, sparing a glance at Nate who was sitting on a chair, scratching the back of his neck. Tommy was looking back and forth and nodded as I came over.

"Looks like a garden or something that used to be a garden," Tommy said. "That big building is the National Gallery of Art if that helps orient you any."

I nodded. "That helps a lot, thanks. That means this is the Sculpture Garden and we're actually across the street from the National Archives."

"Seriously?" Duncan asked from his spot. "We did pretty well, all things considered."

"Don't get ahead of yourself, we're not there yet." I cautioned. "We still have to get across the garden, across the street and into the building, which hopefully will be open, secure the documents and get out without getting shot or bitten."

"Buzzkill," Duncan said, looking back out the window.

"Let's get ourselves moving. We're going to use the garden as much as we can, then it's a straight sprint to the archives," I said.

"John?" Tommy spoke quietly. He had walked back to check out the window in the back of the shed, which had placed him directly behind Nate. Tommy motioned to me to come over. Nate was sitting with his eyes closed and his breathing was deep, like he was sleeping.

I went over to Tommy and he pointed to the back of Nate's neck. There was a small ring of teeth marks on the back of Nate's neck. I looked closer and saw that none of the marks broke the skin, which was good for Nate. But the marks went right across a mosquito bite that Nate had scratched open and that was bad for Nate. The wound was dark red, with deep red lines radiating out from it. A dark, nearly black line disappeared into Nate's neck as it traced higher into his head.

My heart sank into my chest as I realized what had happened. The little Z that had surprised Nate had killed him too.

I motioned Tommy away and he went over to Duncan to tell him what had happened. Duncan's head snapped around and his eyes immediately found mine. I shook my head and saw both men shake their heads in disbelief.

I circled around to face Nate and I squatted down in front of him. His eyes were closed and his breathing was becoming labored. I touched his knee and his eyes snapped open. He looked balefully at me with bloodshot eyes in a pale face.

"Hey, Nate," I said.

"Hey, John," Nate rasped. "The little shit got me after all. Wonder how he did it. He didn't break skin."

"Mosquito bite," I said.

Realization hit Nate like a bucket of water. "Son of a bitch," he said, shaking his head. "Son of a bitch."

Nate stood up slowly and took off his pack. "You'll need the supplies."

"Nate…" I started, but he cut me off.

"John, you know I'm right. Don't get sentimental 'cuz you're gonna have to shoot me soon, anyway." Nate's voice was a whisper. He slumped back into the chair, gathered himself and stood again. He held out his hand and I took off my glove to shake it, trying hard to hold back my emotions.

"Been an honor to know you, John. You made these last couple of years worthwhile." Tears filled Nate's eyes.

"Thanks for all you taught me, Nate," I whispered back, my voice cracking. "You've been a great friend."

"C'mere you two idiots, before I try and take a chew outta you," Nate growled.

Duncan came over first and shook Nate's hand. "You stupid bastard," Duncan said, wiping his eyes.

"Love you, too." Nate grinned.

Tommy shook his hand, too choked up to speak.

"Watch after John," Nate said. "Chances are he's gonna go a little nuts for a while." Nate dropped Tommy's hand and sat back down. "Gettin' tired. Guess this little virus wants me bad."

"Nate…" I started, but he cut me off.

"Finish this, John and kill that cocksucking piece of shit. After that you make this country again, you hear me? You make it a whole country again." Nate looked slowly around and said, "So long, boys. You're the best sons of bitches I ever met." He tumbled out of his chair and fell through the hatch, landing heavily on the floor.

"Nate!" I yelled, hurrying to the opening. Tommy and Duncan were right behind me.

Nate's pained voice drifted up to us. "Stay there! No time left, boys and I wouldn't ask any of you to kill me. Wouldn't want you to live with that. Tell Jake his Uncle Nate will be watching him. I'm going to be with my family now, John. No regrets."

There was a pause and then a single shot. I couldn't see Nate in the darkness and I'm glad I couldn't. I sat for a long time at the edge of the dark hole that had claimed my friend, not knowing what to do next. Tommy and Duncan were silently behind me, each man lost in his own thoughts.

I thought back to the first time I had met Nate, the gruff survivor who taught me how to survive, how to fight, how to reclaim what was mine. Nate did more than teach us to fight, he taught us to not be afraid. I remembered how Jake loved Nate and knew it was going to be hard to tell Charlie and Sarah that our friend was gone. I burned Nate's words into my mind, promising him I would make this country again. Even if I had to do it alone, I would do it.

I reached over and closed the hatch, slowly sealing Nate Coles into the tunnels of D.C..

CHAPTER 18

"Anything on your side?"

"Just a thing about Alexandria."

"What about Mount Vernon?"

"What about it?"

"Didn't Washington live there?"

"Who cares?"

The two soldiers pawed through several scattered pamphlets and dozens of overturned bookshelves and magazine racks. The U.S. Capitol Visitor Center was a disaster, with papers and garbage and backpacks everywhere. There were a couple of corpses in the corner and they looked like they had been trampled in a rush and tossed aside as casually as an empty can. This was on the upper level. The lower level just had a couple of theaters, an exhibition hall and a curious collection of corpses in the Emancipation Hall that looked suspiciously like former representatives and senators. Each one had been neatly shot in the forehead, yet they didn't look like they had been infected. The soldiers wondered if some sort of coup had been attempted.

The two had been assigned the task of finding the location of the founding documents and that required searching for information through piles of tourist pamphlets. It was a telling testimony of the former country's educational system that not only did Major Thorton not know where the documents were, but none of his men did, either.

Private Hickson overturned a large rack of pamphlets, causing a cascade of paper because he picked up the wrong end and managed to dump all of the information on the floor.

"Nice work, dumbass," Corporal Dodge called from across the room. He was browsing an information desk and was turning up a lot of stuff on the Smithsonian exhibits and memorials, but nothing that stood out as definitive proof of the location of the Bill of Rights and the Constitution.

Hickson ignored the comment and continued looking. He was actually happy to have this detail, since the Visitor Center was free of zombies and he didn't have to worry about getting killed. They'd lost enough men as it was.

"Got it!" Dodge yelled, shining his light on a glossy pamphlet.

"You sure?" called the private.

"Definitely," Corporal Dodge replied. Even as he sounded confident, Dodge checked and double checked the brochure to the National Archives. He didn't want to present the information to the major, take the risk of getting there and discover he was wrong.

"All right. Let's get back to the major." Corporal Dodge put the brochure in his breast pocket and waved his flashlight at the stairs. Private Hickson went up first, quickly and quietly. Even though the place was clear, only stupid people assumed it was safe.

At the top of the stairs, the two men walked past a gift shop and Corporal Dodge veered inside. The shop looked remarkably untouched and there were still some packaged food and drinks at the counter. The other gift shop, on the opposite side of the center, was a looted disaster.

"Well, what have we here?" Corporal Dodge queried. He ran a hand over several bottles of water and expired soft drinks, settling on a bottle of fruit punch. Private Hickson stuffed candy bars and chips into his pack.

Corporal Dodge opened the bottle and said, "Cheers," to the other man. As he raised his anticipated joy, Private Hickson shouted suddenly.

"Look out!" he yelled, raising his rifle.

Dodge glance back to the counter and watched with no small amusement as a skeletal hand came up from the darkness and gripped the edge of the display. A grey-haired head slowly rose from behind the glass and glowing eyes looked repeatedly back and forth between both men. As the zombie stood up, the two men could see it had been a person who had worked there, as evidenced by her uniform and name tag which read 'Elizabeth'. She didn't seem to have any serious trauma to her, so she probably had gotten sick by her exposure to thousands of people, any one of which might have had the early sleeper virus.

Elizabeth let out a rasping moan and lunged forward, hitting the counter and bouncing back slightly. She lunged again with the same result, over and over.

"Sad," Corporal Dodge commented. "She'd do that until she broke a hip and then where would she be? Nursing home for zombies." Dodge grinned at his own joke, as he raised a hand and waved it front of the zombie's face, laughing as she snapped futilely at the tender morsels just out of reach. He avoided her clumsy attempts to clutch his hands and stood inches outside of grabbing distance.

"Let's get moving, you're asking for trouble." Private Hickson worried that other zombies might be hidden nearby and he kept looking into the dark corners, of which there were plenty.

"Relax, private. It's not like you've never seen one of these things before. Whoops." Corporal Dodge reached down to pick up the extra bottle of tea he had dropped. When he straightened, he was staring right in the face of Elizabeth, who had managed to walk around the edge of the counter and was now face to face with Dodge. She already had her hands up and grabbed two fistfuls of hair, hauling Dodge's face to hers.

Corporal Dodge had a full second to try and scream, but Elizabeth the zombie covered his mouth with hers as she tore his lips off his face. She didn't stop with one bite, she kept his head in a death grip and tore and chewed most of Dodge's face off.

Corporal Dodge shoved as hard as he could, dislodging Elizabeth who paused to stuff an errant piece of cheek into her mouth, before heading back to her meal. Dodge turned blindly around, finally finding his voice. He screamed for all he was worth.

"Jesus!" Private Hickson shined his light on Dodge's shredded face and bloody clothes. Elizabeth reached up from behind and grabbed Dodge by the hair again, pulling him backwards and bending him over the counter. His hands battered uselessly at her back as she tore out his throat, blood spraying over the display.

Hickson fired once, his bullet entering Elizabeth's head and knocking her to the floor. Dodge twitched on the counter, already bleeding out. Hickson took careful aim and fired again, this time blowing out the top of his corporal's head.

"Stupid fuck," Private Hickson growled. He moved cautiously to the now-dead corporal and retrieved the pamphlet about the National Archives. He checked to make sure it was untouched by blood and zombie gore, then hurried up to the entrance to the Capitol Building where Major Thorton and the rest of the men were waiting.

As he rounded the corner and disappeared up the stairs, a door silently opened on the other side of the Visitor Center. Careful eyes looked for threats as the door to the tunnel leading to the Library of Congress opened wider to reveal many anxious faces.

Private Hickson rejoined Major Thorton and the rest of the men who were lounging about, taking a rest. There were signs of violence everywhere, bullet holes in the walls, bloodstains in the corners. The room reeked of death but the major didn't seem to notice.

"What have you got?" he asked as soon as the private appeared.

The private handed over the brochure. "National Archives, just up the road a bit."

Major Thorton looked over the information, then an errant thought occurred to him. "Weren't there two of you?" he asked.

Private Hickson nodded. "Corporal Dodge was bitten by a zombie he was playing with. She tore his face off." Hickson's voice was devoid of emotion, emphasizing how little he had cared for the late Dodge.

"Shoot them both?" Major Thorton asked, tucking the brochure into his pocket.

"Yessir."

"Good man. You're a corporal now."

Corporal Hickson smiled slightly.

"And you just inherited Indiana." Indiana had been Dodge's domain to govern.

Corporal Hickson's smile got a lot bigger.

"All right! We found out where they are! Let's get moving. We have a couple of blocks to run and then we are there!" Major Thorton yelled to his men. They replied in cheers, but it was difficult to tell by their faces as to whether or not they were glad to find the documents,or if they were glad to be finally finishing this mission. Out of the forty men who had left Bodie, only thirteen remained. The men had no idea that the ten men that had been dispatched to Starved Rock were dead and buried.

As the group moved towards the exit, one of the men thought he saw movement in an adjacent chamber. He looked over his shoulder, saw no one was watching him, so he jogged back to take a quick peek.

Private Schroder entered the rotunda viewing room and looked around at the statues accumulated there, as well as the huge murals painted on the immense ceiling. As he looked up, there was more movement he could see out of the corner of his eye. He walked deeper into the room and shined his flashlight around to see if he could find out what was going on. He didn't worry about catching up with the other men; they would take a while to assess the situation before they moved anyway.

A pale leg showed behind a desk and Private Schroder carefully walked over to it, circling wide in case it was attached to something undead. Getting closer, he saw that it was indeed attached to something larger, a woman wearing a business suit and with a name tag that read "Kristine." The tag also had the symbol of the capital on it, so Schroder figured she must have been some sort of guide. Her eyes were closed and she was slumped over, like she had hidden and died of fright.

Private Schroder straightened and was about to head back when Kristine suddenly reached out and grabbed his ankle. He was so surprised he fired his weapon and the bullet went into his own left knee.

Pain lanced through his leg as he dropped to the floor, his weapon clattering out of reach. He watched in horror as Kristine slowly turned her head his way, his ankle still gripped in her fist. Kristine smiled at Schroder, but it was not a smile of gratitude or recognition. It was a leer of hunger as she slowly pulled his foot closer for a deadly bite.

Private Schroder kicked out with his foot, knocking Kristine back into the desk. She fell, but immediately began getting to her feet, her eyes locked on her target like a laser-guided missile.

Schroder grimaced in pain as he tried to crawl away. He grabbed a statue to try and stand, but his leg gave way and he crumpled to the ground. He clawed at the marble floor, but it was difficult to pull himself along.

Meanwhile, Kristine was on her feet, moving slowly to her prize. For every step she took, she got closer and closer to the stubborn meat that just wouldn't sit still and be eaten.

Private Schroder frantically crawled at the door and his friends, but when he looked back, he realized Kristine was getting closer and closer. In a few steps she would be on him. Desperation fueled his efforts and he scrambled as best he could across the floor, leaving a zig-zag pattern of blood from his wounded knee.

Behind him, Kristine bared her teeth and hissed, hunger making her move just a little bit faster. She was within just a few feet of her prey when suddenly she slipped on the blood on the floor, tumbling her sideways to the marble.

Schroder looked back and saw that his pursuer had slipped and he dragged himself closer to the entrance. His knee was a mass of pain and he felt himself getting slightly dizzy from blood loss, but he couldn't stop and tie up his knee because his ghoulish girlfriend would be on top of him in a heartbeat.

Kristine managed to get back on her feet and paused to lick the blood off of her fingers before continuing her pursuit. She lurched back and forth, regaining the ground she had lost and the two of them were within spitting distance of the doorway.

Private Schroder managed to reach the doorway, and as he did he grabbed the door frame to try to propel himself, hopefully reaching the doorknob so he could pull himself to his feet.

Just as he grabbed the frame, a dead weight fell on his back and Private Schroder arched his back in pain as Kristine bit down hard on the junction between his neck and shoulder. Jerking her head back, she tore out a huge chunk of flesh, spraying blood all over the doorway. Private Schroder closed his eyes and died quietly as he bled out from his two wounds. Kristine fed on his body for a long time, covering herself in blood and gore.

Outside, Private Schroder's absence was noted, but only briefly. Major Thorton wasn't overly concerned at this point whether or not he had ten men or a hundred. He was going to do what he wanted and reap the rewards. Men could be found anywhere to follow him. All he had to do was show them how much they had to gain and they would be his. The men were assembled under the Ulysses S. Grant statue on the west side of the capitol building. A pile of sandbags and a pile of brass casings were silent tribute to the men who tried to defend the building.

Major Thorton looked at the brochure map again and realized they were a little farther from the Archives than he thought. If the map scale was correct, they were a little more than half a mile from the Archives, a decent distance during normal times, an impossible one during a zombie infestation.

As he looked out over the sandbags, Thorton watched the zombies as they moved about the mall. There were some that were still headed over to the Natural History Museum, but for the most part, many of them had settled down and were in dormant mode. They would amble about aimlessly, or just stop altogether, waiting for stimulus.

Thorton thought for a minute, then gestured for one of his Sergeants to come forward.

"You still have those road flares?" the Major asked.

"Yes, sir, I have one left," the sergeant replied.

Ken mulled that one over. They needed to set it off on the far side of the mall, but there was no way anyone could throw it that far. Time to get creative. Since they needed to move on the right, something on the left had to happen. Thorton looked over the terrain and saw a lot of buses and cars stalled out on the road. Maybe, maybe.

"All right. Hand me the flare. You men wait here." Thorton took the flare from the sergeant, noting with amusement the shocked looks on his men's faces as he volunteered himself for what might be suicide.

Thorton moved quickly around the reflecting pool and over to the line of trees that were on Jefferson Street. None of the woods were occupied, all of the former visitors having fled long ago. Thorton ducked quickly in between the trees and ran low to keep mostly out of sight. When he reached a spot in front of the Air and Space Museum, he lit the flare and tossed it into the window of a tour bus parked there. Using the trees for cover again, he made his way back to the statue and the relative safety of his men.

"All right, let's sit tight and see what happens," Ken said as he watched the bus.

Sure enough, the flare managed to catch a seat on fire and as one went up, another went up and soon black smoke was billowing out of the windows of the bus. The flames worked their way back to the engine, where a gas line lit and there was a muffled 'whump' as the tank blew. It wasn't very loud, but it was loud enough to get the attention of a majority of the zombies on the mall. They began wandering over to where the smoke and flames were, attracted by the commotion. The ones in the front were pushed into the flames by the ones behind them and several zombies caught fire and wandered about as candles, setting fire to whatever flammable thing they bumped into, the resulting conflagration attracted the attention of even more zombies and when a car exploded, the resulting distraction was precisely what Thorton and his men needed.

The men waited until the general drift had thinned out from the north and then they made a break for the nearest cover. The grove of trees that lined the mall on the north side near Madison Avenue were just the thing to avoid easy detection by the zombies and Major Thorton and his crew made the most of it.

They ran through the trees, taking care not to run into any zombies that might be lost on their way to the barbeque and quickly found themselves across the street from the National Gallery of Art Sculpture Garden. Thorton checked out the area, then led the way across as his men followed in small groups. They crossed the ring of bushes and circled the pool of stagnant water, stopping only when they reached the other side. Major Thorton looked ahead and saw the National Archives Building and he was impressed. The building was massive, with tall columns protecting a huge bronze door. That door looked to be formidable, so unless they could open it right away, they might have to find another way in.

Ken signaled his men to join him and as he looked back at a shed, he thought he saw movement in there. *Probably the groundskeeper who got trapped. Nothing to care about.* He thought as his men circled him.

"We need to get across the street and into that building. There are a lot of zombies in the cars, so watch carefully. See that door? The men nodded. "That's our goal. Move it." Thorton threaded his way through a couple of cars and his men spread out to find their own ways. One man passing could get through, but you didn't want to be second or third in line when the zombies woke up.

The men passed through the stopped cars without incident, until the second to last man passed too close to a minivan. As he skimmed past, a dark arm shot out of the open window and grabbed him by the hair. The soldier was dragged screaming into the open window by several pairs of undead hands. His hands and feet beat on the side of the van until, after being bitten and torn at enough, his body fell to the ground, minus it's head.

The last man to cross saw what happened and promptly turned around and fled. He ran for all he was worth through the garden and onto the main grounds of the mall. He ran as hard as he could, not realizing he was passing zombie after zombie. When he finally stopped to catch his breath, he was surrounded by hundreds of ghouls, who first looked at him curiously, then hungrily.

He had time for one thin scream as they moved in and tore him to pieces.

Back at the Archives, Thorton and his men just stood in shock as they lost two of their number in a matter of a minute. Thorton quickly recovered and ordered his men to the door. They scrambled up the steps and tried the door without success. The big brass doors were designed to act like vault doors and there was no way they were going to finesse their way in from that entry.

"Plan B," Thorton said. "There has to be an employee entrance around here somewhere. Let's move." Ken led the way from the front of the building to the west side, looking for the door that would let him in and fulfill his destiny.

Across the street, several eyes watched him and his men move down the street and quietly began their pursuit.

Chapter 19

I sat for a long time, just staring at the hatch. I didn't feel like moving, not just yet. On the other side of that chunk of metal, one of my closest friends lay dead. I just couldn't wrap my mind around it. I had killed people I had known, people I was friends with, but Nate's death just hit me in a place that wasn't used to getting hit. I knew that Nate wouldn't want me to make a fuss, but it was hard, knowing he was gone.

A noise behind me caught my attention and I turned to see Tommy looking carefully out the window. Duncan was back in the middle of the shed, his rifle up and ready.

Suddenly, Tommy stepped back into the shadows and he brought his rifle up as well. Curious, I picked up my gun and moved over by Duncan, keeping low as to not be seen by whatever was outside.

"Zombies?" I whispered, unsnapping the flap on my vest that kept a spare M1A magazine in place.

"Thorton." Came the reply.

I immediately went into battle mode. I ducked back down and went over to the far window, making sure I couldn't be seen from the outside. I checked which way Tommy was looking and turned slowly that way. Out of the far corner of the window I could see stealthy movement making its way through the sculpture garden. From our hiding place, I could see the men as they emerged from the bushes, headed towards the Archives.

A large blond man in front caught my eye and I realized this was my first look at an enemy I had pursued across half the country. He was a huge man, easily inches over my six feet, two inches. His broad shoulders and thick neck spoke of enormous strength and as I watched him move through the cars and lightly run up the steps, I saw an agility, which combined with his strength, made him a very dangerous man.

Added to what I knew about what he was capable of and what he had already done, quite possibly I was looking at the living embodiment of evil.

I raised my rifle and trained the sights on his broad, unsuspecting back, but instinct kicked in and I lowered the barrel.

Across the room, Tommy whispered "If that's him, shoot! We got the rest of them!"

"Look at the walls, gents," I said, shifting back to observe the majority of the men make their way through the cars.

"What are you talking about—oh." Tommy argued then fell silent.

"Yeah. How many rounds do you think these walls will stop?" I asked. "Half our shots would be through thick cover. We might aim well but still miss. Our best move right now is to stay out of sight."

"We could shoot and duck into the tunnel," Duncan suggested.

I looked over at him. "Nate's last shot probably attracted some more Z's. And in all honesty, I'd rather not have my last memory of Nate be what he looks like right now."

Duncan looked down, then over at the hatch. I knew he missed Nate terribly, but we needed to stay focused on what we were about.

"I miss him too, guys. Hold on." I looked closely out the window. "Whoa!" I just watched as a man got decapitated by a van full of ghouls, which caused the last man in line to lose his mind and go running full tilt in the opposite direction. Tommy ducked under the window and looked out from the other side to track the man's progress.

"He's across the street, still running. Still going. Passing a lot of Z's. Still going, going. Okay, now he's stopped. All right, they got him." Tommy ducked back under the window and resumed observing in the original direction.

I watched as Thorton approached the big bronze doors that used to be the main entrance. This was interesting, because those doors hadn't been used for entrance in years. Several years back, probably around 2001, the tourist entrance was changed to a door leading under the main stairs, up a hallway and into the main viewing room. By the looks of things, Thorton had no idea there was a different way in. I watched as the group of men, now only ten strong, quickly worked their way across the building and disappeared around the corner.

I waited a full minute before I motioned to the other two. "We gotta go. Thorton doesn't know how to get in the building, so we still have a chance to beat him to the punch."

The other two nodded and we snuck out the door, keeping to the bushes and trees, working our way to the north and the street. We reached the same opening that Thorton and his men had used, but since their passage, there was a lot of activity in the cars. The van had arms sticking out of the window, trying to reach the headless body lying on the ground nearby.

I moved to the left, skirting the worst of the cars and crossed the street with Tommy and Duncan directly behind me. We reached the other side without difficulty and hurried to the tourist entrance doors on the street level. The doors were just made of tempered glass and held in place by an electronic lock. One of the advantages of the Upheaval and lack of general power was electric locks were all but useless. Most of the time we just strolled right in where before we would have been screwed. This door had no handles on the outside, which made things a little more difficult, especially since there were about thirty zombies moving in our direction. With us moving across the street and Thorton moving around, it was a wonder we hadn't already caused a drift.

I grabbed the side of the door and pulled, making absolutely no progress at all. Tommy and Duncan took aim at a couple of faster zombies that were going to be on us in about fifteen seconds if I didn't get this damn door open. The good news was there was a pathway that funneled the zombies into smaller groups. The bad news was the pathway still allowed for zombies to march four across, which was way too many for comfort.

"Anytime, John," Tommy said as he took aim at the nearest Z.

"One thing to try and then we're just busting in," I said, pulling off my pickaxe and jamming the broad end into the space between the frame and the door. I worked it like a crowbar and managed to pop the lock, just enough to open the stupid door.

"Got it! *In!*" I shouted to Tommy who was trying to hold his fire to the last, but in a couple of steps the first zombie was going to be within reach. Tommy spun and followed Duncan, who was already sprinting through the door. I held it open for them then slipped inside, pulling it shut as several Z's slammed against the glass. I wasn't worried about the glass breaking, since I noticed when I opened it that it was at least a half-inch thick. It wouldn't stop a rifle bullet, but it could hold off the zombies with relative ease.

We moved past the screening station and carefully checked the area for more zombies and more importantly, Thorton and his men. We found neither and held a powwow in the Archives Shop, under busts of Jefferson and resin molds of the sights of D.C..

"Okay, guys, we need to make a guess and hope to hell it's the right one. When the shit hit the fan, did the documents stay on display, or were they sent down for storage in the lower vaults?" I asked.

Duncan put down the Madison bust he was picking the nose of before replying. "Tough call. If things happened here fast enough, did anyone have the presence of mind to properly store them? Or were they more concerned about the collapse of society and the rising wave of Z's?"

"I guess we're going to have to find out either way and deal with whatever tries to stop us," Tommy said, checking his rifle's magazine.

"All right. Here's how we work it. I'm going to head to the workrooms downstairs and see if I can find the documents. If I can, I'll bring them back here. You two check the rotunda and if the documents are there, radio me and I'll hightail it topside. We'll use this as our rendezvous point, otherwise," I said.

"What are *we* doing?" Duncan asked, checking his own magazine and indicating himself and Tommy. He obviously hadn't been listening.

"Making sure we don't have any more surprises," I said. "These men declared war on us. They attacked our home and have tried to kill us once already. Finish them."

"What about Thorton?" Tommy asked.

"Dead is dead," I said, although I have to admit I was hoping to be the one to put a bullet in that son of a bitch. "Let's be back here in less than an hour, one way or the other. We're going to need daylight to get ourselves back to the Smithsonian."

"We still taking those people out?" asked Duncan.

"I said I would, so yes." I hadn't considered *not* taking them, but we'd have to burn that bridge when we got to it. "Thorton is probably going to get in on the north side, where the employees usually get in. They will likely make straight for the rotunda, so stay sharp."

"Mind yourself," Tommy said. "We've been here before."

I shook my head at him. "I'm not losing any more friends. You two take care of yourselves." I shook hands with both, hoping desperately I would see them again.

We split up at the stairwell, with me going down and the two of them heading up. With luck, they would hit the rotunda before Thorton. If the documents weren't there, I imagined they would probably set up an ambush. That's what I'd do.

I went down the stairs, passing signs that indicated Charters Café and the William McGowan Theater. I went past the ropes that still said 'Employees Only', tunneling deeper into the Archives. I had never been down here before, so I was running blind. Hopefully, I would find something.

I reasoned that the best place to start was the bottom and work my way up, figuring that was the most logical way not to miss anything. Contrary to the level of importance of the country's founding documents, the National Archives Building was relatively small, by D.C. standards, anyway.

I passed through a security door that was unlocked and found myself in a storeroom filled with documents and boxes. The whole place smelled like dust and I knew this was storage for lesser documents. Still, some important things were there if you wanted to look. I remember someone finding a document with Lincoln's signature on it just hanging out with the rest of the notes, once upon a time. Maybe in the future we'd have the time to go through this stuff, but unless some dope lit a match, it was safe enough where it is.

The whole floor seemed devoted to storage, so I climbed up the other stairwell to the next flight up. A quick look and I saw that this floor was devoted to storage as well. I headed up the stairs again, only to duck down as a bullet zipped by my cheek.

"Get him?" yelled a voice.

"Not sure. Couldn't see too well. Maybe."

I cursed and waited for a sound to be made. I had doused my light after the shot, but then I realized I could use it as a lure. I turned it back on, hiding the light with my hand, then dropped it out in the open where it could be seen, groaning slightly, then exhaling deeply. I was hoping they would think I was down and had dropped the light.

I didn't hear anything for a bit and I waited for what seemed to be a long time. But I soon began to hear slow footsteps, like someone was trying to move quietly in the dark, using the light from my fallen flashlight to show them the way. They couldn't see a body, which was making them cautious. I eased my rifle back quietly and pulled my SIG. This was going to be close in work and my M1A was too big.

I waited on the stairs with my gun pointing upwards. They wouldn't able to see me until they were on top of me, but I would be able to take a shot as soon as they cleared the landing. I just hoped they came together and not one at a time.

After an eternity and much sweating on my part, a head finally peeked around the corner. Resisting the urge to shoot, I waited until I could see another head materialize next to it. It was still very dark and the ambient light from my flashlight wasn't very helpful, but it kept me in the dark and allowed me to see, albeit poorly.

Right before they reached the landing with my flashlight, I fired upward at them. Years of fighting zombies leaves an impression on your skills and I fired instinctively at their heads. The first one died on the stairs, the top of his head erupting in blood and brains as the forty caliber bullet added a skylight to his skull. I shifted to the other man who ducked and before he could get his bearings, I fired again. This time, the bullet entered his face and blew out the back of his head, dropping him down on top of his friend.

I grabbed up my flashlight and didn't look back, sprinting up the stairs to the next level. Just as I reached the door, my radio crackled.

"John. Duncan. They're not in the rotunda. Over."

I grabbed my radio and spoke quickly. "Roger that. Downed two of our friends. Watch yourself. Over."

"Will do. Tommy got three, I got two. Over."

"Then there's three left. Good hunting. Out." I turned the radio down and made my way through the security door. This area was a hallway with several offices located on it, so I figured I was moving in the right direction.

About midway down the hall, I saw a side hallway that led to another doorway. This doorway had some fairly sophisticated mechanisms for security, but with all power turned off long ago, I reached for the door and walked right in. It was funny, because a simple padlock would have kept me out for a while, but all this electronic hardware was useless.

Inside was a large room with several tables off to the side. On pegs along one wall were several environmental suits, presumably for handling the historic documents. There were a lot of tubes and air hoses and such and a large glass walled room over to the side. On the back wall of the glass room were four large cases and in each case was what appeared to be a sheet of parchment.

I moved over quickly and was inside the room without a hassle. I walked over to the documents and looked them over. Each one was in a large case, protected by a thick pane of greenish glass. They looked heavy and I was not looking forward to carrying them across a field of zombies, if it came to that.

I went to the Declaration of Independence and removed the case from the rack which took it up to the display room. It weighed about thirty pounds, so it was manageable, but it was awkward as hell.

I took the document and made my way back to the stairs, heading up to the rendezvous point. I didn't encounter any more of Thorton's men, although I thought I heard firing when I was in the Archives Shop. I put down the Declaration of Independence and went back for the Bill of Rights. After retrieving the Bill of Rights I went back for part one of the Constitution.

It was when I was returning for part two of the Constitution when I ran into Thorton. He and another man were in the glass chamber, inspecting the spots where the other documents were, looking up to see if they had gotten stuck in the tunnels to the rotunda. The second part of the Constitution was sitting on the table. They had their backs to me and I was in the process of bringing up my rifle when Thorton turned around and saw me.

His eyes went wide as they connected with mine and I was nearly firing my rifle when he started firing from the hip. The big forty-four slugs punched through the glass like it was paper, scattering shards all over the floor.

I returned fired with my rifle, the heavy caliber bullets ramming through the air. I got lucky with my shots, one of the slugs connected with the man with Thorton and he went down screaming, holding his bloody hands against a hole in his abdomen.

I ducked around the corner and when I peeked out I saw that Thorton had taken cover behind the heavy table. The man I had shot writhed in agony for a few seconds, then went still as he died.

It was a long moment, then Thorton spoke.

"John Talon, I presume?" The voice was deep, but I could easily detect the contempt hidden behind the baritone. It was instantly mocking and condescending

In my former life, I called people who sounded like this bullies. I hated bullies.

I stayed quiet, figuring it would annoy Thorton not to be acknowledged. I waited, sure he would speak again. I didn't have long to wait.

"Figured it was you. You're a long way from home. Too bad, they probably could have used you at Starved Rock." The tone was reproachful and touched a sore point. I answered in a way I was sure he could understand.

I shifted away from the corner and fired the remainder of my magazine at the table Thorton was hiding behind. The .308 bullets shredded the metal and skipped sparks off the equipment. I didn't even aim.

I saw the bolt lock back, so I ducked around the corner, and reloaded the rifle. The smell of primer and cordite was heavy in the air and my firing had created a small gunpowder fog.

I waited to hear if I had connected and much to my dismay, Thorton spoke again and he didn't seem to be hurt.

"Well, well. That was quite the tantrum. You know, you have to be careful. You might have shot the Constitution."

I heard a shifting sound and figured he was trying to get out of the corner he was in. There was only one exit and I was in the way. I could wait him out, but if there was another man here somewhere, he would be able to come up behind me while I was entertaining Thorton. This had to end and quickly.

"Tell you what, Thorton. Step out, drop your weapons and surrender," I said, getting down on one knee and aiming my M1A at the corner.

"You'll let me go? How noble."

I replied honestly. "Actually, no. I was just wanting to shoot you without the risk of getting shot in return."

Thorton was quiet as he digested this little tidbit. I needed him off balance and out of his comfort zone and having an opponent readily admit they were willing to lie to kill you would throw off anyone.

In reply his gun roared, the bullet' ripping through the walls above my head. Had I been standing, I would have been killed instantly. The second he stopped, I rolled out and fired back, causing him to dive for cover behind the vacuuming equipment.

"Son of a bitch!" Thorton cursed at me. "You're a pain in the ass to kill, you know that?"

"Likewise, shithead," I said. "Why don't you save me some ammo and just shoot yourself? You're not going to live with me blocking the exit."

Thorton said nothing and I moved cautiously around the corner, my rifle leading the way. Just as I cleared the corner, Thorton fired from a new position, striking the forearm of my rifle and knocking it clean out of my hands. I dropped quickly and drew my SIG as I swung back around my cover. I looked down at my rifle and saw the bullet had ruined the forearm, but seemed to have missed the barrel and the gas tube. It should still work, but there was no way I could get it now. It looked worse than it was, which was probably why Thorton hadn't shot it again to render it useless.

"So much for your advantage," Thorton taunted. "Why don't you come and get me? Is it too dark? Maybe I'll have a fire. Let's see, where can I get some paper? I know, I saw a big piece right here."

I fell out of my position onto my right shoulder with my SIG already pointed. I saw Thorton standing by the Constitution with his gun up waiting for me to come out. It took a half second for him to realize I was out but on the ground. I fired once and Thorton threw his left arm back, his handgun flying off to the corner. I jumped up, covering him as he knelt down, holding onto his arm. My bullet had struck him in the left forearm, travelled down the bone and exited near his elbow. It was a nasty wound and his left arm wasn't going to be very useful for a while. He held his arms close, his eyes burning with hatred at being bested.

"I think that should just about wrap things up," I said, aiming my SIG at his face. I was in the process of pulling the trigger when suddenly Thorton struck out with his right hand, holding a huge curved knife which struck the side of my SIG and sent it spinning out of my hands.

Thorton lunged after me with his knife, trying to disembowel me, but I jumped back, pulling my own knife in the process. Somehow, I knew it was going to come down to this. Nothing is ever easy.

"Cute little toothpick." Thorton taunted, waving his blade in front of himself.

I shifted my grip. "Come closer and I'll pick out your fucking eye with it," I snarled. I had seen how agile this man was, so I was not going to take things lightly. If he was even remotely decent with that knife, I could get seriously hurt.

Thorton lunged suddenly, a low stab that turned into a high slash. I had turned to the side to avoid the thrust, but the slash nicked my pack strap and drew a thin red line on my cheek, under my eye.

The major danced back, grinning at his first attempt. "Sure you want to play, Talon? Remember, mine's bigger than yours." He slashed again, cutting the air between us.

This time I was ready and as his arm swung out, I struck, flicking my wrist and cutting a two inch gash on the back of his hand as it passed by.

"Try that again with your neck, if you please," I said, waggling my black blade at him. I needed him angry and unfocused. He was too strong to try and face squarely.

Thorton bared his teeth and I readied for the rush, figuring he would try to barrel into me and use his size to an advantage. He didn't disappoint and I ducked under his cut, which probably would have sliced me in half had it connected. I reached out with my knife and stabbed him about an inch worth in the calf, pulling the blade out as I avoided a reverse stabbing move that missed me by a fraction. He was fast, but not as fast as Charlie, who would have pounded me with that move.

I kicked back and managed to connect with his thigh, barreling him into the table with a large crash. I had to keep up the pressure, otherwise this was not going to go well. I followed him to the table, my blade held a little back behind me, to maximize thrusting ability.

Thorton roared and spun quickly around, his knife raised to stab. My knife was suddenly too far away to do any good, so I struck out with my left fist, mashing his nose and stopping his forward rush as pain exploded in his face. His hands reflexively came up and his knife connected with mine, blocking the thrust which would have ended the fight right there. The major backed up and struck out blindly, missing my head by a fraction. I rammed my knife forward and stabbed him deeply in the leg. I stepped back and let him fall.

As he went down, Thorton slashed downward, slicing my arm open. I recoiled and whipped out my bandanna, wrapping up my wound to be treated later.

"Fucker. I'll kill you for that!" Major slashed my way again, but I danced out of reach. I must have cut something useful in that stab; when Thorton tried to stand, using the table as a crutch, he crashed back to the ground. I had to give him credit, he kept his knife between us and I wasn't going to try to finish him off. Not now, anyway.

I left him bleeding and retrieved my SIG. There was a deep scratch on the slide, but nothing that affected function. I was relieved, since that SIG had been with me at the beginning and I was so used to it I wouldn't know what to do with another gun.

Thorton eyed me as I rearmed myself. I'm sure he figured I was just going to shoot him, but I had another idea, one that was worthy of his level of depravity. I skirted wide around him and removed the second part of the Constitution from it's cradle and carried it over to the doorway.

Major Thorton scoffed as I turned back. "Couldn't finish me hand to hand, huh? Gonna do it the easy way, right? Go ahead, gutless. At least I died a man." He tried to look tough, but like any beaten bully, he was just noise.

I shook my head at him. "Nate Coles was a man and he died well. You, you're just going to die." I shouldered my burden, picked up my rifle and walked away as Ken Thorton screamed at my back.

"I'll find you, Talon! You'll never get this country back! You will fail! I'll find you!" Thorton spat and cursed as he realized he was going to be alone in the dark.

I made my way back to the Archives Shop to find Duncan and Tommy waiting for me. Tommy had a wound on his arm and Duncan had a bandage on his head, but they seemed well enough. Tommy noticed my arm and pulled out the first aid kit again, taking a moment to stitch me up and bandage my cut. Thorton's blade had been sharp as hell.

"Did you find the major?" Duncan asked, eyeballing my rifle.

"I did, thanks for asking," I said, looking around the shop. I needed a satchel or something to carry the documents with. The frames were rather bulky.

"Did you kill him?" Tommy asked, wrapping up my arm and putting a bandage on my face.

I could hear Thorton's yelling and cursing still coming up from the stairwell.

"Not yet," I said, smiling at their curious scowls. "You'll see." I went over to a display of D.C.-themed shoulder bags and tried one out on the big frames. The documents went in, but it was a tight fit and there was a good portion still sticking out. I put my backpack on my front and was able to get my arms through the straps. The frame hung awkwardly, but I was able to walk and keep my arms free.

Duncan and Tommy followed suit, with Duncan carrying two since he didn't have a backpack. He looked like a guy wearing a sandwich sign. We moved with our burdens down to the tourist entrance area where there were still ghouls on the other side of the glass. We went over to the other side where the tourists normally exit. That way was clear, but probably wouldn't be for long. Tommy cautiously looked out and signaled it was all clear for us to make a dash across the street, back into the sculpture garden. Duncan exited first and I brought up the rear. Just as I was about to leave, I pulled my rifle and fired three shots at the other entrance, shattering the glass and allowing the zombies to stumble inside. Several of them were young and they first came at us, but then heard something that caught their attention and went inside the building.

It was awkward firing with a broken stock and I thought I felt something shift inside the gun. I'd have to look closer when I had the chance. I darted outside and closed the door behind me, following Tommy across the street.

At his look, I smiled. *"Now* I've killed Thorton."

Tommy grinned and we joined Duncan back at the shed we had used just hours before. We unburdened ourselves and each one of us took a long look at the grey hatch in the corner. It was the best way to get across the mall, but none of us wanted to be the first to say it.

Finally Duncan broke the silence. "You know, Nate would call us a bunch of sniveling fuckheads if he knew we didn't want to take the path of least resistance because we were squeamish."

I chuckled and Tommy joined me. Duncan was right. What made Nate was gone and even though we might not like what we saw down the hatch, Nate wouldn't want us to give a damn about him when it came to seeing this thing through.

"You're right. I'll go first," I said, pulling out my flashlight and SIG. I opened the hatch and made my way down, scanning both ways, looking and listening for anything unusual or undead.

It was a while before I looked down at my dead friend and when I finally did, I was somewhat surprised. Nate had indeed managed to shoot himself in the head, but the wound was small. There was a lot of blood under his head, but it framed him almost like a halo. *Sure got that one wrong,* I thought. I motioned for the other two to follow and they dropped down the documents first, then themselves. Each one took a long look at Nate and Duncan said goodbye by placing a hand on Nate's still chest.

"Let's go," I said, hoping to get moving before we were discovered by things bigger than rats.

We moved quickly back the way we came, keeping a sharp eye out for any more quick little ones, like the bastard that got Nate. We approached an intersection and I was past it when Tommy stopped me.

"Whoa, hold on," he said, taking off his sack and bringing up his rifle.

I took off my sack and pulled my SIG, keeping my light off for the time being. Duncan gathered up the other sacks and moved them down the passage. In case we needed to run we didn't want to lose seconds finding our prizes.

I didn't see anything, no glowing eyeballs or lights of any kind. It was dark as hell underground, yet I didn't want to raise my light just yet.

"What's up?" I whispered very softly to Tommy.

"I heard something I shouldn't have heard down here," he said cryptically.

"Follow your gut, I'm behind you." I turned to Duncan. "Get those documents to the Smithsonian and see about transportation. If Mike found a working bus, you have my permission to kiss him."

"He'll need bigger tits before I do that," came the murmured reply out of the dark, but I could hear the sounds of Duncan moving away.

Tommy flicked his weapon light on and the narrow beam illuminated a thin patch of the hallway. He scanned up and down and we didn't see anything out of the ordinary. We were about to leave when the sound came again, this time a little louder. We looked at each other and I nodded at Tommy. I had heard it this time too. It had been a while since I had heard a sound like that, but every father knows it.

It was a muffled baby's cry and it sure as hell didn't belong in this darkness.

"Could be coming from anywhere, especially in these tunnels," Tommy said as he moved forward.

"We've covered the area back and forward from this point and it didn't come from behind. It's ahead or we're hearing things," I said, flicking on my flashlight to help search. "We'll go to the end of this path and if we don't find it, we leave it."

Tommy looked hard at me and I ignored him. Sometimes tough choices had to be made, as much as I hated to make them. But we had a lot of people counting on us and chasing noises in the dark wasn't getting anything accomplished, it only increased our chances of getting killed. For all we knew, it was a baby zombie and I had no desire to kill any more of those.

Fifty yards down the tunnel, we came to another intersection. I flashed my light around a corner and leaped back, bumping into Tommy who stumbled backwards, catching himself on a utility pipe.

"Shit!" I cursed, bringing up my gun. Several figures walked slowly around the corner and I was about to open fire when I realized something. They were shielding their eyes from my light. Zombies don't do that.

Tommy saw it as well and he aimed his light to center on the survivor's chests. It kept them lit without blinding them, but allowed us to be mostly unseen.

The first person stopped and I could see he was in a bad way. His clothes were threadbare but clean and he was thin from lack of proper nutrition. His eyes were sunken and his face was gaunt.

"That's far enough," I said. "Who are you?"

The man raised a weak hand. "Please help us. We've been out of food for days, maybe a week or more. We wouldn't have left our sanctuary, but the kids are starving and we couldn't stay."

I didn't move. "Who are you and where are you coming from?"

The man replied slowly. "I'm Brian Graf, my wife Irene is back there with the rest of the group. We took refuge in the Library of Congress when the city fell to the dead and we've been doing okay, but things took a turn for the worse. We saw the men come by the building earlier and we thought we could reach them, but they always seemed to be a step ahead. Once we were out of the library, we decided to try and make a run for our friends in the Smithsonian, but we got lost down here and by luck, you two came along."

I stepped around Brian and took a look at the frightened group hiding in the dark. A young mother was holding a wiggly baby and he let out another squawk that she tried to shush. I shook my head at her and smiled. "Your little one let us know you were down here. Otherwise we might have passed you by." The mother looked at me and then at her baby and held him close, big tears coming out of her eyes.

I stepped back and addressed the group. "I'm John Talon, this is Tommy Carter. We're not going to hurt any of you; we're going to get you out of here."

Excited murmurs started in the tunnel, but a single voice called out. "Once we get out of the tunnel, what then? We'll be stuck in another building, just waiting to die or be eaten."

I looked back and said, "You misunderstand. I'm taking you all out of the city."

The voices got louder but the single voice spoke again above the din. "How?"

I smiled unseen in the dark. "Damned if I know. I make this shit up as I go along. Follow me." I led the way back down the tunnel with a procession of about thirty people following slowly. Tommy brought up the rear and I could hear each person thanking him as they passed. It was funny, because this actually saved me the trouble of having to figure out how in the hell I was going to get to the Library of Congress and rescue these people. I didn't often catch a break, but I was grateful for this one.

We moved well through the tunnel and I had the chance to talk with Brian and get the story. He and his wife had been visiting relatives and were caught inside the city when martial law was declared and no one was allowed in or out. Things got ugly fast and people started to fortify the buildings when the army was overrun. He said there had been people in the American History Museum and Natural History Museum, but they hadn't had any contact for months. The only ones left it seemed to them was the group at the Smithsonian Castle. The hotels and buildings that had people trying to survive were eventually overrun or the people gave up and left, to be eaten by the dead. They had followed the destruction of city after city while they still had power and internet access, but when that went down they were truly on their own. They had rescued a few people here and there, but Brian assured me he was no fighter like me.

I laughed. "Like me? Hell, I was a school principal before the Upheaval. Circumstances make us and I'd say you did just fine." We reached the end of the tunnel and I knocked on the heavy door.

"John?" came a voice.

"Yes. Open up," I said.

"What's the password?"

"Open the goddamn door or I'm going to start shooting through it."

"Correct!" The door opened and light flooded the tunnel. Duncan grinned at me, but his smile faded when he saw all the people behind me. "Holy—"

"Yeah," I said, stepping into the basement. "Get Jason and Rita and Katie and tell them we have the people from the Library. They are in bad need of supplies. Go."

I helped the people through the door, noting how thin and pale most of them were. I directed them to the stairs to go up and they all thanked me as they passed. I gently disengaged the ones that hugged me and gave reassuring pats on the head to the little ones too shy to say anything.

Tommy was the last one through the door and he closed it with finality. He turned to me and asked, "Now what?"

I sighed. "Now we figure out how in heaven we're going to get these people out of here."

"Never ends, does it?"

"Not on this trip, it seems."

CHAPTER 20

We spent the rest of the day retrieving our supplies from the RV which was still sitting in the garden. I had half a hope that the silly thing might actually start, but Duncan reminded me that Nate had the keys, so I dropped that notion. Tommy, Duncan and I went over half a dozen maps, trying to figure out the best way to get out of the city. Once we had a route planned, we would go to one of the towers and see what kind of obstacles we faced. Increasingly, it was looking like we were not going to be able to make a run with a bus. We would be able to get only so far and then abandoned cars and dead people would stop us.

More and more I was looking at the river, wondering how bad it would be to just stick to the water. A river journey would take a month or more and I wasn't looking to stay out that much. I was getting homesick something fierce and I knew Tommy was fidgeting about Angela. We needed to make a decision and we needed to do it now.

Interestingly, it was Duncan that came up with the best idea. Tommy and I were arguing about rivers when Duncan poked his head in and said, "Something wrong with going south?"

I stopped arguing long enough to look at the map and I realized we were going in the wrong direction. If we headed for the coast and simply sailed south, we could cruise around Florida and pick up the Mississippi without too much difficulty. It would take about the same amount of time, but we'd not have to worry about locks and Niagara Falls and irritating things like that. Plus, there would be no worries about zombies.

I started to say good idea, but Tommy stopped me.

"Don't compliment him. It will just make things worse. Trust me," he said.

I thought about it and decided it was probably for the best.

With half a plan, we decided we needed to find a boat or several boats. Tommy suggested the Navy Yard, but I didn't think a warship was the answer. We needed river boats that could survive a short ocean jaunt. We also needed to get there alive.

Mike had produced a bus, but the windows were all broken out and the door was busted off. It ran, but at the first mess of trouble it would be a coffin. We'd have to make a fast push then evacuate in a hurry.

"Okay, here's what we'll do. We'll take the bus as far as we can and ditch it when we reach water. We'll have to scavenge for boats, but we haven't got much choice. Once we leave the city proper, we can find better transportation." I was gambling like hell that we could find anything that floats, but it was better than swimming. We'd do that only if we had to.

Tommy agreed and we decided to leave first thing in the morning, right before the sun came up. Experience taught us that zombies had trouble seeing in the dawn and dusk hours, mostly because their eyes had a hard time adjusting to the light of the sky and the dark of the ground.

We packed up everyone onto the bus in the morning and with as many people as we had, it was extremely crowded. I had talked to the groups the night before, explaining that any fighting or shooting was to be done by myself, Tommy or Duncan. When Mike asked us what happened to Nate, Duncan just stared at him until he shut up.

We moved out quickly, following the path of destruction the RV had created in getting to the castle. But it became apparent that we were going to have to take a divergent path, when we discovered the huge throngs of zombies that had converged on the mall. We reached the Washington monument, but had to veer south. The zombies were too thick even for this bus and we had already sustained a good deal of damage from plowing into several groups. The only good news was we were using a tour bus, which put the windows higher than normal and the engine was in the back, so we could take a good deal of damage before we had to stop.

The bus tore through the brush and trees, eliciting a few gasps and small screams from the group. The kids looked like they were enjoying themselves, probably this was the first time they had been out in a long time.

We lurched over a larger than normal speed bump and I thought I heard something snap as we landed. About fifteen feet later, the front of the bus tilted sharply and skewed to the left.

Tommy jumped out of the driver's seat and I joined him to check the damage. The front axle had broken. We were done with this bus.

I looked around at the zombies that had taken an interest in us and calculated the odds of making a stand. In short, we were dead.

"Everyone out! Go! Go! Go! Follow Tommy! Go!" I yelled, pulling out my pickaxe and advancing on two zombies that were much too close. "Duncan, take the side, get to the river!"

"Which way is the damn river?" Duncan asked, helping a woman out of the bus.

"That way!" I pointed south with my pick then swung high to crush the skull of a suited zombie. *Probably a lobbyist*, I thought as I lined up the second one. This one was a woman in a pantsuit, at least it was a woman once. Her neck was a ruined mess and her left hand was chewed to the bone. Probably tried to defend herself with that hand and got it eaten for the trouble. I buried the point of the pick in her temple and jerked it loose once she was on the ground.

Just as I freed it, ten more zombies came around the rear of the bus. Later for this. I turned and ran after the group, slipping between two zombies who gave a grab in my direction but were too slow by half. I caught up to the group and took a position at the rear. Tommy lead the way and we kept up a hurried pace. Duncan was kept busy on his side, knocking over zombies which I would finish off as I reached them. It was a decent system, but we were running out of luck.

Suddenly, everyone stopped. I ran to the front, worried about the rear because we were being chased by a growing number of zombies. It was like the call had gone out and they were converging from all over.

"Why have we stopped?" I asked Tommy, who was staring down his rifle barrel at a grove of trees.

"There's a group of about forty in those trees, cutting us off," he said grimly.

I looked and sure enough, the vegetation was alive with zombies. "Come on," I said, "We have to keep moving. The basin is right over here." I moved slightly east, followed by a large group of increasingly anxious people. I needed to find a place to make a stand, somewhere we could hold off a horde.

As I moved south again, I saw what looked like a rooftop sitting out on the water. Curious, I hurried to the side to clear my line of sight and I saw a building sitting on the water, with a narrow walkway leading to it. Perfect. As I led the people over that way, I saw some curious white things on the docks. As we got closer I saw what they were and laughed out loud.

"What the hell?" Tommy panted, coming up alongside me.

I didn't answer, I just pointed to the building and kept moving. A shot rang out, then another. I spun around and saw Mike had shot two zombies that were getting close to the group. The heavy report echoed across the lawns and through the buildings. Everything was still for a second, then it seemed like the entire city moaned at once.

"Shit." I urged greater speed, hurrying people onto the causeway of the Tidal Basin Boat House. For defense, it was perfect. The boat house was forty feet from the edge of the basin and the walkway was barely six feet wide. We could hold this place all day. But what made it even more perfect were the rows of paddle boats. We had our escape. It wasn't exactly first class, but it was transportation until we could find something better.

Tommy looked over the boats and started laughing and Duncan grinned like he had just eaten the last piece of pie. I stood on the walkway and just waited for the zombies to try and get across. "Get the boats in the water, make sure they float. Don't overload them. You kids with the documents, you're on that four-seater." I paused to knock a Z into the water. "The youngest kids go on the other four-seater, they can all fit with two adults. Get moving, it's gonna get busy in a second." I could see a large horde moving this way and there was no way I could take a rush like that, even with a narrow bridge to defend.

Several splashes told me boats and people were getting in the water and I took a second to drag several benches across the causeway. It wouldn't completely stop the zombies, but it would slow them a little and every second counted right now.

"You got three minutes, Tommy!" I said, taking aim with my rifle. Two shots later and two dead zombies added to the barricade.

"Almost there!" came the reply. I couldn't look over my shoulder, since the zombies were at my barricade trying to climb over. Slavering mouths and hungry dead eyes stared at me like they'd never seen anything so delicious. I fired twice, then my bolt locked back. I switched magazines and fired again, spinning a dead TSA agent into the murky basin. The benches moved back against the onslaught of so many bodies and I gave ground, firing judiciously. I tried to make my shots count in terms of barricading the walkway, but there was getting to be too many.

Suddenly, my rifle stopped firing. I pulled the handle back, figuring I had a bad round, but the bolt was stuck. I looked at the stock and saw Thorton's bullet had damaged the gas tube after all and this gun was an anchor now. The zombies looked at me and if I didn't know better, I swore the lead ones smiled. I tossed the gun aside and just as I pulled my SIG, a voice called out from behind me.

"John! Move it, right side!" Tommy yelled.

Bless you, Tommy, I thought as I spun around and raced down the pier. Behind me the benches crashed over and the zombies came pouring down the dock. Several fell into the water, but far too many were at the Boat House. On the land behind the entrance, hundreds of zombies had converged and behind them were thousands more. I reached the end of the pier and stepped into the paddle boat, placing my pack on the small bench between the seats. Tommy and I pedaled quietly for a moment, joining what had to be the weirdest flotilla known to man. We steered around the thirty or so boats, taking the lead and moving slowly but surely away from the shore.

Tommy looked over at me as we passed the Jefferson Memorial. "Where to now?"

I laughed. "Let's get out of the city first, then we'll see about better transportation. There has to be bigger boats somewhere."

Tommy labored on the pedals for a second. "God, I hope so."

Behind us, we could hear the splashing of paddles as the Paddle Boat Armada made its way out of the former District of Columbia.

CHAPTER 21

We paddled and drifted and paddled and drifted for a while, not really caring how we went, we were just happy to be going. I was watching the riverbank go by, paddling occasionally, looking back to see how well we were doing. The paddle boats had strung out in a two by two line and were keeping up pretty well. We sure couldn't paddle our way back to Illinois, so eventually we were going to have to find some serious water transportation.

Along the shore numerous zombies slowly watched our passage, too many for a quick trip ashore for supplies or a look-see. It matched with what we had felt crossing the Appalachians, that for the most part the east coast was a zombie wasteland. I'm sure there were pockets of survivors here and there, but not enough to make a real difference.

About four miles out of D.C., Tommy nudged me and steered the paddle boat over to the east bank. It looked like there was a harbor for river and ocean craft and I could see at least five boats resting quietly in the water. Three of the boats were sailboats, so they would be handy when the gas ran out, but I liked the look of the big fishing boat. If we could get that sucker up and running, we could ride that all the way back home.

A quick look around showed the boats to be usable and there was a quick transfer from the paddle boats to the sailboats. The people from the Library of Congress split up into groups of ten, shook our hands, extended their thanks and shoved off. Duncan, Tommy and I shared a look, but I was never one to make anyone stay when they wanted to go. We had brought them out of the major danger zone, so they were free to do as they pleased. I never assumed anyone owed me for anything.

The rest of the people and the kids from the Smithsonian opted to hang around for a bit longer. They were from Missouri and would appreciate a ride until we got there. I thought that was fine, but unless we got these boats running, we weren't going anywhere. I wasn't worried about transportation anymore, since across the water there looked to be another harbor with several boats still there, so we had some choices.

Duncan dug around the harbor office and when he came back he had a handful of keys. Tommy had spent his time checking out the two boats and making sure the engines at least looked like they might be coaxed into working. I stood guard on the dock, watching with interest as dark shapes moved among the houses in the subdivisions to the north and east. I was tempted to start a little fire, but I had no way of knowing for sure who or what might be in the houses and after our experience with the burning houses in Ohio, that little zombie cure didn't sit well at the moment.

A cough and sputter caught my attention, then a deep throated purr as the big fishing boat started up. Tommy poked his head out of the engine compartment and grinned. Duncan hopped off the boat and took his handful of keys over to the smaller craft, a decent sized lake boat. After an hour of fiddling, that boat had started as well.

"Looks like we're in business." Tommy declared, helping kids get onto the boat and tossing their gear blow. We could fit twenty on this boat and the other boat was tight with seventeen, but we managed. The refrain I kept hearing was "Beats paddling."

"Excellent. I'll steer this one, Duncan can manage the other one," I said, settling into the chair. I had never captained a boat this big, but I figured it couldn't be all that hard.

We moved out across the river and I went immediately to the other side to the other harbor. This was a place for sailboats only, but I wanted to try and top off the fuel tanks, which according to the gauge were only a quarter full.

While I pumped gas for the boat, several kids wanted to have their own sailboat and be towed by the bigger craft. I didn't care and it meant less crowding on the boat. Duncan's group wanted the same thing, so by the time we pulled out, we both were trailing sailboats full of teenagers.

Tommy was up in the bridge with me, checking charts and maps. It was oddly relaxing and I allowed my mind to drift to thoughts of home. I looked over at Tommy and his face wasn't as lined as it used to be. I guess he was feeling a bit relaxed as well.

"Well, we did it," I said.

Tommy looked up. "Yeah. Wish Nate could be here," he said sadly.

I knew how he felt. It was bitter irony that we had made it across the country intact, only to lose one of our number within sight of our goal.

"He's here," I said. "Probably screwing around with our lines and hoses right now."

Tommy laughed. "Not here. He's over on Duncan's boat messing with the rudder."

I laughed and figured it to be true, considering how badly Duncan was steering.

We kept a steady pace, pausing to try and refuel at a place called Colonial Beach. We found a goodly store of gas, but I had to take out a ghoul to get it. We pushed on and by nightfall we landed at Lake Conoy, which was on the southern tip of Maryland. There was a boat dock and we looked for fuel, but came up empty. We had enough for a while if we didn't run too fast, but these things weren't meant for long travel.

Duncan and I explored a bit and found a handful of supplies in the boat house, but with night coming soon, it wasn't worth it to run into zombies unless we got seriously low.

We pushed off in the morning and passed by several islands on the sides. We got lucky at another harbor and refueled both boats to capacity. This was fortunate, since we did not want to come too close to Norfolk.

Even from a distance, it wasn't pretty. People must have flocked to the naval base in the hopes the navy could somehow save them. The ports had become jammed and two ships had run into each other, sinking just enough to keep other boats from leaving. After that it was just slaughter. Zombies were everywhere, crawling all over the big grey ships, now becoming rusting hulks. What could have been havens for thousands became tombs as the ghouls scoured the ships for survivors. Several Z's saw us and fell into the murky water, not understanding how far away we were.

I moved us past the scene and I was cognizant of how quiet my passengers were. Millions of people lived here before the Upheaval. Now none lived at all.

Chapter 22

We finally reached the Atlantic as we passed Virginia Beach and I gratefully steered the boat south. We had a long trip ahead of us still, but I finally felt like we could make it. Of course, with my luck, we'd get hit with a hurricane which would blow us to Europe and then we'd be in a world of crap. Sarah would never believe me.

We avoided the major cities and steered around dozens of boats whose occupants had long since gone over to the other side. We passed many boats crammed with refugees, all of them undead. Out on the horizon a big cruise ship sat at anchor, but I wasn't curious to see if we could secure some supplies. As I put it to Tommy, who wanted to try, how was he planning on getting up one hundred feet to the railing?

About a week later, we rounded the southern edge of Florida. We encountered a lot more live people on boats and the Florida Keys were actually living communities. They had realized what was happening and took the drastic step of destroying the bridge that linked them to the mainland. One of the men we talked to said it was the worst thing he had ever done, blowing that bridge. He could see the people on the other side, screaming and crying, holding up their children as if they could appeal to his pity. But he had to protect the people who were here and so in the end, turned his back on the refugees. Every once in a while he would come out to the edge of the bridge and pray for forgiveness, but he never knew if they heard him.

The kids held a conference and between them and the chaperones, they decided to stay in the Keys. I couldn't blame them; it was as safe a place as could be found, provided the infection didn't ever become airborne. We left the smaller boat and filled the larger with supplies, topping off the tanks and carrying three five-gallon drums as reserve. The people on the Keys were very happy about us, once they knew what we had done and promised to send a duly elected rep to the new convention which was going to be getting underway soon.

With goodbyes said and grateful hugs exchanged, Tommy, Duncan and myself shoved off once more for the trip home. As we left, I noticed a man standing in the back of the crowd, his eyes fixed intently on me. He looked familiar, but I couldn't place his heavily bearded face. I put it out of my mind and as we put the horizon behind us, I focused on getting us to the Mississippi and finally home.

Finding Louisiana wasn't hard, finding an entrance to the Mississippi River was. Since the stoppage of everything because of the rise of the dead, the river was actually on its way to being near drinkable. Since there wasn't as much sludge and silt pouring out of the river, it was hard to figure out which entrance to take. Some would say that it should be easy, just find New Orleans. But New Orleans actually sits back sixty miles from the Gulf of Mexico and there are at least nine ways to get to the Mississippi. The Big Easy wasn't so damn easy.

We got our bearings and finally headed north. I had to admit that when I was on the wheel, I tended to give the engine just a tad more throttle. I was anxious as hell to see my son and my wife, praying that they were okay. We still didn't know anything and for all we did know, they could already be dead. I didn't want to think about that, but Thorton had been a sure-fire bastard and the men who followed him were on par as well.

I was surprised at the number of living communities we passed. We stopped in several, taking on supplies, trading information. Everyone we spoke with was supportive of what we had done and thanked us for the effort. To a person, they all wanted to see the documents and nearly everyone touched the glass with a kind of reverence. It was during those moments I knew I had done the right thing. People brought out their children and showed them what we had and every man who saw them took care to shake each of our hands.

I spoke with several communities about the need for a new central government and the gathering that was occurring north. They all agreed to send someone to speak for them and I was getting hopeful about our prospects. Many communities spoke of additional survivor towns and they promised to send word to them.

I caught Tommy watching me as we passed by Memphis. That city was as dead as a hammer and I thought the Elvis impersonator zombies were way over the top, even for God's sense of humor.

"What's up?" I asked, steering around an errant sandbar.

"I have to ask and I need you to take me seriously," Tommy said.

That was unusual. "Fire away," I said, giving the boat a little more throttle through a swift current area.

"What's your plan? We have all these people coming to us, from all over the place, risking their necks through zombie territory, just for a meeting?"

I thought for a moment. I had, over the past three weeks of travel on the water, given a great deal of thought as to what we were going to do. I hadn't tried to frame it into a coherent plan before now.

"Well, I'll tell ya," I said. "As a species, we damn near bought the farm, lock, stock and henhouse. We got shoved to the brink of extinction and all the technology, weaponry and ability didn't do us a lick of good. We'd built our defenses around a living enemy that would stop once we pounded them hard enough. We weren't prepared for a foe that was already dead." I paused, working on how I would phrase this next part.

"Those of us that survived, did so by a shitload of luck, will and a determination not to go quietly into the dark. Some, like me, had reasons to fight. Others, like you, fought because it wasn't in you to just quit."

I looked over at Duncan who was lounging on a couch below us. "Lastly, there were the guys like Duncan, who fought to live because it gave them a sense of purpose they might not otherwise have had.

"So what we have left over is a large group of independent-thinking, hard fighting, surviving people who know what the dark looks like, who the enemy is, and what the promise of the future could be if they are strong enough to reach for it."

I paused again, steering around another sunken obstacle. The river was full of stuff, especially around the bridges. It wasn't unusual to find several stacks of cars under major bridges.

"That sound like any group of people you might know, or remember from your history books?" I asked, looking sideways at Tommy.

Tommy frowned in thought, then he punched me on the arm. "I'll be dammed."

I laughed. "Already there, welcome to the club."

Four days later, I docked the big boat quietly at the pier at Starved Rock. It was a little past dusk when we landed and I was happy to see the boat we had sent Janna home in tied up to the dock. At least someone made it back safe.

We decided to leave the documents on the boat. They would be safe enough and since we were going to be transporting them north anyway, it was silly to carry them out only to bring them back on board.

Walking up the pathway to the lodge, a shadow disengaged itself from the woods. We reacted on instinct, spread out, and I took point, holding my pickaxe low and to the left, while my other hand held my SIG. I didn't know who it might be and if it was one of Thorton's men he was going to die slowly.

The shadow stopped and through the still night air I heard Charlie's voice.

"Hey, guys. Nate with the boat still?"

Relief flooded through me as I moved forward and was fiercely hugged by my friend. I thanked God and returned the favor and then Charlie gave Tommy and Duncan the same treatment. When we had calmed down, Charlie looked back at the boat and when I caught his eye I shook my head. Charlie frowned and dropped his head, his big shoulders moving with the sound of his breathing. When he looked up his eyes were wet with one question.

"How?"

I steered Charlie back towards the lodge and as we went up the trail stairs, I filled him in on the events surrounding Nate's death. Halfway up the stairs I stopped and stared in wonder at the lodge. Tommy and Duncan stared as well and it took a moment before Charlie realized what we were staring at.

"Oh, the lights? Yeah, we've had power for a few weeks now. Turns out the little dam was a power plant for the locks and I just diverted the power up here. Attracts all kinds of attention, but this way the Z's come to us and we just finish them easily."

I had to admit it was nearly the most beautiful thing I had ever seen. I hurried up the stairs and stopped on the patio. The big hall was lit up and Sarah and Jake were reading on one of the couches. My eyes filled with unbidden tears as I took in the scene, all of the fear and worry vanishing in a moment and I swore right then I would never leave these two again.

I didn't move and something must have warned Sarah, because she looked up suddenly and stared out the window. Her eyes found me standing there and with a suddenness that elicited a startled yelp from Jake, she rushed out onto the patio, carrying my son in her arms. I wrapped them both up and held on tight, letting my eyes water their faces as I cried with joy and relief. Sarah was crying as well and Jake wrapped his little arms around my neck in a tight hug, refusing to let go. I kissed them both repeatedly, barely noticing that Tommy had gone to seek out Angela, or that my brother and his family had come out to see us.

Duncan stood apart for a second, then out of nowhere Janna jumped on him and he was as happy as I had ever seen him.

We all moved inside and for the next hour we talked about the trip. Everyone was sobered when we talked about Nate and we spent a good deal of talking about him and the things we remembered most about him.

We all went to bed after a while, but for a few of us, we weren't going to be sleeping for a while longer.

CHAPTER 23

In the morning, I called a quick meeting, outlining what we still had to do. Tommy talked about the communities we had been to see and the reps that were coming. Charlie grunted, saying he had seen a lot of movement on the river and all of it heading north. We agreed to get up there as quickly as we could, but we decided that it could wait for a few days.

I met privately with my brother and gave him the letter and box our father had left for him. Mike's eyes misted over when he read the letter and he asked me about the house in Virginia.

"It's just a house, dad's not there," I said. "I think he may have survived the outbreak and aftermath and headed for safer pastures."

"What about Mom?" Mike asked.

I looked down. "She's buried in the backyard with the gardens she loved so much."

Mike exhaled loudly and said, "She loved those gardens. It's the perfect spot."

I nodded and changed the subject. "So Dad decided I needed a 1911 to face the world with. What about you?"

Mike shrugged and opened the long case. It was a Smith and Wesson X-frame in .460 S&W. It had a ten inch barrel with a compensator on the end. A scope was included with the weapon. We looked at it for a long time before either of us spoke.

"I think he meant well..." Mike started.

"Yeah." Was all I had to say. I guess Mike could reach out and nail something fairly far away now. If he could see it, he could shoot it. If he shot it with that cannon, he would obliterate it.

We left Starved Rock a week later and sailed north to Leport. Tommy stayed behind with Angela and Rebecca, since Angela was too pregnant for a trip on the river. Charlie was a little apprehensive about leaving, but Tommy assured him that all of Thorton's men had been accounted for.

We were past Joslin when Sarah snuggled up against me in the chair I was using to steer the boat with. "Penny for your thoughts," she said.

I sighed. "Just thinking about all this. How are we going to ever going to secure the country?"

"You'll find a way, John." Sarah replied. "You always do."

"I don't know, babe. This one's pretty big. I never realized how big this country was until I went through half of it. We had gotten so used to instant communication and fast travel that the thought of it taking a month to reach a destination was unheard of. There's hidden places everywhere and literally millions of zombies," I said. I tried not to sound defeatist, but when I looked at it from a big picture standpoint, it was fairly daunting.

Sarah gave me a little punch in the ribs. "You're such a downer. Remember when we used to get into a tight spot and people would be worried about getting overwhelmed by the zombies, what would you say to them?"

I thought it over. "I'd say kill the zombie in front of you and after a while there won't be any."

"Exactly. So how does that apply now?" Sarah asked.

I smiled. "You're right. It does apply." I wrapped an arm around her and gave her a quick kiss. She gave one back, but had to leave quickly because Jake was attempting to climb the railing and touch the water. That's my boy.

Passing into Leport was both joyous and sad. It was good to finish the journey we had started, but it was sad since the community had lost such a valued member. The people held a wake that evening for Nate, walking across the bridge with candles that were dropped into the river on the other side. It was as nice a send off as I could have wished for the old cuss.

The following day, after a brief visit with the doctor who wanted to give Jake a checkup and talk with Sarah for some reason, we had another meeting. The town had grown and I recognized a couple of kids that Janna had brought back. They found her and surrounded her in a flurry of hugs and she beamed in the attention. I looked over at Duncan who gave me a sly smile and the look I gave him was an order to take care of business.

Sarah saw me looking and added her stare and Duncan got nervous enough to shift in his seat. Funny way my wife has with men.

As the meeting finally came to order, I outlined what had taken place and what we had seen and done. There were cheers when Charlie brought in the founding documents and the meeting was delayed as everyone wanted to take a closer look. We'd have to figure out some place of storage, since the old writing couldn't take too much exposure to light.

I got around to the governing part and everyone listened carefully. I explained that because of the Upheaval, we had gotten a second chance, something that rarely happens in human history. We knew what mistakes were made and we knew how to keep them from happening again. Before we could have a functioning society, we had to get some things settled first.

"First and foremost, we need to get the power back on, one way or the other. We know where the power plants are, we need to send people to them to figure out how to get things working again. Second, we need to have our communications up and running. I figure a cell network might be the best way to do that. Third, we need to have reliable transportation. That means clearing the roads, one way or the other. This is not a thing we have to do alone. Every community should be responsible for as much as they can do around their area of safety.

"That's the job for the communities. Always push out further, always expand. Push your borders however you have to. If a town is dead, eliminate it. Burn it down. Don't give the bastards any place to hide. This is our country and by God, we're taking it back."

The cheers were deafening and the meeting broke into smaller planning groups. The representatives from other communities had been here for a while, with others still coming in. I let them work out the governing details, figuring they knew what they were doing.

I walked with Charlie for a time and we headed out onto the bridge. We didn't say much for a while, then Charlie filled me in on the assault at Starved Rock. I was stunned at the story of the cougar, not really believing it but taking Charlie's word for it. I thanked him for keeping my family safe and he said that it was his pleasure.

We watched the river go by for a bit when a small boy ran up to us. He looked like he had a message with him. We waited for him to catch his breath, then he handed me an envelope. I recognized the handwriting as belonging to the doctor here at Leport. I opened the letter and read it quickly, then handed it to Charlie to read, since he was mentioned as well. We exchanged a look and forgot about the boy, lost in our own thoughts of incredulity. It wasn't until a timid hand touched my arm that I remembered the lad.

"What's up, son?" I asked.

The boy panted. "They sent me to find you and to tell you that a president has been chosen and everyone says it should be you. Mr. James is your vice president."

I expected a lot of things, but that certainly hadn't made the list. I figured the group to go with a leader of some sort, but I had no thought it would be myself or Charlie.

I tried to argue, but Charlie held up a hand. "We've heard it all before, John and this time its official. Tag, you're it."

I thought about it and figured what the hell, somebody had to do it. We walked back to the town and passed a number of people who congratulated the two of us. Word spread pretty fast around here. We went up to the church where most everyone had gathered and I thanked the them as their new president for their confidence. I said I would try not to let them down, but not to get their hopes up too high.

"What's the first order of business?" One of the representatives asked.

I thought about that one for a bit, then Charlie answered for me. "We get busy living. Everything else is details."

Amen to that, brother. Amen.

The End

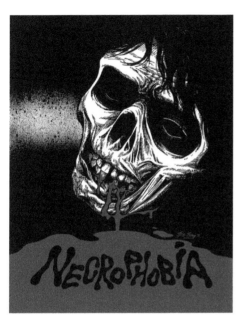

NECROPHOBIA
Jack Hamlyn

An ordinary summer's day. The grass is green, the flowers are blooming. All is right with the world. Then the dead start rising. From cemetery and mortuary, funeral home and morgue, they flood into the streets until every town and city is infested with walking corpses, blank-eyed eating machines that exist to take down the living.

The world is a graveyard.

And when you have a family to protect, it's more than survival.

It's war.

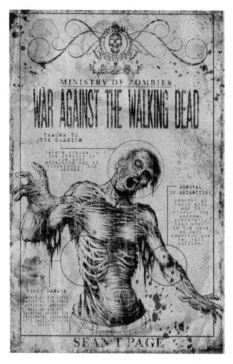

More than 63% of people now believe that there will be a global zombie apocalypse before 2050...

So, you've got your survival guide, you've lived through the first chaotic months of the crisis, what next?
Employing real science and pioneering field work, War against the Walking Dead provides a complete blueprint for taking back your country from the rotting clutches of the dead after a zombie apocalypse.

* A glimpse inside the mind of the zombie using a team of top psychics - what do the walking dead think about? What lessons can we learn to help us defeat this pervading menace?
* Detailed guidelines on how to galvanise a band of scared survivors into a fighting force capable of defeating the zombies and dealing with emerging groups such as end of the world cults, raiders and even cannibals!
* Features insights from real zombie fighting organisations across the world, from America to the Philippines, Australia to China - the experts offer advice in every aspect of fighting the walking dead.
Packed with crucial zombie war information and advice, from how to build a city of the living in a land of the dead to tactics on how to use a survivor army to liberate your country from the zombies - War against the Walking Dead may be humanity's last chance.

Remember, dying is not an option!

Available at www.severedpress.com, Amazon and most online bookstores

THE DEVIL NEXT DOOR

Cannibalism. Murder. Rape. Absolute brutality. When civilizations ends...when the human race begins to revert to ancient, predatory savagery...when the world descends into a bloodthirsty hell...there is only survival. But for one man and one woman, survival means becoming something less than human. Something from the primeval dawn of the race.

"Shocking and brutal, The Devil Next Door will hit you like a baseball bat to the face. Curran seems to have it in for the world ... and he's ending it as horrifyingly as he can." - *Tim Lebbon, author of Bar None*

"The Devil Next Door is dynamite! Visceral, violent, and disturbing!." *Brian Keene, author of Castaways and Dark Hollow*

"The Devil Next Door is a horror fans delight...who love extreme horror fiction, and to those that just enjoy watching the world go to hell in a hand basket" – *HORROR WORLD*

DEMONMACHY
Brant Danay

As the universe slowly dies, all demonkind is at war in a tournament of genocide. The prize? Nirvana. The Necrodelic, a death addict who smokes the flesh of his victims as a drug, is determined to win this afterlife for himself. His quest has taken him to the planet Grystiawa, and into a duel with a dream-devouring snake demon who is more than he seems. Grystiawa has also been chosen as the final battleground in the ancient spider-serpent wars. As armies of arachnid monstrosities and ophidian gladiators converge upon the planet, the Necrodelic is forced to choose sides in a cataclysmic combat that could well prove his demise. Beyond Grystiawa, a Siamese twin incubus and succubus, a brain-raping nightmare fetishist, a gargantuan insect queen, and an entire universe of genocidal demons are forming battle plans of their own. Observing the apocalyptic carnage all the while is Satan himself, watching voyeuristically from the very Hell in which all those who fail will be damned to eternal torment. Who will emerge victorious from this cosmic armageddon? And what awaits the victor beyond the blood-drenched end of time? The battle begins in Demonmachy. Twisting Satanic mythologies and Eastern religions into an ultraviolent grotesque nightmare, the Messiah of Death Saga will rip your eyeballs right out of your skull. Addicted to its psychedelic darkness, you'll immediately sew and screw and staple and weld them back into their sockets so you can read more. It's an intergalactic, interdimensional harrowing that you'll never forget...and may never recover from.

Available at www.severedpress.com, Amazon and most online bookstores

BIOHAZARD
Tim Curran

The day after tomorrow: Nuclear fallout. Mutations. Deadly pandemics. Corpse wagons. Body pits. Empty cities. The human race trembling on the edge of extinction. Only the desperate survive. One of them is Rick Nash. But there is a price for survival: communion with a ravenous evil born from the furnace of radioactive waste. It demands sacrifice. Only it can keep Nash one step ahead of the nightmare that stalks him-a sentient, seething plague-entity that stalks its chosen prey: the last of the human race. To accept it is a living death. To defy it, a hell beyond imagining

"kick back and enjoy some the most violent and genuinely scary apocalyptic horror written by one of the finest dark fiction authors plying his trade today" HORRORWORLD